SWAY
WITH ME

SWAY
WITH ME

SYED M. MASOOD

HODDER &
STOUGHTON

First published in Great Britain in 2021 by Hodder & Stoughton
An Hachette UK company

1

Copyright © Syed M. Masood 2021

Mandala © by ViSnezh/Shutterstock.com
Decorative border © by Katika/Shutterstock.com
Cover art copyright © 2021 by Fatima Baig.
Cover design by Angelie Yap.
Cover copyright © 2021 by Hachette Book Group, Inc.

A CIP catalogue record for this title is available from the British Library

Trade Paperback ISBN 978 1 52931 138 9
eBook ISBN 978 1 52931 139 6

Typeset in Sabon by Manipal Technologies Limited

Printed and bound in Great Britain by Clays Ltd, Elcograf S.p.A.

Hodder & Stoughton policy is to use papers that are natural, renewable and
recyclable products and made from wood grown in sustainable forests. The
logging and manufacturing processes are expected to conform to the environ-
mental regulations of the country of origin.

Hodder & Stoughton Ltd
Carmelite House
50 Victoria Embankment
London EC4Y 0DZ

www.hodder.co.uk

For my friend
Saad Saifuddin Ahmad,
who is good for the heart

Chapter One

"Everything's going to be okay, Arsalan. You'll be fine."

That was a lie and, unfortunately, deceiving yourself when you already know the truth about something is almost impossible. As a result, I'd been standing in front of a full-length mirror in my bedroom for quite a while, struggling to convince my reflection that the quest upon which I was about to embark was no big deal. All I had to do was be cool.

But I knew that in my seventeen years on Earth, I had managed not a single moment of cool. Also, the task before me was actually daunting. Momentous. Herculean, even. Today, after school, I was going to talk to a girl about love.

"Are you quite done preening?"

I jumped at the sound of Nana's voice. My great-grandfather rarely came by my room. Stairs, like everything else in the world, irritated him. When I turned toward the door, I saw that he was hunched over his cane, still in his fraying velvet dressing gown, looking rather miserable. He was never agreeable until after I'd made him his morning tea.

"I wasn't preening...exactly," I protested. "I was making sure I was presentable."

Nana's critical gaze traveled from my freshly polished—though hopelessly scuffed—dress shoes, to my zealously ironed khaki pants, to my green blazer, and then to the laboriously perfected knot of my dull yellow tie. When his eyes fixed upon my hair—I'd made certain the side part I'd had since kindergarten was flawless—he asked, "Since when do you care about what you look like?"

That was a good question. Nana had a habit of asking those.

"And are you aware that you're running half an hour late?"

Nana also had a habit of asking a second question before I could answer his first. I wondered, sometimes, if I'd find him as endearing as I did if I hadn't spent almost all of my life with him.

I looked around and realized there was a lot more sunshine in my room than I was used to in the mornings. I'd lost track of time. That was unusual in the extreme. I had, in fact, never been late for school—not that this was all that much of an accomplishment. I'd only been going to Tennyson High for a few weeks. Nana had homeschooled me before that.

"I got distracted."

"Like Narcissus," he said.

I shook my head. That particular figure of Greek mythology had nothing in common with me. Narcissus had been so enchanted by his own beauty that he had spent his life staring at his own image. I knew perfectly well that I was not a pretty face. I'd just been trying to look a little better than I usually did, less like the definition of the word "dweeb."

"So," Nana asked, "I assume a young lady is responsible for your newfound vanity?"

"There is no—"

He raised his extraordinarily bushy eyebrows.

"Fine," I muttered, surrendering to his disbelief. Shoving my hands in my pockets, I admitted, "I was going to talk to a girl after school."

"Excellent," Nana cheered. "You will do marvelously with the fairer sex. After all, you have an exceptional vocabulary."

I rolled my eyes. "Right. As if that is relevant."

"Oh, but it is. Girls like nothing better than a strapping lad who sounds like he reads the thesaurus every night before bed."

I wasn't exactly a "strapping lad," and in my experience—limited as it was—Nana's theory about what impressed girls was more than a little incorrect. Either that or every single one of them at Tennyson was a brilliant actress in the making, pretending to be totally uninterested in my mastery of language.

I'd tried explaining this to Nana before, but he was nearly a hundred years old now and held the opinion that he had outgrown being wrong.

"You see, the size of your vocabulary tells a girl the size of your most precious organ."

I frowned, genuinely confused. "How?"

"It lets them know you've got a large brain, Arsalan."

Oh. Right. The brain. Also important.

"Syllables, my boy," he declared, "are irresistible."

"If you say so."

"Come, now. You look positively dejected. Muster some confidence."

"That's what I was trying to do when you walked in."

Nana waved a dismissive hand in the direction of my mirror. "You cannot rely on your looks. You have to show off your strength. What is the most impressive word you can think of?"

I shrugged. " 'Incomprehensibilities'?"

He made a face to show what he thought of that effort.

" 'Impedimenta'?"

"Adequate," he conceded.

" 'Sesquipedalianism.' "

Nana grinned. "There it is! Who would not be impressed with such brilliance, hmm? Tell me, do you not feel better about yourself?"

I had to admit that I did, actually, though maybe that was because Nana almost never gave out compliments.

Leaning heavily on his cane, Nana made his way over to place a hand on my shoulder. "Everything is going to be okay, Arsalan," he said, repeating what I'd been saying to my reflection. "You'll be fine."

At the end of the day, after classes were over, I made my way through the deserted corridors of Tennyson High and tried not to think about how deeply alone an empty school could seem. It was like walking into an abandoned mosque or a mall that had shut down. It felt wrong somehow.

It wasn't as if I didn't like being by myself. I was used to that. But there's something sad about stumbling upon solitude in places you don't expect to find it. It makes you miss strangers you've never met and friends you've never had.

Anyway, I didn't like it, so I walked as quickly as I could.

As the gym—not my natural habitat—neared, handmade signs told me I was drawing close to the dance audition where I knew I'd find Beenish Siraj. I'd waited until almost all the other students had gone home before seeking her out. This way, if I embarrassed myself, at least it wouldn't be in front of a large group of people.

My worries felt entirely justified. Beenish was terrifying. I didn't know her personally, but I'd heard tell. Apparently "Beans," despite being the younger sister of a teacher, had been suspended last year for punching some guy and breaking his nose. She was rumored to be prickly, stabby, and sharp. Definitely the kind of person I would usually avoid.

Why was I about to talk to her, then? Because Beenish was the daughter of Roshni Siraj, the premier matchmaking aunty of the Greater Sacramento Area. There was no one better at setting up arranged marriages in all of California.

Unfortunately, Roshni Aunty likely wouldn't help me if I reached out to her on my own. She had an exclusive client list. The men she did business with were always in possession of a good fortune and in need of a wife.

I was not a man, though I was scheduled to become one within a year.

Also, I didn't have a fortune. My total net worth was around twenty dollars.

Finally, I didn't really want to get married. I was too young for that. I needed a rishta aunty to work her magic on my behalf because I wanted an assurance—a guarantee—that no matter what happened, I wouldn't end up alone in the world.

I needed an engagement, and if I impressed Beenish maybe she'd convince her mother to find me a match.

"Clinomania," I whispered to remind myself of my conversation with Nana that morning. "Mellifluous. Surreptitious."

Never having been to a dance audition before, I'd imagined an event with music and lots of frantic activity. That wasn't the case. The gym was empty except for a single table at the exact center of it, where Beenish Siraj sat.

I took a deep, bracing breath, stepped toward her, and pasted on the biggest smile I could manage. I probably looked like the Cheshire Cat had escaped Wonderland.

"Greetings," I said—squeaked, actually—and bowed my head a little. "I would very much appreciate the opportunity to converse with you."

Not bad. The bow had been unnecessary, and I hadn't used any really big words yet, but it was a decent start.

Beenish, however, seemed distinctly unmoved by my performance.

For my part, I thought her rather remarkable. She had the darkest eyes I'd ever seen. They were pretty in an "is there even a soul inside this person" kind of way. I noticed also her black hair and her T-shirt, which said THE NIGHT in bold, capital letters.

"Maybe stop perving out and look at my face when you're talking to me?"

I blushed and yanked my gaze away from her shirt.

I'd *never!*

Okay, so perhaps "never" is overstating things a bit, but in this case I definitely hadn't been staring at . . . I hadn't been staring *there.*

"I was looking at what you're wearing. Honest."

"Sure."

"It's true," I insisted. "What does that mean, anyway, 'The Night'?"

"It means I'm dark and full of terrors."

There was a pause as she waited for me to react to what

she'd said. This happened a lot. People made pop culture references and then waited for me to get them. I usually didn't.

"Well, anyway, if it is not too much of an inconvenience, I was hoping to procure your assistance in a delicate and confidential enterprise. You see—"

"Why are you talking like that?" Beenish demanded.

"Like what?"

"Like you just stepped out of a Dickens novel."

I frowned. "I endeavor only to make a good impression."

That earned me a puzzled look. "Why would you want to impress me? I don't even know who the fuck you are."

I gasped. It wasn't so much her awful language that was shocking. It was the carelessness with which she'd used it, as if she said words like that all the time.

"Dude," she said with a grin. "You're a trip."

"I am, in fact, Arsalan Nizami," I corrected with as much dignity as I could manage in the circumstances.

"Uh-huh. And does Arsalan Nizami dance?"

"Not when people are watching. And also not when no one is watching."

She pointed to a sign saying this was a dance audition.

"That's not why I'm here," I explained. "I need your help finding a girl."

"You lose someone?"

"Yes. I mean...we've all lost someone. But I haven't lost any girls, no."

"Who'd you lose?" Beenish asked.

I blinked. That wasn't the kind of thing you asked people

8

you'd just met, was it? It was private. I'd come here to discuss completely impersonal things. Like marriage.

"I need your mother's help finding a girl," I clarified, hoping to get our conversation back on track.

"Oh. You're one of *those*. Look, Nerd Scout—"

"Nerd Scout?"

"Because of your outfit. What are you wearing?"

I adjusted the knot on my tie and tugged at the lapels of my sport coat. "It's my uniform."

"Tennyson doesn't have a uniform."

I shrugged. "The school doesn't. But I do."

Beenish didn't seem to know how to respond to that. "Whatever," she ultimately decided. "Look, my mother doesn't do that arranged marriage crap. My stepmother does."

"What difference does that make?"

That earned me a look that threatened to scald my soul. Apparently, it made a great deal of difference. "Sorry," I said, though I wasn't really sure what I'd done wrong.

"Why are you even bothering me?" Beenish asked. "Just have your parents call Roshni and set things up for you."

"This wasn't...This isn't an idea my parents came up with, exactly."

She looked at me as if I were completely incomprehensible. "You actually *want* to meet a rishta aunty to ask for an arranged marriage?"

I shrugged again. "I need help."

"Obviously. Listen, I'm sorry, all right? I don't get

9

involved in anything Roshni does. Ever. Now, as you can see"—she gestured expansively at the massive gym—"I'm super busy with this audition."

"No one is here," I pointed out.

"There's time," Beenish said. "People could still show up."

"Is this for cheerleading or something?"

"Do I seem like a cheerleader to you?"

I laughed at her dark tone. "Not even a little."

For some reason, that caused her eyes to narrow.

"What?"

"Get," she snapped, "out."

So I did.

In the school parking lot, I put my head down on the steering wheel of my great-grandfather's ancient Cadillac and closed my eyes. That had sucked. Not only was Beenish not going to help me, I already knew that some of the things she'd said with casual, thoughtless brutality would bother me for a long time.

I don't even know who the bleep *you are.*

Nerd Scout.

What are you wearing?

I'd remember it all for years.

I wondered if other people were like me, if small hurts haunted them the same way. Maybe I was the only one who obsessed over every faux pas I made and cringed at the memory of every minor slight I'd endured. I often felt bad for things that had happened forever ago and, at the same time, felt petty for obsessing over what were, after all, minor bruises. Surely the rest of humanity was better than I was. Surely.

I sat back up and glanced over at the passenger seat, where the beat-up briefcase I carried—Nana thought backpacks were juvenile—sat mocking me.

You are different, it said. *You're strange. Everyone laughs at you.*

I sighed and turned the ignition. The old car gasped, sputtered, sounded like it was preparing to perish, but then rumbled to life.

Before speaking to Beenish, I'd planned on going back to Nana's. Now the long silences my great-grandfather and I shared seemed like too heavy a burden to bear. My heart and mind were full. I needed to speak to someone who would listen to me without trying to offer advice, and without interruption.

There was only one person like that, and I always knew exactly where to find her.

"Hi, Mom," I said.

She didn't answer, but she never did.

Not anymore.

It was a nice autumn day. The sun was playing

hide-and-seek with a few scattered clouds. Birds I couldn't see chirped in trees that were still hanging on to their leaves. In a few months, the cemetery would no longer be full of their song.

"How are you?"

A cool breeze picked up slightly. I knew that it was not a response from my mother. And yet...

I lay down next to Mom. Up above, in the light blue of the sky, I thought I could just make out the moon, which was always there, but often veiled by the brightness of the sun.

"I finally spoke to that Beenish girl I told you about. It didn't go great."

I really shouldn't have to do this, I thought. *You should be here.* But there was no reason to be unkind. As a general rule, I tried not to complain about my life when I visited my mother. Whatever my troubles, she had it worse, being dead and all.

"Anyway, what about you? Anything interesting happening?"

I closed my eyes and listened to the silence around me.

Two years ago, I'd have been freaked out by the thought of being in a graveyard as the sun began to fall from the sky. Now I knew it was a peaceful place where I could be around the only person who'd ever really known me.

Of course, she wasn't actually present. This was just where her body was. Her spirit was elsewhere. I wondered what that felt like. Maybe it felt like a dream.

I don't remember the room. I want to say it was cold and clinical, but I've forgotten a lot of details about that day, even though it ended up being the most important one of my life.

I remember holding my mom's hand as she lay on the hospital bed. I remember how little it seemed to weigh. There were deep, ugly, purple bruises on her face, but they didn't look so bad. Not bad enough to die from.

It's internal bleeding, doctors told me. *You can't see it.*

Where's your father?

I didn't know.

Do you know if your mother has insurance? Are you eighteen yet? There are these forms that . . . We'll give you a moment.

A moment. A moment to hold her hand.

Allah said he made human beings from clay.

You forget that, until they break.

Then she opened her eyes and I dared to hope.

She managed a smile. It was small, but it was the world.

"Hey," she said, very, very softly, her parched lips struggling to part.

"Hi, Mom."

"How much time do I have?"

"What are you talking about? There's nothing wrong with you."

"You know you shouldn't lie, Arsalan."

I remember crying and crying and crying and not being able to stop.

I remember her stroking my hair as best she could.

"Everything's going to be okay, Arsalan," she whispered. "You'll be fine."

"I don't know how to live without you, Mommy."

She was in tears too now. Her hand dropped away; her breathing came faster. "You will. Search for love and you'll see. Life is beautiful."

Her eyes closed and she couldn't open them.

They sedated me and darkness fell upon me too.

I woke up.

She never did.

Chapter Two

The moon was bright when I woke. I got to my feet, brushed myself off, said goodbye to Mom, and rushed to the Cadillac. I would have called Nana if I'd had a phone, but he wouldn't allow it. He was a Luddite and believed that technology wasn't to be trusted.

It wasn't that he would worry about where I was. Nana wasn't the worrying sort. I just needed to make sure he took his many medications before he went to bed because he forgot them sometimes. That had caused a couple of emergency room visits in the two years since my mother had passed. Each had ended with him complaining about how all he wanted was to die in peace and that my insistence that he continue to live was irritating.

He was being selfish. I needed him. He was all the family I had left—well, almost. When I told him that, Nana asked me if I knew what irony was.

He was a lot of work.

When I got back to his place—well, the place he still thought of as his, anyway—the lights were on. At least I wouldn't have to wake him. I parked in the driveway. The garage was full of boxes, the contents of which Nana probably couldn't even remember anymore. The entire house was like that—a storage space full of mementos and memories, which Nana never wished to leave. It was his entire universe.

He was slouched in his favorite overstuffed, worn burgundy leather chair, a smoking pipe dangling lazily from his lips. His wild, Einstein-like hair cast a funny shadow in the glow of his reading lamp as he pored over a book. The deerstalker hat he usually wore was sitting in his lap. If he didn't die in a hospital, this was probably the pose his maker would find him in one day.

"Salaam, Nana," I said, and got no response.

This was typical. Nana didn't entertain any interruptions to his reading time.

I went to the kitchen, where he kept his medications, and saw the breakfast I had rushed to leave him—a fried egg, sunny-side up because something in life should be, and a piece of toast—still on the dining table. I sighed, warmed up some milk with a dash of turmeric, honey, and a few bits of saffron, and took it to him with his pills. It was the one thing he never refused. Something to do with the fact that his mother used to make it for him.

I had to wait for him to finish the sentence he was in the middle of before he acknowledged me. He carefully removed his glasses with trembling hands, set them aside, and traded his book for his drink.

"You're home late."

"I had an . . . unusual day," I told him.

"Ah, that's right. You were going to talk to a girl. How'd it go?"

I considered telling him everything that had happened with Beenish but couldn't. Nana wouldn't react well to my seeking out a rishta aunty to set up an arranged marriage. No one in our family had ever had much luck with committed relationships. Nana didn't think very highly of them.

"Poorly," I told him.

An anxious shadow appeared momentarily on Nana's face. It wasn't much, just a slight wrinkling of the brow that was gone in an instant, but I knew his expressions well. "You did fine, I'm sure," he said, before pausing to take his pills and drain a large portion of the milk I'd given him. "Tell me, did you utilize your full vocabulary?"

"She didn't give me the chance. It went sideways fast. Like I've told you before, I don't think using big words works anymore, Nana. She seemed to think it was weird."

He swatted my experience away dismissively. "You are

young. You are supposed to be weird. You know where the word comes from, yes?"

I shook my head. Nana could turn any conversation to Old English. "You're going to tell me, I'm sure."

He ignored the snark. "It comes from 'weorthan,' which means 'to become.' It is the natural state of being a teenager or, at least, it should be. Young people who are not weird, who have already become what they are going to be—they are the ones who ought to be a little concerned. Weird, my son, is good."

"It doesn't impress girls much, though."

"Give it time. Girls are weird too. Was the one you spoke to not?"

"I guess she was."

Nana nodded approvingly. "Excellent. The next time you speak to her—"

"I don't think there's going to be a next time."

"The next time you speak to her," he repeated sternly, "make sure you are wearing a hat."

"A hat?"

He chuckled at my skepticism. "Of course. There is nothing more appealing to a woman than a man in a hat. Trust someone who has danced a tango or two in his life, won't you?"

The next day, during lunch break, Nana's theory was put to the test as Beenish Siraj declaimed, "Seriously, dude, I know

I asked you this before, but I've got to again. What the ever-loving fuck are you wearing?"

I flinched, not just at the language, but also with surprise. No one ever spoke to me during lunch, probably because I never ate in the cafeteria. There was too much pressure, too many places to sit where I didn't know if I'd be welcome. My lunch spot was a little nook I'd discovered on the second floor, a snug space between two sets of lockers, where no one would tell me to go away.

As I looked up from my ketchup sandwich, I was struck by the fact that even though Beenish was a small person, she took up a lot of space in the universe, like a kitten with the roar of a much bigger, much more dangerous cat.

Today she had on a T-shirt printed with the words WHITE SAVIOR.

"What are *you* wearing?" I countered.

"I help white people break free of their biases because of how awesome I am. I save them from their own prejudices. That means I am a . . ." She pointed at her shirt.

"That isn't what that means. At all."

"I'm making it my own. Anyway, this is about you. You're the strange one here."

With a grimace, I looked down at my own clothes. I was wearing exactly what I'd had on the day before. "I told you, this is my uniform."

"On your head, Dorkus Maximus."

"Oh." I adjusted the wide-brimmed fedora I'd borrowed from Nana's collection. "This is a hat."

"Obviously. Why do you have it on?"

"My great-grandfather says that girls like hats."

"Seriously?" she demanded, dropping her backpack onto the linoleum floor and leaning back against the lockers across from me. "Why are you taking advice on how to be a player from a fossil?"

"That's not very nice."

She took a deep breath. "Right. Sorry. Let's start over. This isn't going like I thought it would."

I knew the feeling, so I nodded sympathetically before realizing how strange it was that Beenish Siraj had actually planned out a conversation with me. Now that I thought about it, she must have had to search for some time to find me here. That was incredible.

"I felt bad about yesterday," she said, "in the gym. I wanted to say that I'm sorry. I'm not usually—"

"A porcupine?"

That drew a grin from her. "Was that you trying to make a joke? Nice. You also don't look like you're going to puke just because you're talking to me. This is progress."

I shrugged. "I'm not trying to dazzle you anymore."

"Good. Because you have no shot with me. You have like a negative zero shot."

"I didn't want..." It occurred to me that saying I had no interest in her might be hurtful, so I said instead, "I wanted you to feel like I was cool enough to recommend to your mother—your stepmother—for her business."

"You don't need to be cool for that."

"Really?"

She held out her hands in a half shrug that clearly meant *What the hell is wrong with you?* "How many cool people do you think need help from middle-aged desi aunties to find themselves someone to marry?"

I hadn't done the math on that before. "Negative zero?"

"Exactly. You never needed me to like you. That was terrible planning. Also, no offense, but you're an awful arranged marriage prospect."

I frowned. "Saying 'no offense' doesn't automatically give you the right to be rude."

Beans flipped her black hair over her shoulder. "I'm pretty sure you're wrong about that," she said breezily. "Anyway, trust me, I hear about this stuff at home all the time. I know exactly what families looking for matches for their daughters want."

"Someone with a kind heart?" I ventured.

She snorted. "That's hilarious. First thing, always, is a good education. You"—she pointed at me—"are in high school."

I looked around us. This was undeniable.

"It can't just be any education either. Having a PhD in English literature isn't going to get you anywhere."

"Disappointing," I murmured.

She ignored me and went on. "So, really, a good education that'll probably lead to a high-paying job is the most important requirement. Doctors get the best girls, of course."

"What do you mean 'the best girls'?"

"Most guys want hot white girls," Beenish said.

I frowned. "Do white girls even have arranged marriages?"

The look she gave me left me convinced she thought I was an imbecile. "No. They all want desi girls. They just want them to look white. They want light skin."

"That doesn't make any sense."

Her smile was swift and warm. "That's right. It doesn't. I like that you see that, Olive Oil."

"Olive Oil?"

"Because you're extra virgin."

Also undeniable.

"Anyway, don't get me started on how ridiculous Roshni's job is. As far as you're concerned, I mean, you have good grades, and all aunties fantasize about guys with 4.0s, but— oh, don't look so surprised, Arsalan. Even if my sister weren't teaching you physics, I'd have guessed. That's why you dress like you do, right? To let everyone know you're smart?"

I shook my head. I'd never thought about how I dressed. I just wore what I had, which was what was already in Nana's house. He didn't believe in spending money on things that weren't books.

Beans scratched the back of her head. "Then why do you wear..." She seemed to be searching for words to describe my ensemble, but eventually just waved vaguely in my direction. "...all of that?"

"Is there a point," I asked, "anywhere in our future?"

"I'm just saying you haven't got an education or a fancy profession. Is your family rich? Didn't think so. Plus we're

22

so young. Barely anyone gets set up before they're out of college. Except sometimes people who are really conservative. Are you religious, Arsalan?"

"God, no."

"Then you suck as a potential rishta. Sorry to break it to you, but even if I talked to Roshni, even if she tried to help you, it'd be pointless."

I nodded. I'd considered most of what Beenish Siraj was telling me. What I hadn't realized was that Roshni Aunty's requirements were not her own, but rather a reflection of the demands of the people she was trying to match up. That made perfect sense.

It was still disappointing, though.

"I guess it was foolish to hope anyone would ever like me," I said after a moment.

"What? No. Dude, that's not…Aww, now you look like a super-nerdy puppy who was begging for food and got turned away."

I squared my shoulders and sat up straighter. I was not sure what such a creature would look like, exactly, but it didn't sound dignified. Nothing was more important, I'd always been taught, than a gentleman's dignity.

"Why do you want to get an arranged marriage anyway?"

I hesitated. Another very personal question. I wasn't about to tell her that my mom had asked me to find love. Acquiring it as part of an engagement and eventual marriage contract seemed like the only realistic way to fulfill her dying wish.

23

After a moment, Beans added, "And why aren't your parents handling this for you? It isn't your job. That's the one benefit to the whole system, right?"

I took a deep breath. There was no way to answer her inquiries without revealing something deeply true about myself. I was tempted to try to make a joke or to change the subject, but there was a sudden intense earnestness in Beenish's dark gaze that was arresting. Answering her just...it just felt like the right thing to do.

Luckily, you can keep things a secret while still telling the truth.

"I'm afraid."

"Of what?"

"Of being alone."

She tilted her head to one side to look at me, as if she could figure me out if she saw me at just the right angle. "Why do you think you'll be alone?"

I shrugged and glanced away.

After a moment, Beenish declared, "I'll help you. That's what I came to tell you. I'll set you up with someone."

"You called arranged marriages crap yesterday."

"Not someone to marry," she clarified. "Someone to hang out with. Cuddle with, if that's what you are into. A girlfriend."

I couldn't help but laugh. "I think my odds are way worse if I try to find someone on my own."

"You won't be on your own. That's the whole point. I'll be on your side and, trust me, I usually get what I want."

I could believe that. "You are undeniable."

"Exactly," Beans said happily. "I should put that on a shirt. Like I was saying, your approach was all wrong yesterday. You said you were trying to impress me. You didn't need to do that. What you needed was for me to owe you."

"What could you possibly want from me?"

As soon as I asked the question, an image of her sitting alone, in an empty gym, holding an unsuccessful audition flashed in my mind.

"You want me to be your partner," I said. "You want my body."

Beenish snorted. "I definitely wouldn't put it that way. But yes, Arsalan Nizami, I'm here to ask if you'll dance with me."

I had a hard time focusing in physics, which was unusual because it was my favorite subject. A lot of people didn't care for it much. They complained about how difficult it was to remember all the formulas we were required to know.

That wasn't my approach. Physics, like chemistry and biology and all the sciences, really, was about relationships. Once you understood the basic elements involved, you could extrapolate the formulas yourself. There was no reason to memorize them.

Besides, it was fun. Learning physics was like figuring out how the universe speaks to itself. Who isn't interested in that?

Me, apparently, at least after talking to Beenish Siraj. I couldn't get her offer out of my head long enough to pay attention to Newton.

The bell had rung before she could explain exactly why she needed a dance partner, but no matter what the reason, I was a horrible choice. For one, there was no evidence that I could dance. I'd never really tried. People say that you should "dance like no one's watching," but that is not something Muslims can do. Allah is always watching, and He isn't doing so without judgement. Judging people is kind of His thing.

It would be mortifying to meet the Creator of All Things and have to explain to Him why, despite being desi, the only dance move you could pull off was the white man's shuffle.

Besides, as we were walking toward our respective classes, Beenish had admitted that she'd never actually set someone up before. So there was also no evidence to support her claim that she'd be a good matchmaker. But she seemed to think that if Roshni Aunty could do it, she could too.

I barely knew Beenish, but I could already tell that she did not suffer from a lack of confidence. She probably thought she'd be as good at carrying the Earth on her shoulders as Atlas or as great at writing poetry as Mir Taqi Mir. Her certainty that she had the capacity to overcome any obstacle was a little impressive and a little daunting and, frankly, just a little envy inducing.

"Arsalan?"

Startled, I looked up at the kind face of Qirat Siraj,

Beenish's sister and the woman charged with teaching physics at Tennyson High. "Yes?"

"I seem to not have your attention." She spoke sweetly, but then Ms. Siraj always spoke sweetly. She was the opposite of her younger sibling that way. "Am I terribly boring?"

I shook my head.

"Then perhaps you wouldn't mind focusing a bit?"

"Sorry," I muttered, slinking down in my seat.

She managed to glare at me for a moment before her stern expression melted into a bright smile. Happiness was her usual state, or so it seemed. It was why even though a lot of people seemed to hate physics, everyone liked her. It helped, I think, that she was the youngest teacher we had. She was probably no more than twenty-four.

If I hadn't known better, I would have never guessed that she and Beenish were sisters. It was as if God had sculpted Ms. Qirat Siraj out of sunshine, while Beenish had been carved out of the moon.

"What was I saying? Right. The extra credit assignment. If you read the syllabus, you'll know that a voluntary assignment is going to be handed out soon. It'll be one question. Answer it without discussing it with anyone or reading anything. I want you guys to think and figure the solution out for yourself. Thought experiments have been vital to the progress of this science, and you should try at least one while you're in my class."

The bell went off at that moment, and there was a mad dash for the exit. Ms. Siraj, with a grin, threw her hands up in the air. As I was in the front row, I was able to hear her say, "Though I guess that's not going to happen today. See you soon, guys." Raising her voice a little, she added, "Arsalan, hang back, will you?"

I stayed in my chair, carefully putting my books into my briefcase. When we were alone, she said, "I guess my sister spoke to you."

"What?"

"Beenish talked to you, right? I assume she's the reason why you were distracted in class."

I wasn't really sure what a safe response to that was.

"I hope she wasn't...well, herself. Beans can be a lot."

"She's fine," I said. Then, realizing that might sound like a comment on Beenish's appearance, I hurried to add, "She's bearable, I mean."

Ms. Siraj grinned. "I'll tell her you said that."

Well, that was just excellent.

"I wanted to make you sure didn't feel obligated to dance with her," Ms. Siraj said, "even if it was my idea. I didn't make that suggestion as your teacher. I was being her older sister."

"Beenish didn't mention you at all."

"Oh. Well, in that case, you can forget we ever had this conversation."

I nodded and started to get to my feet as she made her way back to her desk. Then I stopped. "Why?" I asked.

"Why did I think you two would make good dance partners? Because of physics, of course. Opposite forces—"

"Attract?"

Ms. Siraj raised her eyebrows. "I was going to say that opposite forces balance each other out."

I could feel my ears burning a little. "Right. Of course."

"Besides, Beans is pretty determined to take part in some dance contest she's found. One way or another, she is going to find a partner and, whoever that ends up being, she's going to spend a lot of time with him. It'd be nice if he were someone I knew she'd be safe with."

I blinked. "Thank you. I mean, you haven't known me for very long but—"

"I am an excellent judge of character, Arsalan. I just wasn't sure if you'd agree to her proposal. Did you, by the way?"

"Beenish told me I could think about it until the end of the day."

"She's very magnanimous," Ms. Siraj said dryly. "Anyway, whatever you decide, it won't change your standing with me, which is great, by the way."

"Did—did she happen to mention..."

That earned me a bemused look. "The fact that you wanted her to ask Roshni to set you up? Yes. Do you know how long it took me to convince Beans to agree to speak to Roshni if you dance with her? It isn't a small cost for her."

I hesitated. Clearly Ms. Siraj didn't know that Beenish had decided to play matchmaker herself. I chose not to mention it. Nana always said words are eternal, that once you say something, you can't take it back. It's good to be careful when you're dealing with forever.

29

There could be a good reason Beenish hadn't been entirely forthcoming with Ms. Siraj. But there was no good reason, just then, for me to reveal what she had chosen to conceal.

So, instead of correcting my teacher, I asked, "You could talk to your stepmother on my behalf, right? That way I wouldn't have to dance."

Ms. Siraj leaned back in her chair and gave me a small smile. "You didn't come to me first, even though Beans and I have the same relationship to Roshni. Why?"

"It didn't seem like an appropriate thing to ask of a teacher. A gentleman tries not to ask acquaintances for favors that may have to be denied. It puts them in an awkward position."

She nodded. "Right. And are you still a gentleman?"

"Yes. Of course."

"Then," she said, "you're excused."

Chapter Three

As I stepped out of Ms. Siraj's class, two people walked toward me. I recognized Annika Bryzgalova, who was at the top of almost every class at Tennyson. We hadn't spoken much, though we had exchanged nods a few times. I fully intended to be where she was academically by the end of the year, and I suspect she recognized that we were in competition.

Nana did not much care for grades. He said the purpose of an education was to elevate and nurture a mind, not to rank it. Nevertheless, I wanted to do well. If you're going to be forced into an arena, you might as well try to win. Words to live by for gladiators and high school students alike.

The guy with Annika was desi. I didn't know him, but

I had definitely noticed him in the halls. His wardrobe consisted of astonishingly tight-fitting clothes in loud colors, and chains with religious imagery on them. He wasn't exactly inconspicuous.

Today he was wearing a silver chain with a crescent moon dangling prominently from it, along with a bracelet that looked like it was made out of repurposed prayer beads. The whole look was completed by Jesus-length hair slicked back with heavy gel, and expensive-looking yellow sneakers.

"Hi, Arsalan," Annika began. "This is—"

"No introduction needed," her friend cut in. "I'm sure he knows me." My face seemed to tell him that I didn't, because he added, "You don't know Diamond Khan?"

"No. Who's Diamond Khan?"

He held his arms out to his sides. Their alarmingly over-developed musculature made it clear that he worked out more than necessary. Then again, I worked out a lot less than necessary, so I wasn't one to talk. For a brief second, I wondered if he wanted to hug me, but then realized Diamond Khan was merely allowing me the opportunity to admire his full magnificence.

Apparently, he'd been speaking about himself in the third person. I didn't know that was something people actually did.

"Nice to meet you," I told him. It came out sounding uncertain.

"Of course it is. We're bros, yeah? You and I are brothers in the deen. You are Muslim, right?"

"Nominally."

He looked like I'd told him there was a way to figure out the location and momentum of a particle at the same time. "What does that mean?"

"Nominally is defined," Annika volunteered, sounding professorial, "as—"

"Doesn't matter," he said, waving her off. "Your last name is Nizami, right? You mind if I call you Niz? It's shorter. Errssaalllaan. Nobody's got time for something like that. Maybe you should translate it to English. My name was Heera but that's not as cool as Diamond."

"It's shorter, though," I pointed out.

Annika chuckled. Diamond ignored us both. "What does Errssaalllaan mean in English anyway?"

"It means 'lion,'" Annika answered. When we both looked at her in surprise, she shrugged. "Like Aslan from Narnia, right?"

I smiled. "Yeah."

"Narnia?" Diamond repeated. "Never saw that movie. Anyway, that's badass. Maybe you could go by Leo." He stepped back and looked at me critically. "But you don't look much like a lion. You look like a tree. A thin, sad, old tree that's about to die. Doesn't fit."

I wondered if I ought to be offended, but Nana had always taught me that one shouldn't be offended by the truth. Besides, Diamond hadn't said it in a mean way. His tone was, if anything, aggressively friendly.

"So, anyway, Niz, I asked Annika to point you out because Beans said you needed help."

33

I frowned. "With what?"

Diamond reached over and slapped my shoulder hard. I winced, but he was entirely unapologetic. "With building that up. She said I should teach you how to properly work out."

I shook my head, trying to make sense of what was happening. "Work out?"

"A workout," Annika began, "is a session of—"

I rolled my eyes. "I'm aware. Why does Beenish think I need help?"

"We spoke in history class," Diamond told me. "And she thinks you need help because...I mean, look at you, bro. Now give me your number so that I can text you. I'll let you know when we can meet up to get started on building that body."

All of this was so strange and happening so quickly that I didn't really know how to react. It was as if I was in a play where everyone knew the lines, but I hadn't yet seen the script. "I just have a landline. I can't text."

Annika and Diamond stared at me like I was a Kafka protagonist, like I was transforming before their eyes into something curious.

"That's bizarre," she finally judged.

"Weird," Diamond agreed.

"It's fine," I protested.

They looked at each other, then back at me, their expressions full of pity.

"It is," I insisted. "Anyway, Diamond, thank you for

your offer, but there is no reason at all for me to alter my appearance."

They looked at each other again.

"Stop doing that!" I flinched at my own volume. "Sorry. It's just—"

"It's cool," Diamond declared. "We all get sensitive about stuff we're not good at. I'm very sensitive about…" He trailed off, apparently trying to figure out his flaws for the first time in his life and failing to come up with any.

"Listen," Annika said, with the air of a doctor dispensing very important medical advice. "Have you seen the show *Queer Eye*? You really, really need to watch it."

I ran a hand over my face. "I don't understand what is happening."

"If you're going to be around Beans," Diamond Khan said, "you'll get used to that. Never forget, Niz, the world belongs to her. We're just living in it."

Beenish—or "Beans," as everyone apparently called her—was perched on the massive hood of Nana's car, waiting for me after school ended. She'd obviously want to know what I'd decided. It was a good question. I had one of my own. "How'd you know which car was mine?"

"It was the weirdest thing in the lot," she said. "Not exactly a mystery. So you've had time to think things through. You in?"

"Why'd you send that Diamond guy to see me?"

Beans shrugged. "To get you to a gym. Didn't he tell you?"

"Yes, but why?" I asked.

"As part of your makeover."

I raised my eyebrows.

"It's going to be really hard to get anyone interested in you if you look like you stepped out of an issue of *Dorks Weekly* from 1947. We're going to have to work on your image."

"You're exaggerating a bit."

"Yes," she agreed, "but not by much. You don't have to become Diamond. In fact, please don't. He needs to turn it down a *lot*. Your look has to be updated, though. I'm right about this."

Her dark eyes had that dangerous, urgent earnestness in them again. Their ability to go from playful to fervently serious was quite…disarming. Half the time it seemed that Beenish didn't really care about anything, that she was laughing at you and everything in the world around you. However, when her eyes got like that, warm and sober and resolute, it was impossible to not be convinced that your concerns were the most important thing in the universe to her.

"Trust me," she said.

"I do," I told her, because it was true.

She clapped her hands together, her face breaking into an irrepressible grin. "Excellent. This is going to be so much fun. I've always wanted to give someone a makeover. I never thought it would be a boy, but life is full of surprises."

"So it would seem."

Beans held out a hand. "We've got a deal, then?"

I thought about it. I really didn't want to dance. I had no experience or skill in that department. It was possible that I'd end up making a fool of myself. However, it was in Beenish's interest to do well in whatever competition she wanted to enter. Therefore, it followed that she would help me practice and get better. Plus, even if everything did go wrong, and I did end up looking like an idiot in front of other people, they'd all be strangers. It was one of the benefits of not really knowing anyone. It wasn't like I'd be hearing about any potential horrible performance for years.

The fact that Beenish was clearly taking her end of the bargain seriously helped make up my mind. Besides, if she failed in finding me a romantic match, at least I wouldn't be as weird as I was now by the time she was done trying. The makeover she was planning would make sure of that.

Her hand had been waiting for mine almost longer than good manners could bear, so I took it. It was warm and soft. It wasn't until we'd released each other that a question that should have occurred to me sooner came to mind.

"How come you didn't ask Diamond to dance with you instead of asking him to help me get in shape?"

She didn't answer. Instead, she said, "I'll see you at the Arden Mall on Saturday at ten in the morning. Don't be late."

Chapter Four

"There is a letter for you, Arsalan," Nana told me as soon as I got back home. I didn't need to ask who it was from. The sourness in my great-grandfather's tone was enough to give that away. There was also the fact that, aside from Zeeshan Nizami, there was no one else in the world who would write to me.

My thoughts, which had been about how Beenish Siraj's hand had felt in mine, curdled. I'd left school feeling like the day had been strange but good. The arrival of a letter from my father was a drop of arsenic for my mood.

He had always known exactly how to ruin everything.

"You don't have to read it. What can that man have to say that is of any consequence?"

I shrugged and went over to the small console table on which Nana kept his mail next to an old gramophone. Letters and vinyl records were both, he said, ways one could hear "the still, sad music of humanity." I picked up the thin envelope that had been mailed from Arizona but did not open it. I never read my father's letters in front of Nana. There was always the chance they might contain information he wouldn't like.

"Don't you wish your mother had never married that rascal?" Nana asked.

"Sometimes," I admitted. "But then I think about it and am glad she did. It may be selfish, but I do rather like existing."

"A fair point," he conceded. "For what it is worth, I sometimes like the fact that you exist as well. I assume you will now disappear into that room of yours to brood?"

"Do you need anything, Nana?"

"No, no. Go. Be miserable. God knows you have reason enough."

I started making my way upstairs, but then realized I still had Nana's fedora on. I took it off, went over to him, and placed it gently on his head. "Thanks for the hat. It worked. A little."

He reached over and grabbed my left wrist. "Stay away from things that stress your heart, my child. Prophet

39

Muhammad told us that worry is half of old age. Don't let the pain of the world steal away your youth, if you can help it."

"Imam Ali," I corrected him.

Nana frowned. "What?"

"Ali ibn Abi Talib told us that worry is half of old age."

"Are you sure?"

I nodded.

He made a face. Nana had never gotten very good at being wrong. He said it was because he'd had such little practice at it. "This is why you rarely hear me quote holy men. I don't know what it is about religion, but I've never quite managed to get it right."

My room—like almost all my possessions—had once belonged to someone else. It was where my grandfather had grown up and, more recently, where my uncle had lived. And it felt like the space they had inhabited still remembered them, even if I couldn't.

The posters that had survived Rayyan Uncle were gone, taken down by Nana before I moved in, but I could still see their absence in the discoloration of the walls. I'd found a dusty old guitar in his closet, which Nana said Rayyan had never played; and a worn, black leather jacket, which Nana said he had never taken off. You have to be committed to a leather jacket to wear it in the summer in Sacramento.

I'd also found some less-than-delicate magazines buried

40

under a stack of comic books, an old computer keyboard belonging to a Commodore 64, and a decidedly unscientific smoking apparatus.

I hadn't told Nana about the magazines. I didn't know what kind of relationship he and Rayyan Uncle had shared, but I knew Nana would almost certainly resent the presence of such magazines in his home. A little ignorance never hurt anyone. "He that increaseth knowledge increaseth sorrow," as the Bible says.

I went to sit at the massive, solid oak desk that had apparently been in this room since the house had been built. In the lower right-hand corner, Rayyan Uncle had carved a heart with his initials, along with someone else's. It always made me smile.

Of my mother's father, there were fewer vestiges. There was an old, barely stable bookshelf that was still standing, laden with musty, outdated books about chemical engineering. On the table beside my bed, next to the dictionary Nana insisted I read every night, sat a model of an atom my grandfather had made when he'd been younger than I was.

When I was in my room, when I actually thought about it, I could see the true value of this house. It wasn't just a soulless wooden box, especially for Nana, who had actually known and loved these people I had never met. It was the canvas on which the story of his family had been painted.

I reached for the bottom drawer of the desk that was currently mine. This shot my smile dead. In it were my father's letters, along with a few other belongings of his, like medals he'd won as a sniper in the army, killing people whenever he'd been ordered to do so. His country had trained him to fight. I wondered sometimes if it had forgotten to train him to stop fighting.

With a deep breath, I tore open the envelope containing his newest letter and skimmed it, like someone ripping off a bandage to examine a wound. It didn't say much this time. It just let me know that he was doing well, that he'd been sober for three months now, that he'd been reading the Quran more and was becoming a better Muslim. He said that he was working on getting a job so that he could get an apartment of his own. I could go live with him then. We could be a family again.

Shaking my head, I dropped the letter into the growing pile, closed the desk drawer, and walked over to slump on my bed.

That hadn't been so bad. He hadn't gone on about how he was convinced that Nana and Mom, when she'd been alive, had poisoned my mind against him. He hadn't threatened to kick Nana out of his home.

That had become Zeeshan Nizami's go-to threat whenever he wanted me to do something.

It was why I wrote back to him.

It was why I'd started going to public school this year. My father thought it would get me away from Nana's constant influence.

A few years ago, when battling a long illness that had almost taken him from us, Nana had signed his house over to Mom. He'd recovered his health, but never thought to recover his property. I don't think either he or my mother imagined she would die before him. Now that she was gone, my father claimed that her house—this house that Nana and I lived in—belonged to him.

We were at the mercy of Zeeshan Nizami, and Nana didn't even know it.

By the time I went down to make dinner, Nana was napping in his reading chair. After Mom died, I'd slowly taken over cooking for the household—such as it was. As a result, we mostly ate eggs, a couple of basic salads, a few salans, and ramen. I would have liked better food, but even with Nana's mother's translated collection of recipes, I couldn't make anything taste like it was supposed to.

Nana didn't seem to mind, at least not enough to complain. That did not change when I walked into the living room with a plate of cucumber sandwiches. He did grumble about being woken up, though.

We ate without speaking for a while, which was unusual, as meals were the one time Nana usually wanted conversation. The Prophet had said it was best not to eat alone or to eat in silence.

On that night, however, my great-grandfather was quiet but restless. He was tapping his feet, flipping his sandwiches around to examine them from every angle, and sighing occasionally.

I couldn't help but smile. Nana was dying to know what had been in my father's letter, but the impeccable manners he insisted were the hallmark of a civilized individual made it impossible for him to ask. One didn't inquire about the contents of private correspondence, as he'd told me more than once in the past. He'd always been talking about his own letters, though.

Finally, apparently unable to bear it anymore, he cleared his throat. "So, Arsalan, is Zeeshan doing well?"

"I didn't know you cared," I replied. "I'll be sure to tell him you asked when I write back."

"Do no such thing," Nana commanded, entirely unnecessarily. "You know it makes no difference to me if that man is living or dead."

I shrugged. "You asked."

Nana scowled and jammed an impressive amount of food into his face, possibly to keep himself from saying anything further.

I decided to give him a break. "The letter was fine. My father says he's doing better, getting help. Things will be different the next time we meet, he says."

"That's what he always says," Nana reminded me.

"Yes. Anyway, I don't want to talk about it. I was actually having a pretty good day before the mail came."

"Were you? It's unfortunate that your day was ruined, but you can't say that Shelley didn't warn you."

He was talking about Percy Shelley's poem "Mutability." I ignored the reference. If Nana got started on the Victorians, he'd be intolerable for a month. "Do you have any other tips for how to be around girls?"

Nana frowned, then realized I was talking about his advice that I ought to wear a hat. He found a grin. "The fedora really worked well, then?"

" 'Worked' might be overstating it a bit, but...things got more interesting."

"If you're not careful," Nana said, "that'll become a habit."

"Would that be so bad?"

He shrugged. "Perhaps not. But boredom is a blessing too. People often forget that. Still, you have both the luxury and the hardship of being young, so I suppose a little excitement is in order. As long as you cover your excitement, if you take my meaning."

I frowned as I finished my sandwich. I should have used more cream cheese. I'd have to remember for next time. "I shouldn't seem too eager around girls, is what you're saying?"

"I'm saying to use a condom, Arsalan."

"Nana! That's just...gross. And it's not like that at all. Also, I'm trying to eat."

"You're done eating," he pointed out, "and I'm done with children, do you hear me? I am done with babies, with diapers and the mess and the toys and the potty training and the whining and—"

I held up my arms in surrender. "I assure you that there are no children in my future."

That seemed to irritate him even more. "I didn't say *ever.* Children aren't entirely without merit, you know. Some of them grow up to make passable cucumber sandwiches."

"There are no children in my *immediate* future," I amended.

"Good."

There was a new silence. This one felt really awkward, so I added, "But I swear by Allah, nothing like that is happening at all. I mean, Beans is... There is no way a girl like that would be interested in me, so you don't have to worry."

Nana didn't say anything for a moment, then held up a finger. "First, as you know, you are not supposed to swear by Allah. It is an oath not to be taken lightly."

I managed not to shake my head. For someone who wasn't a practicing Muslim, Nana had a lot of vestigial hang-ups. Oliver Wendell Holmes once said that we are all tattooed with the beliefs of our tribe as children and, try as we might, we can never be fully rid of them. My great-grandfather was proof that this was true.

"Second"—Nana raised another finger to join the first— "why do you suppose this young lady you are spending time with was named after a legume?"

Chapter Five

I wasn't nervous about going to the mall, which didn't make sense. The entire venture ought to have made me uncomfortable.

I don't find sprawling collections of stores unnerving, of course. In fact, they represent one of the great comforts of a capitalist society. If there is a chance you are willing to spend money, you'll always be welcome in malls. People will smile at you, ask how you are, make you feel like you belong, and hope to see you again soon. Basing the value of a person on money, as Hemingway once sardonically noted, simplifies the world considerably.

Of course, if people can tell you don't have much money

to spend, you get treated a little more rudely. That's one of the great curses of capitalism. If the utility of people is easily assessed, their worth often goes unconsidered.

All this is to say that I do not find shopping centers disconcerting. However, the thought of meeting a girl, on my own, in the wild—well, as wild as Sacramento gets—ought to have been at least a little frightening.

But it wasn't.

I wondered if this was partly because being around someone who was both Muslim and desi, even if my connection to those identities was tenuous, was unlike meeting a perfect stranger. It was more like being from a very small town and moving to a big city. When you come across someone from home, even if you don't really know them, you know the landmarks they know, you have encountered the trees they've encountered, and you've met the people they've loved.

So while Beans and I didn't know each other, on some level, we understood how the other had been taught to see the world. That was familiarity of a sort.

There was also the fact that Beenish was less of a girl and more of a hurricane. When I was around her, everything was so frantic that there was rarely time to feel awkward.

As soon as she saw me that day, for example, she said, "You're killing me, Arsalan."

Just like that, there was no time to search for things to say. She demanded that the world react to her. She was, in a sense, a Newtonian force.

"I haven't done anything," I told her. "I just got here."

Enunciating each word more than was necessary, she asked, "What. Are. You. Wearing?"

"My school uniform. Same as always."

I could have asked her the same question, but I probably wouldn't have gotten a satisfactory explanation for her shirt, which had a picture of a yellow rubber duck next to the letter "U."

"It's Saturday," Beenish reminded me.

"So?"

"There is no school on Saturday."

"I know," I told her. "That's why I left out the tie."

"Excuse me one second," Beans said. She walked up to the nearest wall and dramatically pretended to bash her head against it. A few people gave her curious looks. I tried to shrug and wave at them at the same time and failed at doing either.

"You can stop your one-woman play. You've made your point."

"Good," Beans said, shoving back her straight black hair, which had fallen forward onto her face. "We're going to start over, okay? This"—she gestured grandly around her as if she were an angel unveiling heaven for the first time—"is a mall. Welcome. It is a place where—"

"I know where we are, thank you."

"Where," she pressed on, "normal people buy clothes. Actually, I don't like that word—'normal'—because it doesn't really mean anything."

I understood her perfectly. "I agree. 'For there is nothing either good or bad but thinking makes it so.' That's Shakespeare, of course."

"Of course," Beenish agreed, but in a tone that made me pretty sure that she was dying to roll her eyes. "Anyway, I didn't mean 'normal.' I meant...regular, I guess?"

"Conventional?"

Her eyes brightened. "Yes. Exactly. Conventional people shop at the mall. That's a good word."

I couldn't help but smile. What do you know? Girls *do* appreciate a nice-sized vocabulary.

"If that's true, then what are we doing here?" I asked. "What is good about being conventional?" I wasn't familiar with current fashion trends, but I doubted Beans got her "funny" shirts off a rack. "You don't shop here, do you?"

"No, but that's because I'm kind of snooty about clothes."

I tsked. "I'm never snooty."

"Right," Beans said. "People who quote Shakespeare randomly are known for being down-to-earth."

"I don't know what you mean."

"Never mind. Look, I've agreed to help you hook up with a girl, and you'll have a much easier time getting a date if you don't look like you have plans to meet up with Alexander Hamilton to help draft the Declaration of Independence later."

I cleared my throat. "Actually, it was Thomas—"

"Jefferson," Beans interrupted. "I meant to say Jefferson."

"I'm sure you did," I conceded.

She narrowed her eyes at me, as if suspicious that my

magnanimity was not entirely genuine. However, she decided to move on. "Obviously, the most important thing to do is to avoid the places you buy your clothes from now." She looked at my brown blazer and khakis with the same disdain that Jane Austen had for mercenary marriages. "Where did you get that stuff anyway? Some place that sells antiques?"

"Nana doesn't care about appearances, so I just wear whatever old stuff he has lying around. My mom had a brother who died young, so..."

"So your school 'uniform' is your dead uncle's actual school uniform?"

"Yes."

"That's ridiculously sad. But then, that's you, I guess."

I frowned. "Do you really think I'm sad?"

"Arsalan...I didn't mean that. It's...You're going fishing, okay? You need good bait."

"I'm not crazy about that metaphor. It doesn't end well for the fish."

"I don't care. Let's go and find some things humans wear this century."

"I don't have any money, Beenish."

"Don't worry about it. I have a credit card that doesn't have a limit."

"Really?"

She shrugged. "It's my father's, but he doesn't ask any questions, not about money anyway. Guilty rich parents are the best parents. And since he's the reason I have to do any of this, I think it's only fair that he finance us, right?"

"Your father is the reason you're helping to set me up?"

"Um...no, obviously, that's...not important. What's important is that we're morally justified in spending his money."

I shook my head. "I don't see how that could possibly be the case."

"Ohmygod. Fine. Whatever. You can just owe me."

"I'm also not comfortable taking loans," I said. "The Bible says that the borrower is slave to the lender."

Beans raised her eyebrows. "You've read the Bible?"

"Hasn't everybody?"

"Not most Muslims," she pointed out.

"I've read the Quran too." It came out sounding defensive. Her remark felt like it had been a swipe at something that was a part of me, which I guess maybe it had been. "Nana says it is impossible to understand the Western literary canon without being familiar with both the Old and New Testaments."

"Why would you even want to understand all that stuff? The 'Western literary canon' was written by old white men for old white men, and all of them are dust. There are so many new books out now that actually speak to *us*."

"Like what?"

"I read this one recently—something something *Pretty Face*—by a desi uncle who's actually from Sacramento—"

"There are authors here?"

"Yeah? Aren't they everywhere?"

I hadn't thought about that. Every book I'd encountered

in school and in Nana's library had been written by someone who had already passed away. Somehow, in my mind, being deceased had become a prerequisite to being published.

"Anyway, we're burning daylight. Let's focus. We're going to Express first. This way."

"Wait," I said, hurrying to follow her. "What exactly are we going to express?"

Halfway to Express—which happens to be the name of a store—Beenish decided that my "makeover" had to begin with a haircut.

"It'll change your face."

This made no sense, but I suspected that arguing with her would be pointless. It would be like trying to argue with an earthquake. The end result, always, was going to be the same.

So we went to a salon, where she used her phone to pull up a picture of a model who had the kind of hairstyle I was to get. I was informed that it was a "low skin fade with a spiky side-swept fringe." Try saying that five times fast. I did, in fact, until Beans told me to stop being peculiar, though she said it with more emphasis and her word choice was not as nice.

I was also told that this look required that I put product in my hair, which wasn't something I'd ever done before. Whenever I had some hair poking out at an unfortunate angle, I'd always just used water to smooth it down. It had worked. Mostly.

By the time we were done, I'd been erased and redrawn in the image of some random person on the internet. I had to admit, somehow, my face did look different.

Beans simply said, "Wow."

At Express, she and I argued over skinny jeans. She thought they looked good. I could see no reason why any item of clothing needed to be that tight. Eventually, we compromised on a "slender fit," which was supposed to be different than a "skinny fit." I explained to the store clerk that these adjectives were virtually synonymous and, therefore, not the best way to differentiate products from each other. He didn't seem at all concerned.

"It works, man," he said.

I had to admit this appeared to be true.

We purchased a pair of sneakers, some khakis, something called Henley shirts, tees, and a couple of button-down oxfords that I was forbidden by Beenish to ever tuck in. These we got from the only banana republic in the world not in need of liberation.

I was badly in debt by the time our trip was over. I also looked like a different person.

"Dude. This is amazing. Arsalan, you're a *doll*."

"I've definitely been dressed up like one."

She laughed. "I mean you look good."

No one had ever said that to me. It took a moment to figure out how to respond. "Thank you."

"Just remember that life is easier if you aren't wearing stuff that belonged to some kid who died ages ago."

"I didn't have a choice."

"You probably did," Beans said, "but didn't fight for what you wanted. The world is rough, dude. It doesn't just give you stuff."

"Your world is rough?" I couldn't keep the amusement entirely out of my voice.

"What?" she asked defensively.

I started to tell her that she had no idea what she was talking about; that I had experienced sorrow the likes of which she probably never had; that there was cruelty in the world one could not negotiate with; that there was, at times, no fighting with destiny.

But I said none of that. The things that had made my life difficult...they weren't something I ever talked about, except—in part—with Nana.

So, instead, I tried to be funny. "You've got your dad's credit card. The world doesn't give you stuff? You can just buy what you want."

"Is that all it would take to make you happy, Arsalan?" Beenish asked. "Money?"

"No," I admitted. "I mean, I suspect not. I haven't exactly had the opportunity to experience that."

She smiled a little. "Well, it doesn't make me happy. I mean, you're right. We are more fortunate than a lot of people. We don't have to worry about how we'll get access to life's basic necessities. But that doesn't mean I have to be okay with the life I have. The pain we all suffer...it isn't a contest, right?"

"Well"—I was unable to resist pointing out, even though

I thought her point a valid one—"we are called the human *race*, so..."

Beenish shook her head. "You absolutely have to have the last word, don't you?"

"It's a hereditary condition. Anyway, what would?"

She frowned. "What?"

"You just said money doesn't bring you joy. What would?"

"Me? I don't know. I guess it'd be nice if, when someone told me they loved me, I could believe them."

I wasn't sure how to respond to that.

But Beenish Siraj, being who she was, did not give me a chance to come up with a thoughtful response. "Whatever," she said. "I don't want to talk about my mom. You're completely ruining my shopping-spree buzz. You're a real downer, you know that?"

"Yes," I admitted. "I know."

Chapter Six

"It would be very interesting to know what it is you are thinking about, Arsalan."

I looked up from my reading at Nana, who was peering at me from over his glasses. He seemed a little irritated. He'd been that way since he'd seen my new look a few days ago. He hadn't said anything about it, and neither had I, but he kept glancing my way every once in a while, clearly on the verge of making a comment of some sort.

Maybe he was no longer able to restrain himself.

This was "family time," so we were in the same room, reading separately. I wasn't allowed to do homework, though. Nana insisted I do that after he slept, which meant

I'd have to stay up late tonight to get ready for a quiz tomorrow on *Measure for Measure*. I was required, instead, to use our evenings together to improve myself, which was just another way of saying that I had to read whatever Nana picked out for me. I was in the middle of *Meditations* by Marcus Aurelius just then. He'd been a Roman emperor around 1800 years ago, when Nana had been young.

"'Everything that happens is as normal and expected as the spring rose or the summer fruit,'" I recited off the page before me. "That's what I'm thinking about."

This wasn't entirely untrue. I was thinking about how, if Emperor Aurelius had ever met Beenish Siraj, he would never have written that sentence. She seemed to be pretty much the opposite of everything the Stoic philosopher-king had believed in. Beans was proof that not everything in the world was predictable.

I hadn't asked her what she'd meant about not being able to believe that she was loved. She'd let it slip that she was speaking of her mother, but obviously it wasn't the kind of thing one pried into. Still, it had struck me as a sad thing. Despite everything that had happened in my life, I'd never had to doubt that Mom cared for me.

"You're really thinking about what you're reading? You haven't turned the page in quite some time."

"There's a lot to unpack there."

"True," Nana agreed, "but I think it is more likely that you are thinking about that Chickpea you mentioned."

"Beans," I corrected.

"Close enough. You were thinking about her, weren't you? Don't bother denying it. You've always been an abysmal liar. Despite the fact that you've spread out your feathers like a peacock, I presume you have too much sense to fall in love or any other such nonsense."

"Yes, sir," I said. That was the answer he wanted. Besides, God have mercy on whatever poor soul ended up with Beenish.

"Only pain comes from love, young man. If you live long enough, it is a lesson you too will have to learn, if you're not careful."

"Don't worry about me. Like I said yesterday, it isn't like that."

"But she does have you looking not at all like yourself. And you are distracted from the wisdom of Aurelius," he noted. "Failing to give an emperor your full attention is a dangerous business. You might as well not read his work if you're not going to give your entire mind to it."

"Well," I said, "I do have a test on Shakespeare I have to get ready for...."

"Fine," Nana said. "Go spend time with the Bard. There is worse company one can keep. But bring her to meet me, sometime, this Bean of yours."

"Why do you want to meet her? You don't like people."

"For the most part," he conceded, "I've found humans to not be worth the effort to get to know. Every once in a while, however, one finds exceptions to that rule."

"How do you know when you've found an exception?"

A small smile came to Nana's lips. "Exactly."

I wanted to roll my eyes at the one-word nonresponse, but that would've been disrespectful, so I didn't. Conversations with Nana got like that sometimes, when he started giving answers that were short and cryptic. It was especially annoying that I could never tell if this was because what he'd said made no sense or because it had been so wise that it had gone over my head.

When I'd been younger, I'd always thought that I wasn't getting what he was saying, that one day, when I was old enough, I'd understand what he meant. But now I sometimes suspected that even after living for a hundred years, Nana might be muddling his way through life as much as anyone else. Wisdom, I guess, did not keep you from stumbling. It just let you catch yourself before you fell too far and too hard.

I made my way to my room and picked up the play I was supposed to be working on. I started reading out loud, because Shakespeare demands to be read out loud. " 'Ever till now, when men were fond, I smiled and wondered how.' "

"Isn't it fun being pretty?"

I looked up to see Beenish Siraj holding a bag of pretzels that apparently constituted her lunch. While I didn't care for how they tasted, I'd always thought that the shape of pretzels was interesting. They looked like the plot of a Lorenz attractor for some values.

I considered mentioning this to her but decided not to.

My mother had always said that the things I found incredible weren't usually fascinating for other people. This was, she believed, perfectly natural. My father, for example, was fond of football. I didn't see the appeal of watching people in colorful uniforms acting like Neanderthals. It was perfectly fine, Mom had insisted, for people to be interested in different things. But life was supposedly easier if you kept your more esoteric hobbies and observations to yourself.

Then again, I'd been keeping to myself for seventeen years and I hadn't found life to be particularly easy, so perhaps she'd been wrong about that.

Beenish tapped my foot lightly with hers. "Hello?"

"Sorry?"

"I asked you if you're enjoying being pretty. A cute girl just smiled at you."

I frowned and looked around. We were at my usual lunch spot, by the lockers on the second floor. There was no one else in the area. "What girl?"

"She's gone now. And no, before you ask, I don't know her."

I hadn't been about to ask.

"But she was definitely checking you out."

I wasn't really sure what to do with this information. But I had been getting a lot of compliments since my makeover, often from people I'd thought were strangers, unaware of the fact that I even existed. I didn't hate it.

"I suppose that means your efforts to improve my appearance were a success."

"I am incredible," Beenish admitted with what I suspected was all the modesty she could manage. "What were you thinking about?"

"Edward Norton—"

She seemed confused. "The actor?"

"Edward Norton Lorenz. The meteorologist. He discovered that small changes in initial conditions can lead to dramatic alterations in long-term outcomes."

Beenish frowned. "What?"

"Chaos theory. He was the one who figured it out."

"Uh-huh. So . . . you didn't notice that blond make eyes at you because you were thinking about some scientist dude?"

Actually, I hadn't noticed whoever Beenish was talking about because I was usually pretty oblivious to my surroundings unless there was a reason not to be. However, I thought her version of events cast me in a more flattering light, so I let it stand. "He was also a mathematician. Pretzels remind me of him."

"You're hopeless. How'd you get to be this way?"

The words should have stung, but she said them without any venom.

"Most of the credit goes to my great-grandfather. You'll see when you meet him."

"When I meet him?"

I nodded. "Yes. I told him about you, and he'd like to see you. Maybe after school today, if you have time?"

She answered with a question of her own. "Why?"

"He's curious, I suppose. He also worries about me, I think, more than is—"

"No, Arsalan. Why did you tell him about me?"

"There was no reason not to. Nana knows everything about me."

"Must be nice."

I wasn't sure what she meant by that. I must have looked confused too, because she went on, "I mean, it must be nice to be known like that. To be accepted. To not be judged."

"Actually, Nana judges me all the time."

"Oh. Well, two out of three isn't bad, I guess."

"Not bad?" I asked. "That's sixty-six point six seven percent. It's a 'D.' You can't possibly think that's acceptable."

"Ugh. Fine. I'll meet your nana if you want. I'm sure he's less of an uncle than you are."

"You didn't have to open the door for me, you know. Guys don't do that anymore," Beans said as I slid into the driver's seat of my car.

"Why?"

"I don't know," she admitted. "They just don't."

It was weird that so many small acts of kindness seemed to have just stopped being customary. It was stranger still that no one could explain why.

I used to open the door for my mom. I hadn't thought about whether or not I ought to do it for Beans. I'd just done it. It was what I'd been taught.

These days Nana was my only passenger. I opened the door for him too, but that was because he had trouble getting in and out of the car by himself.

Anyway, Beans was going to be a much more distracting passenger than Nana. He didn't smell like flowers I couldn't recognize and bitter oranges. I'd have to be careful to keep my attention on the road as much as possible.

"This thing is prehistoric." Beenish ran a hand over the wood panel on the Cadillac's dash, which had been installed around three decades before either one of us had been born. "When's it from?"

"It's a sixty-nine Eldorado."

She giggled.

I looked at her out of the corner of my eye as I turned the ignition.

"What? That's funny." When I didn't answer, she cleared her throat. "Anyway, can we stop for coffee before we go to your place?"

"Of course," I said. "There's a map in the glove compartment. I just need an address for where you want to go and I'll—"

"A map?" She looked at me like people looked at Nana whenever he broke out his Old English. "You know there's an app for that, right?" Beans then spoke to what she later explained was a virtual assistant called Siri, who seemed happy to guide us toward some caffeine.

I'd never used a GPS device. Nana was scornful of the concept.

It should be required of us all to choose our own roads to the destinations we set, he always said. *Greatness is not found by following the commands of others.*

"I can't believe," Beans was saying now, "that you have to chart a fucking course like a navigator on a ship every time you have to go somewhere. Your nana needs to get with the times."

"Maybe don't say that to his face when you meet him," I said, putting the car in gear. "Also, please tone down the swearing a little. He will say that proper young ladies don't curse."

Beenish held up her middle finger to tell me exactly what she thought of that. Her words, however, were reassuring. "Will you relax? I'll do fine. I can be charming."

"Can you really?"

This time she held up both middle fingers. "Uncles are easy to deal with. It's aunties that worry me. My Aunty Deception Mode isn't always on point. Anyway, how come I'm meeting your nana and not your mom or your dad? Are your parents not okay with us dancing together? It isn't exactly kosher for Muslims."

"Halal, you mean?"

She scowled. "Yes. You don't always have to have the right word for everything."

"True. But it's nice when you do." When she didn't answer, I added, "You don't have to worry about my parents."

"They're cool?"

65

"My father is—"

"Turn left," a disembodied voice with a mechanical twang instructed sternly. "Then stay in the right lane."

"Rude," I muttered, which earned me a wry smile from Beenish. I was, however, glad for the interruption. It gave me time to come up with something true I could say about Zeeshan Nizami. You don't just say *My father is an alcoholic who used to beat me.* That's too personal. "My dad is...not cool. But it doesn't matter. He's in Arizona."

"Is he on a business trip or something?"

I shook my head. "He lives there."

Understanding—misunderstanding, really—dawned on her face. "Oh. Your parents are separated."

"They are separated," I confirmed.

"Is your mom going to be home?"

"Most definitely not. She's..." As much as I didn't like talking about it, there was no way to avoid telling her about Mom. Muneera Nizami's absence would almost certainly come up when Beans met Nana. One can only dodge death for so long. "She passed away."

"Arsalan, dude, I'm so, so sorry."

I didn't have to glance in Beenish's direction to know how her eyes looked just then. I could hear their intense earnestness. I kept my hands on the wheel, my attention on the road, and my voice steady.

"It was a car accident a few years ago. I live with my great-grandfather, my mom's dad's dad." After Beenish's phone instructed me to merge onto the freeway, I tried to brighten my tone and, by extension, the conversation. "Anyway, he won't have a problem with us being alone or dancing together. He isn't all that religious. He doesn't believe in any kind of GPS."

"What?"

"Religion is just a navigation system for your soul, right? Nana, as you've seen, still makes me use maps."

"That's...a take."

"What about your family? Obviously, Ms. Siraj is okay with all this."

Beans snorted. "My sister isn't okay with it. She's like... resigned to it. Qirat is pretty religious. She prays regularly and everything. But she doesn't try to force me to practice like she practices. She doesn't have any high horses."

I nodded.

"I think she also feels bad that I won't ever be allowed to become a dancer. Professionally, I mean. My father is a born-again Muslim, so he's pretty serious about it, and Roshni wears her Islam like a fancy dress."

"What does that mean?"

Beans shrugged. "She wants other people to see it, because displaying it makes her feel good, but she can take it off when she wants."

I winced involuntarily at the bite in what she'd said.

"Not to be harsh or anything," she added.

"Right. Wouldn't want that," I agreed. When Beenish grinned, I asked, "What about your mother?"

Beans rolled her eyes. "Dancing is the one thing she

agrees with the rest of the family on. She was a dancer, and she says it isn't necessarily an easy life for a desi, Muslim girl, especially one from a conservative family. My mom doesn't want me to end up being just another version of her."

"Your mother was a dancer?"

"You may have heard of her. Aiza Begum?"

I shook my head.

"She was a big deal for a while in Lollywood—"

"Lollywhat?"

"It's Pakistan's version of Bollywood, which I guess is India's version of Hollywood."

"I see why Nana says originality in the arts is dead."

"Anyway, my mom made sure we were classically trained, Qirat and I. My sister never cared for it. I did. I do, I mean. It's just..."

"It isn't an easy life for a desi, Muslim girl," I repeated.

Beans flailed her arms around dramatically. *"What will people say? Who will marry you? What will Allah say? You're going to burn in hell forever because you twirled around in front of people."*

"Your family doesn't think God's heard of a proportional response?"

Beans frowned. "What? You know, you randomly say really weird stuff."

"I'm...still getting used to talking."

"Talking?"

Talking differently to different kinds of people is what I meant. These first weeks in high school had taught me that

68

I couldn't speak to everyone like I spoke to Nana. It made them think I was showing off how smart I was or being superior. It was best to sound "normal," which was proving to be an acquired skill.

"Yes," I answered simply. When Beans seemed unsatisfied, I added, "My inner dork comes out every once in a while."

"I get it. You're like the Hulk, except with a thesaurus."

I didn't get the reference but didn't bother telling her that. The sooner I could get this conversation to not focus on me, I figured, the better. "So your family—aside from Ms. Siraj—doesn't know about this dance contest you want to enter?"

She hesitated. "You don't have to worry about them. Anyway, listen, we've still got some practical details to work out."

"Like what?"

"Like where we're going to practice. We can't do it at my dad's place or my mom's. It's not like we're going to start dancing in public. Do you think your nana would be okay with us using his garage?"

I shook my head. "It's full of junk. It has been since I can remember."

"If it's junk," she countered, "then we can just move it for him."

"Nana will never allow it. He is fond of keeping things just the way they are."

Beans interlaced her fingers and stretched her arms in

front of her. "Well, we'll just see about that. Like you said before, Arsalan, I am undeniable."

After Beenish picked up her coffee, the navigation system directed me home. The closer it said we were to our destination, the more uncertain I felt. "This may not go well. He can be a little ornery sometimes. Most times, actually."

"Will you relax?" she asked. "People who don't know me love me. They think I'm super sweet."

"When you're really a little sour all the time."

"I'm sweet and sour," she countered. "I'm a hot pot full of incredibly complex flavors."

"Crackpot is more like it," I muttered under my breath as I pulled into Nana's driveway.

"What was that?"

"Nothing."

Beenish took a moment to glower at me before stepping out. She closed the passenger-side door and began examining her own reflection in the car window. After that, she ran a hand through her hair, pasted a sugary smile on her face, then nodded approvingly. "Aunty Deception Mode engaged."

"There are no aunties here," I reminded her.

"It works on uncles just fine. Now let's go. I can only keep it up for like ten minutes at a time."

I'd never had any guests of my own over before. No friends and certainly no girls...not that Beenish was a girl, exactly. I mean, she was, obviously, but I never noticed.

Okay, sometimes I noticed, but rarely. The point is that if she ever even suspected I was looking at her, she'd make my life into a production of *King Lear* with her as Cornwall, plucking out my eyes. The physical traits of Beenish Siraj were a subject best not to dwell upon.

"Dude? Are we doing this?"

"Yes," I said, walking toward the front door, where I was struck by the realization that I hadn't really looked at Nana's place in a long time. Having Beans with me somehow made me notice it again.

The house was very old but well cared for. The front lawn was freshly cut, and the bright purple chrysanthemums I'd recently planted were in bloom. They were the last flowers of the season, before everything stopped growing and leaves began to fall in earnest. I had decided to plant them because it was what Mom used to do every year. It had been a sad thing, but seeing them now, I was suddenly happy to have done it.

The old wood floor creaked as we walked in. Beenish looked around, her gaze drifting from the worn midcentury furniture to the overflowing bookshelves on almost every wall. It was a warm home that, in an emergency, could double as a library.

"This is nothing like where I live," she said.

"Is that a bad thing?"

Still looking around, she shook her head.

When we got to the living room, Beans seemed confused. After a moment, she asked, "You guys don't have a TV? That's weird. How do you decide which way to face when you're sitting? It's like going to a mosque where no one knows what direction Mecca is."

"Actually, we do have a TV. It's in the guest room. Nana watches his tapes there."

"Tapes?"

"Videocassettes."

"That is so old school. What's the newest movie you've watched?"

I hesitated, not sure if I wanted her to know.

Beans grinned. "Why are you embarrassed? Was it like porn from the fifties? Did you like it? You can tell me. No judgment. Well, a little judgment but—"

"*No!* Nothing like that. It was *Star Trek*, okay? And I did like it. I just didn't want you to make fun of me because it isn't 'cool' or whatever."

"Which one was it?"

"It was *Star Trek*. Wait. There's more than one?"

"Oh, Arsalan, dude, I'm gonna rock your world. I'm going to blow you—"

"Ahem." Nana, having appeared behind Beenish from his study, cleared his throat.

Beans jumped, then scrambled to add, "…away. I was just telling him I was going to blow him away. Not…you know, obviously…"

Nana raised one of his bushy eyebrows at me. I shrugged. I was not about to start explaining this person to him. It was an impossible task.

With his cane, Nana pointed at our guest. "There is an intruder in this house, my boy, wreaking havoc on my solitude."

"This is Beenish Siraj," I told him. "You said you wanted to meet her."

"Ah. Ms. Siraj. Whether or not you manage to blow Arsalan remains to be seen—"

"Away," Beans repeated. "Seriously. Every time you say that, you really need to add 'away.' It's totally critical."

Nana looked at me for confirmation. I nodded. "It is how people talk now."

He seemed unimpressed with this intelligence. "Well, young lady, you have already blown me away. You've transformed my little caterpillar into a butterfly."

Beans gave him a winning smile. "He looks great, right?"

Nana harrumphed. "Did you consider that you were moving his life cycle along by doing so? When a caterpillar transforms and goes out into the world, is it not moving closer to its own death?"

"I guess. Every bug has got to die, though. Not every bug gets to fly around and be pretty."

That answer seemed to surprise Nana. He grumbled incoherently, causing Beenish to look at me, concerned. I tried to wink at her because I knew this was his way of admitting he'd been bested in an exchange.

"Come and sit," Nana said, ambling toward his favorite chair. "I wanted to meet you because this boy of mine is rarely distracted from his books. You, however, have managed it."

It was Beenish's turn to look at me and raise her eyebrows. If everyone could just stop doing that forever, that'd be just fine.

"I would like to know what your intentions are toward my grandchild."

"She doesn't have 'intentions,' Nana," I said. "We're just..." What? Friends? I wasn't sure if that was true. I definitely didn't want to say it out loud, in case Beenish contradicted me. "We're dance partners."

Nana's expression at that moment was a perfect illustration of the word "flummoxed."

I waited for Beans to tell Nana about the dance contest she wanted to enter, but for some reason, she stayed quiet. I was left to explain. "There is a competition, and Beenish needs a partner for it."

"Why Arsalan?" Nana demanded of her. "Surely you have other friends."

"Diamond volunteered, but—"

"Diamond volunteered?" I asked, frowning. Why hadn't Beenish taken him up on his offer? Now that I thought about it, I'd asked her exactly that before. She hadn't answered.

"Who?" Nana asked.

"Diamond Khan," she told him. "He's...a family friend."

Nana made a face. "Children these days have such strange names. Diamond indeed. You didn't want to dance with this sparkling family friend of yours?"

"He talks about himself in the third person most of the time."

"We simply can't have that," Nana said, glancing at me sideways. "Aren't you valiant for rescuing Ms. Siraj from having to spend time with someone that noxious."

"Also," Beans added, "he knows my stepmother, Roshni, and my family does not approve of me dancing, so..."

"For religious or cultural reasons?"

She shrugged. "Does it matter? Both, I guess. Besides, the way Arsalan moves, I think he has the potential to be good."

My great-grandfather snorted. "He moves like a baby deer learning to walk."

"There's a lot of grace there," she countered. "It waits for practice before showing itself."

That earned her a smile. "You have an answer for everything, don't you?"

"I try."

"Very well. You may dance with Arsalan, if only because I believe that dancers ought to have the freedom to dance and singers to sing and painters to paint. 'Religion,'" he said like a spiteful wine critic holding a glass to the light, "is a word that comes from Latin."

I groaned.

"Its root is in *religare*, which means 'to tie up and bind.' I haven't ever subscribed to that way of thinking. I've always believed people should be free to make their own choices, right or wrong, as long as they don't hurt anyone." He fixed Beans with an intense look. "You're not going to hurt anyone, are you, Ms. Siraj?"

She shook her head solemnly. "We're just going to dance and rebel against the patriarchy."

"Ah, well, a long time ago I might have approved of that

second bit. However, I find I've now become something of a patriarch myself. Though I'm not oppressing anyone."

Beenish looked at me as if she expected me to say something to that. When I didn't, she sighed, and said, "There's just one more thing...."

I got dinner together after Beenish left. Somehow she'd managed to convince Nana to let us use his garage as a practice space. Actually, "convince" is overstating it a little. She'd just asked, very nicely, in a tone coated with caramel, if it would be okay. Nana, who never approved of any changes, had simply said yes, on two conditions:

First, we had to be careful with any boxes we moved out of the garage.

Second, we weren't to open them.

He had, in other words, actually agreed—basically without protest—to change something about the house just because she'd asked. I slammed the lid down on the salan I'd made and a metallic clang sounded through the house like a bell. It was unclear what salan it was or what it was supposed to taste like. But it was edible. Probably.

"You're scowling, Arsalan," Nana said, limping into the kitchen. He was leaning on his cane more heavily than usual. "Is something wrong? I thought the visit with Ms. Siraj went rather well."

There was no reason for me to be irritated with Nana.

If anything, I ought to have been happy that he'd agreed to Beenish's request.

But it had been *her* request. Nana never did anything *I* wanted to do. Last winter, I'd tried to get him to buy a space heater for his room because he complained it was always cold. He'd answered by saying that, as much as possible, things should remain how they were.

He'd said the same thing when I'd suggested we get a microwave, a computer, and an internet connection. He made me use fountain pens because they were more cultured than ballpoints. No one at school even knew what fountain pens were. Pulling out an inkpot in the middle of classes definitely drew stares.

No wish of mine, no matter how reasonable, was to be granted, apparently, but Beenish Siraj waltzes in and asks him for his garage, and he just says yes? The last time I'd asked about the boxes in there, he'd snapped, "They are ghosts and ought not to be disturbed."

"I asked you a question," Nana said. "You haven't responded. What's the matter?"

"Nothing," I muttered. "I'm fine."

"Sullen and churlish. You are being a real teenager right now, young man. You know that is not something I appreciate."

I threw my hands halfway up in the air before letting them drop. I didn't know what to say. Beenish, I think, would have told Nana exactly how she felt. She knew how to roar.

I didn't.

There had been times in my life when I'd talked back. I remembered my father slapping me across the face. I remembered how he used to threaten me if I raised my voice to him. I remembered the bite of his belt against the skin on my back, which had bled rebellion out of me entirely.

Well...no, not entirely. My heart was still defiant, even if it could no longer find the words it needed to tell the world so.

"Surely you can do more than shrug at me," Nana pressed. "You are more articulate than that."

"Let it go," I told him.

"*You* let it go," my great-grandfather insisted. "Say what you want to say."

I ran my hands through my hair. Did he want us to fight? Why? Maybe he just wanted an argument. He got like that sometimes. "It's nothing," I said. My voice was so tired all of a sudden that it actually surprised me. "I'm just being stupid."

Nana gave me an appraising look, then shrugged. "Very well. May I suggest you don't make a habit of it?"

"I'll get you a plate," I said as he made his way to the table. When I turned away from him, however, the dam of my common sense broke a little, and before I could stop myself, I spoke. "You would've said no if I'd asked to use the garage to practice dancing, right? You would have said no if Beenish weren't involved."

"If she weren't involved, would you have even wanted to dance?"

78

"That's not the point. I…" I inhaled deeply, then slowly exhaled. "You know what? It's not important."

There was a heavy silence, interrupted only by the sound of a spoon moving against the salan pot as I dished out Nana's food. After a few minutes, he said, "I like your haircut."

"No, you don't."

"I really don't," he admitted with a smile, "even though it does look good. I was used to the way you had it before, and you know how I feel about change."

"Yes," I said. "I know all about that."

Chapter Seven

Beans showed up at Nana's home the next day wearing a blue sweatshirt that had a closed skeletal fist on it, with the zipper acting as the extended middle finger.

I sighed as I let her in. "Really? You made such a good impression on Nana yesterday. He's not going to like that"—I waved in the general direction of her torso—"if he knows what it means. I'm not sure he does."

"Relax," she said. "I'm going to take it off."

As she did what she'd said, I saw that she was wearing a simple white tank top to match her tights. I couldn't help but notice the goose bumps on the skin of her bare shoulders and the steady rise and fall of her...

I cleared my throat and directed my attention up to her face. She was looking directly at me. Had she realized what had caught my attention? She had. I was sure of it. My life, such as it had been, flashed before my eyes. I stepped back a little without meaning to, surprised at how completely unprepared I was to meet my maker.

"Better?" Beans asked mildly instead of laying into me.

"What? Me? Oh. You mean your outfit. Yes. It's great. I mean, it's fine. Absolutely."

"Good. So, let's get moving? If we get the boxes out quickly, we might even get a practice session in."

"That's...optimistic," I said, both relieved and confused that I'd been spared the mortification I'd had coming to me. I gestured for Beenish to follow and led her through the house.

"Your nana isn't here?"

"He's always here. But he's taking a nap, I think." Knowing how much Nana hated company, it was equally likely that even though he seemed to like Beenish fine, he was curled up in bed with a book, with no intention of coming out to be hospitable. She didn't need to know that, however.

At the door to the garage, I intoned, " 'All hope abandon, ye who enter here.' "

She frowned. "What?"

"It's from *The Divine Comedy*—"

"Okay. You read," she said, reaching past me to open the door herself. "I get it. Stop showing off for—holy shit!"

It was pretty much the only way to react. We were standing before an Everest of cardboard. Boxes were piled up to the garage's ceiling, with barely enough room for two people to move.

"What is all this stuff?"

"I don't know. Nana has always said not to touch it."

Beenish looked at me like I was a newly discovered alien life-form. "And you just listened?"

"Of course," I said.

"So you've been ignoring a mystery that's right under your nose for what? A couple of years?"

I nodded. In truth, the prohibition keeping me away from the garage had been in place since I was a child, and most of my days had been spent at Nana's home. Mom had to work, and he'd always been available to watch me. But I wasn't sure Beenish Siraj would believe anyone could follow a rule for that long.

"I moved in two years ago," I explained, "after my mother passed."

She still seemed amazed by my restraint in not exploring the garage. "We're lucky Allah didn't make you first instead of Adam, otherwise humanity would've never left the Garden."

I chuckled. "Wouldn't that have been a good thing?"

"I don't know," Beans said, stepping into the garage. "I mostly like my life. Don't you?"

There wasn't enough room to stand too far behind her. Even before my bare feet touched the cool concrete floor, I could smell bitter oranges again. I noticed also that she had her own climate. It was definitely warmer around her than anywhere else. "It's okay," I answered. "Some days are better than others."

Beenish clapped her hands together. "All right. Let's get to work. Laser focus, Arsalan. It'll go by fast if we don't get distracted."

"Easy for you to say," I muttered, still mustering the will to ignore our proximity.

"What?"

I shook my head. "Nothing. Let's get started, yes?"

Beenish got distracted first. We'd managed to move about five or so cartons to the study when a pile of newspapers caught her attention.

"Wow, 1973? You guys don't recycle, huh?"

"Nana likes to read old newspapers. I guess this is where he keeps them. There are tons more tucked around the house."

She blinked. "He likes to do what?"

"Read old newspapers."

"You say that like it's normal. It's super strange, dude. I don't know anyone who does that."

I shrugged. "How many people do you know who are a hundred years old?"

"Okay, fair, but what's the point? He could read the latest news. Why doesn't he?"

"I've never thought to ask."

Beans shook her head. "I don't get you. Honest."

83

"When you only have one person in your life," I told her, "you accept them as they are. You don't ask questions. You can't afford to upset them."

I regretted the words as soon as they were out of my mouth. They revealed more about me than I usually cared to show the world. I wasn't at all prepared for questions probing that sentiment. Thankfully, Beenish didn't launch into an excavation of my soul. She just lightly touched my arm, offered a quick smile, and said, "Makes sense. Hey. Is this one labeled with someone's name?" She gestured to Nana's ugly, barely legible scrawl on the box closest to her. "Who's Rayyan?"

"My uncle. Rayyan Haq. It's his uniform that I used to wear."

"That box says 'Salma.' This one says 'Tareef.' 'Nadeem.' This is all—"

"It's all family," I said. "My grandmother and grandfather and—"

"Your nana has lost a lot of people."

"I guess if you live long enough, that's what happens."

Beenish frowned. "That's terrible. Makes you wonder if it's worth it. A long life."

"You were just telling me you were glad Adam sinned because you like your life."

"I'm not sure if I'd like being the only one left, you know?"

"He's not the only one left," I reminded her.

She inclined her head to acknowledge that I was right. "He's lucky to have you."

I didn't know what to say to that. I'd always thought I was the lucky one, that I was the one who needed Nana. It had never occurred to me that the opposite might also be true.

"Hey," Beenish asked softly after a short pause. "What was your mom's name?"

"Muneera," I said, now very interested in the labels on the boxes myself. "Did you see it?"

She shook her head. "I'll let you know when I do."

Over the next two hours, we cleared out a decent amount of space in the garage, though we didn't find any boxes with my mother's name on them. That didn't make any sense. Being the most recent one to leave us, her things ought to have been near the front.

Was it possible Nana had kept nothing of hers? He was a compulsive hoarder. I wanted to ask him, but given that we weren't supposed to open the boxes, it would've been an extremely suspicious inquiry.

"Let's stop for a bit," Beans suggested.

"Tired already?" I gasped.

She gave me a dry look. She seemed fine. I was the one who was breathing hard and sweating and, though she couldn't know this, feeling like my arms were made of fire.

"Maybe get some water before you faint and I have to give you mouth-to-mouth."

My eyebrows rose pretty much on their own at that image.

"Ugh. Boys. Just go, will you?"

Nana was sitting in the kitchen reading *The Epic of Gilgamesh*.

"Hilarious," I told him.

He looked pleased I'd gotten this "joke." In his quest for immortality, Gilgamesh had been forced to travel to the land of the dead. Spending time in our garage, Nana was saying without using any words, was my equivalent of Gilgamesh's journey. It was the kind of parallel Nana found unjustifiably amusing. He'd be chuckling to himself about it for a month.

"I see you are feeling better about the world than you did last night," Nana said as I went looking for clean water glasses.

"Sorry about that. I was just... having a moment."

"That much was evident." He paused, then added, "You know, it is acceptable to speak up when something is bothering you. One of the lessons in *Gilgamesh*, you'll remember, is that phantoms diminish for one, when two speak of them."

By now, I'd discovered there were no clean glasses around and started washing some. "I don't have time to discuss ancient Mesopotamian poetry with you. Beans is waiting."

"Are you making progress on—is that music?"

It definitely was. I couldn't identify it because Nana believed anything that hadn't originally come out on vinyl wasn't worth listening to. Nevertheless, he got to his feet as

I quickly dried my hands and we moved toward the garage. When Nana opened the door, I saw Beenish Siraj dancing for the first time.

I'd never seen anything like it. The music around her was soft and melodious and thoughtful, before it unexpectedly sped up and jumped; and somehow, impossibly, Beans leapt with it, became one with it, absorbing the grace of the notes and letting the sound flow through her.

As the pace of the music continued to rise, she twirled faster and faster, arms held high, fingers linked, balancing on her toes, in some strange mix between ballerina and whirling dervish, until I was sure that either her ankles would fail or she would trip over herself, but that didn't happen. Everything about her movements was certain and precise and so completely confident that it seemed like God himself was holding her hand.

Nana reached over and pushed up on my chin, closing my jaw for me.

When the song ended, there was a moment when it felt like there was no sound in the world, except for Beenish's hard breathing.

Then, tucking his cane under his arm, Nana started to clap loudly, and the spell was broken.

"Bravo. Truly marvelous, Ms. Siraj," he cheered. "Beautifully done."

Beans's eyes shone with the joy of her own brilliance.

"That...that was incredible," I managed to add. "It was the best thing I've ever seen in my life."

"Thanks," she said with a grin, obviously pleased, but she also looked away.

A moment passed. Then another. Then another.

"I'm not used to giving compliments," I finally admitted. "What happens now?"

"Now," Beenish said, "we get to work."

Work, on that first day, was just Beans showing me videos of shirtless men.

After Nana went back to his room, she made me sit next to her on the garage floor and watch music videos of Bollywood actors like Tiger Shroff, Hrithik Roshan, and Varun Dhawan kick and prance their way across colorful sets, lip-syncing to lyrics in what appeared to be Indian cinema's version of the internal monologue.

"I can't move like that."

"You will," Beans assured me. "It's not that hard."

I snorted.

"Fine. So it's actually really difficult," she admitted. "But, as a dancing instructor once told me, faith is belief in the absence of certainty. And I have faith in you."

"I'd take that as a compliment," I said, "but neither you nor I appear to be very good at faith."

"That's not true," Beenish said. "We suck at *religion*. Faith is different."

I had to concede that was true.

"Any questions about what you've seen so far?"

"Yes. Why does Bollywood hate clothes? They appear to have some kind of vendetta against sleeves, when the performers are even allowed shirts."

She laughed. "Well…I mean, look at the actors. They've got to show off their guns. Can you imagine how much they have to work out to look that fit? It'd be unfair to cover it all up."

"If you say so. Will I also need to dance without a shirt?"

Beans looked me up and down and raised her eyebrows in a manner that wasn't very flattering. "Um…no. That's not necessary."

Understandable. My reed-thin form did not have much in common with the bodies of these actors. Still, she didn't have to react like I'd said something ridiculous.

"Good," I said coolly. "I've got no desire to parade around like that. It's not dignified."

"No one cares about that anymore. It's out of fashion. There are more important things in the world."

"Like what?"

"I'm sorry, did you not see Tiger Shroff's abs?"

I rolled my eyes.

Beans nudged me with her shoulder. "Come on. The actresses don't have much on either."

"I didn't notice, I'm sure," I said…well, lied, to be honest.

"Right." Her voice dripped with disbelief.

"So," I said, deciding to change the subject, "how does this contest work? When is it? Are there multiple rounds?"

"It's on Christmas Eve. We've got months," Beans told me. "We're just going to do one song. That's your only concern. I'll figure everything else out."

"Have you decided what song to use?"

She shook her head. "No. But I was thinking of doing something that'll really catch people's attention. I'm thinking it has to be an item number."

"What is an 'item number'?"

"It's Bollywood speak for like...It's a performance that focuses on the looks and body of the performer. They're typically a little more...um...suggestive than other songs."

"Oh," I said. "Look, Beenish, I'm not sure that I feel comfortable being objectified in such a manner."

She started to laugh.

"What?"

Beans coughed, then cleared her throat. "I'd be the 'item.' Not you."

"That...makes more sense."

She nodded her agreement before hurrying to add, "Not that you wouldn't make a perfectly good 'item.'"

"Your derisive laughter notwithstanding," I muttered.

"I wish there was a way to set you up with some girl who writes SAT questions. She would love you."

I decided to ignore her comment. "Are these videos why you want me to work out with Diamond? So I'll look more like the actors when we do our dance?"

"You're not going to look like them in four months. Or

ever, probably. But it'll help for you to be in shape because our practices are going to get intense. Also, it'll make girls more interested in you."

Her logic there was impeccable. I did, however, have one concern. "When you say practices are going to be intense—"

"I mean you're going to be in some…discomfort. Dance, like love, hurts."

"That doesn't sound like fun. I don't much care for pain."

She grinned. "Don't worry, Arsalan. You'll learn to like it."

After another couple of hours, we'd made more than enough room for dance practice in Nana's garage. We hadn't had to move everything out, but we'd checked every box for my mother's belongings. They weren't there.

"You okay?" Beans asked.

"I'm fine."

Beans narrowed her eyes. "Are you?"

I shrugged and walked her back through the house to the front door. She had to head home. Something about a test in US Government and Politics. Why someone would take that class, I'd never understand. It was the worst science. "Yes. I hadn't even thought about where Mom's things went before. I didn't realize they might still be around. Therefore, getting upset over not finding them now isn't logical. Right?"

"I guess so," she answered. "But if it does upset you—"

"It doesn't."

"But if it did, you could always ask your nana what happened to them."

I shook my head. "Remember his rules for use of the garage? We aren't allowed to open any of the boxes. Where any of them are should make no difference to us."

"Whatever." Beans started putting on her sweatshirt. "Everyone knows rules are like hearts and promises. They're made to be broken."

That made me smile. "I'm not sure that makes sense."

"Not everything has to." Beenish's tone was light and airy, though her words turned grave. "I'm starting to think that's your real problem. It's not the awful clothes, or the weird words, or the complete lack of muscle tone. It's that you use this"—she stood on tiptoe and jabbed her index finger at my forehead—"too much. You're trapped in your own brain."

I wondered, for a moment, if that ought to have hurt me. It wasn't something people just did, point out that you had issues, but there was no sting, no malice, in what Beans had said.

Was this what it was like to have a friend?

"You know," I told her, "Descartes said, 'Cogito, ergo sum.' It means—"

"I know what it means."

I crossed my arms in a manner that challenged her to show off her Latin.

"It means you're fucking hopeless," Beenish said dryly, no trace of humor on her face.

I stared at her until her deadpan expression finally cracked, and she began to laugh, which for some reason made me laugh too.

I hadn't done that for so long, it was a miracle I remembered how.

Chapter Eight

I went looking for Diamond Khan during lunch at school the next day, only to find out that he, along with the MSA—the Muslim Students' Association—had organized a bake sale.

This was less than ideal. I felt a little out of place around religious people. They had a tendency to think I was one of them, and then they were either surprised or disappointed to learn I wasn't. They didn't have the best poker faces either— which I suppose made sense since gambling is forbidden in Islam—so things tended to get awkward pretty fast.

I decided I would wait until the end of the lunch break to approach Diamond. If I stood behind a wall, just out of sight of the MSA membership, I could catch him on his way to class. Feeling a bit like James Bond—though I didn't have any of Sean Connery's charisma—I checked my watch. There were only fifteen minutes left before the bell—

"Brother Niz!"

I jumped at being unexpectedly discovered, and by the very person I was hiding from, no less. My spy craft definitely needed work.

Before I could tell Diamond why I'd come to find him—that I did, in fact, want his help working out—he grabbed me by the arm and began introducing me to Sister This and Brother That and Sister Her and Brother Him, all related to me, I suppose, by being the children of Eve and Adam.

Diamond seemed to fit in perfectly, and it appeared that everyone liked him. At least, until he caught himself about to introduce me to "Sister Beans."

His cheer frosted over under her cold gaze. He cleared his throat uncomfortably. "Obviously, you already know each other."

Beenish ignored him completely and turned her attention to me. "What are you doing here, 'brother'?"

"I *really* would rather you not call me that," I said. "But to answer your question, I came here to find Diamond. To get him to help me work out."

"Okay. But don't become like him and go overboard. Remember that you'll get to keep your shirt on."

"Whoa." Diamond seemed as shocked as Edison must

have been when he finally got a light bulb to work. "Wait. Who has been taking their shirt off? What's going on with you two exactly?" Then he looked around, as if remembering where he was, and added more quietly, "Never mind. You can explain later."

"Or," Beans suggested, "we could not. Seeing as how it is none of your business."

He actually looked a little pained at that. "But we're friends."

She didn't reply, which was both cruel and merciful at the same time, I suppose. I'd certainly been under the impression that they were friends. She had, after all, asked Diamond for a favor on my behalf. Apparently, their relationship was more complex than I'd thought.

"Beenish," he said urgently and with evident concern, "your reputation, bro. You've got to worry about what people think of your character."

She answered him with not one but two flipped birds, drawing a few gasps from people around us who noticed. I doubted very much that this was a common gesture at MSA fundraisers.

Diamond, for his part, just shook his head in response.

"I'll see you later, Arsalan." Beenish paused, then nodded toward Diamond. "Betty Crocker."

I stood where I was for a moment, with Diamond beside me, watching her walk away. "What was that about?"

"Niz, don't even worry about it. It's a long story." Then he took a deep breath, forced a smile onto his face, and suddenly seemed genuinely cheerful again. Was that possible? Could someone just will themselves to be happy?

If not, he was better at lying to himself than I was, because he seemed to be in exactly the same mood as before he'd encountered Beenish.

Diamond grabbed my arm and pulled me away from Beenish's retreating back like I was a dog on a leash. "Welcome to our bake sale. Want to try a brownie?"

"I'm fine," I told him, shaking my head at the table of food he was steering me toward.

"They're delicious and they're Diamond Standard."

"You're saying you made them?"

He grinned. "Yeah, bro. They're Diamond's specialty. Diamond is basically a professional baker. You just have to follow the instructions on the box the mix comes in and they turn out great every time."

"I'm good, really. Thank you."

"Are you sure? They're special brownies."

I knew I was naive, but I wasn't *that* naive. I'd heard of "special brownies" before. Lowering my voice, I leaned closer to him. "You brought marijuana to school?"

He chuckled. "No, of course not. I just read Surah Fatiha over them. Nothing will get you as high as prayer, right?" When I didn't laugh, he added, "It's funny because of the levels of heaven—"

Prayer! I'd completely forgotten about the fact that, it being a Friday, there would be a congregation starting any minute now.

"I get it. Listen, Diamond, I have to run before—I just have to run." I was many things, but a hypocrite I was not. I didn't usually pray, and I didn't like the idea of praying just because the people I happened to be around expected me to. That would mean that I'd be praying for their sake, which didn't sit well with me.

"You don't have to go running after Beans, Niz."

"I'm not. I just...I just wanted to tell you that I actually could use some pointers on how to work out. If you're willing."

"Sure, bro," he said. "Diamond would be happy to help out."

"Great. If you give me your phone number, I'll call to see when you're free? I didn't want to miss you today and then not be able to reach you all weekend."

Diamond frowned. "Don't you have Beenish's digits? Couldn't you have asked her for my cell?"

I opened my mouth to respond, then closed it. That was a fairly obvious solution. I could have avoided a lot of MSA-related anxiety if I'd thought things through.

After giving me his phone number, Diamond said, "Come on. We're going to start Jummah prayer soon."

I shook my head. "No. That's okay. I can't. I...well... I...really have to go to the bathroom. And it's going to be a long, long while, so..."

He wrinkled his nose. "Okay. Well, good luck, brother. Sounds like you're going to need it."

Ms. Qirat Siraj was nibbling on the last bits of a brownie when I got to her physics class. She waved at me a little. That was new. Now that we were connected by Beenish's dance contest, perhaps we were closer to being acquaintances than before. I was surprised enough by this emerging familiarity that my wave back felt ridiculously late. She didn't seem to think anything of it, though.

"All right, guys," Ms. Siraj said, polishing off her snack and getting to her feet. "I'm going to hand out the extra credit assignment I talked about last week. Remember that you are doing a thought experiment. This means that you don't look for the answer on Google or in the library. Don't talk to anyone about it. I trust you all."

I looked around at the thirty or so other students in the room. That was a lot of people to trust. There was no way everyone would prove worthy of it. As Nana always said, *A portion of every human you encounter is fecal matter. Expect them to behave accordingly and you'll rarely be disappointed.*

"Just to make things interesting," she added, "I've made sure none of the questions are the same, so please don't copy off each other. This is voluntary. Either do it right or don't do it at all."

As she walked past, Ms. Siraj handed me a sheet of paper with a single line on it. I took it and read the question posed to me: "Why is the world round?"

I frowned.

I'd never thought about that. It was simply a fact I'd learned long ago. It hadn't occurred to me that there might be a reason behind it.

Of course, what I had learned was that the world wasn't round. Not really. Was that the answer? Could it really be that simple?

I stayed behind after class to find out.

"Can I reject the premise of your question?" I asked Ms. Siraj, holding up the assignment so she could read it.

"Probably not. Tell me my newest star student doesn't believe in the flat Earth theory?"

"There is a flat Earth theory?"

"Yeah," she said, "They have conferences and everything. Anyway, you're not saying the Earth isn't round?"

"I am saying that, actually," I told her. "I don't remember the name for the shape of the world, but it isn't a perfect sphere. It's flat at the poles and is distorted at the equator. So the question—"

"—is poorly worded," she admitted with a wry smile. "Give me a second." Ms. Siraj grabbed her phone from her purse, typed something in, then took my question sheet. She wrote something on it and handed it back to me.

It now read: "Why is the world an oblate spheroid?"

"Happy?" she asked.

"Not really. I was hoping it was a trick question and I'd stumbled upon the answer."

"You'll figure it out," she assured me. "I have faith in you."

I sighed. "People have been saying that to me a lot lately. Being believed in is not comfortable. Makes you wonder why God likes it so much."

"Beans?"

I nodded.

"Don't let her boss you around too much. She's—"

"A steam engine running on rocket fuel?"

Ms. Siraj chuckled. "Sure. But I hope you guys are becoming friends."

"Because I could use friends?"

"She could too. Beenish..." She exhaled, thought about what she was going to say, then went on. "Beans doesn't let a lot of people in. She's friendly with everyone, but she really only has one friend, and that relationship is about to change a bit."

"What do you mean?" I asked.

Ms. Siraj glanced at the door, then back at me. Quietly, she said, "It isn't widely known yet, so don't tell the other kids, but this will be my last semester at Tennyson. I'm getting married and moving out of California."

"That's awful," I said, then realized my reaction wasn't exactly how her announcement ought to be received. "Sorry. I just meant it's terrible for us. You're a great teacher."

She seemed genuinely pleased to hear that. "Thank you, Arsalan."

"But congratulations are in order."

"I suppose. Anyway, Beans is pretty upset. I keep telling her to look on the bright side. Come Christmas Eve, she won't have to share a room with me anymore."

Something about what Ms. Siraj had said didn't fit with what I already knew. It took me a second to figure it out. I must have looked confused, because she added, "You haven't seen our place, have you? She knows better than to bring boys there. But yes, obviously, we don't *have* to share a room—"

"No. I'm sorry. When did you say you were getting married?"

"Christmas Eve. Why? What's wrong?"

Beenish had said the dance contest she wanted to take part in was happening on Christmas Eve. Her sister had just told me that she was getting married that same night.

It was inconceivable that Beenish would miss Qirat's wedding, no matter how important she felt her dance contest was.

It was clear what this meant.

Beans had lied to me.

I didn't know what to do with that information. After convincing Ms. Siraj that everything was fine, I stood in the corridor outside her classroom, trying to figure out where to go or what to think.

People walked past me, around me, giving me strange looks.

That wasn't unusual. I glanced down at the briefcase in my hand.

You are weird, it reminded me, like it had the day I'd first met Beans. *Everyone laughs at you. Why did you think she'd be any different?*

I tightened my grip on its handle, though really, what I

102

wanted to do was throw it somewhere and never see it again. It was my scarlet letter, a symbol of how different I was from who I was supposed to be.

What are you wearing?

Extra Virgin.

Nerd Scout.

You're the strange one here.

My throat felt as though the pressure on it was increasing, as if someone were squeezing it with calipers. My mind flashed back to how sublime Beans had looked when she was dancing. I imagined myself trying to do the same and realized how badly I'd fail and how foolish I'd seem. Wouldn't that make the world laugh?

If this were a prank, that would explain everything.

It would explain why I—as peculiar as I was—had been able to get along with someone so effortlessly for the first time in my life. I'd thought that Beans and I had been able to connect. But that was ridiculous. She was charming and witty and beautiful, and I was none of those things.

It had been a fantasy.

I'd wanted to believe it, so I had.

I was a fool.

"Get off my car," I told Beenish Siraj when I met her by the Eldorado after school. To make sure she understood how angry I was with her, I waited a good fifteen seconds before adding, "Please."

"Okay," she said, hopping off her perch on the hood. "Nice to see you too, Grumposaurus. Rough day?"

I didn't answer. I just made my way to the driver side of the car, opened the door, and tossed my briefcase in.

"Aren't you going to open my door for me?" Beans asked.

I folded my arms across my chest and glared at her.

"What?"

"You are a liar."

"Am not," she exclaimed, all playfulness evaporating from her tone. "What the hell?"

"You lied to me. There is no dance contest, is there? You are going to be busy on the night it's supposed to be happening. Your sister is getting married on Christmas Eve, after all."

Her indignation went the way of her playfulness. "Oh. That. I was going to tell you. I swear. I can explain."

"Was this some kind of joke?" I demanded, my voice rising higher than it had in a long time. "Was Diamond in on it? You guys were going to have fun at the expense of the new nerd, weren't you?"

"Arsalan—"

My chest felt like someone had rolled a boulder onto it. "Let me guess. You were going to tape me trying to dance on your iCell and upload it onto YouTV, right? What a brilliant plan."

"iPhone. YouTube. And, no, how can you even think that? It's not—"

"What I can't understand is how you got Ms. Siraj to go

104

along with any of it. Involving her was genius. I probably would've said no to this whole idea if she hadn't said it was something I should do. I actually thought she liked me." My vision was blurry, my voice a hushed whisper when I added, "I thought *you* liked me."

Beans looked like someone had walked over her mother's grave. Not that her mother had a grave, of course, but we process the world in terms we can understand.

Before she could say anything else, I got into the car and slammed the door shut. If Beenish Siraj tried to defend herself further as I turned the ignition and started driving away, I didn't hear her.

Nana knocked on the door to my room and, without waiting for a reply, walked in. I stepped away from the mirror and finished doing the last of the buttons on one of Rayyan Uncle's shirts.

"It's late," Nana said. "Are you going out again?"

"No. I'm home."

"Why are you wearing your uniform, then?"

I shrugged. "Just reminding myself who I am."

Nana took a deep breath and went to sit at my desk. "You went to see your mother, I assume. That is why you didn't get here in time for dinner."

I really hoped this was not going to be one of Nana's periodic lectures about how my habit of going to talk to Mom was, in his opinion, less than ideal. He saw this *macabre wallowing in grief* as an inability to heal, when he believed I should be trying to move on.

I was not in the mood to hear it. So, to forestall any such diatribe, I said, "Are you hungry? I can make something."

He shook his head. "I ate already. I came to tell you that Beenish Siraj stopped by—"

"Oh."

Nana pulled a note from his pocket and held it out. "She left this for you."

I took it from him. It had obviously been scribbled quickly on the back of what looked like a torn piece of paper from a textbook. That was sacrilegious. I shook my head. Beans.

> Qirat doesn't know anything.
> Please don't tell her or anyone.
> I can explain, I swear. Meet me
> tomorrow at Arden Mall in the
> food court at 11 am. Beenish.
> PS: I like you fine.
> PPS: But you have issues.
> PPPS: Also, you're an ass.

I looked up from the note to find that Nana was studying me carefully.

"Is everything all right?"

"Hard to say," I told him. "Apparently, I'm an ass."

The old man shrugged. "No help for that. You probably get it from me. Arsalan," he continued more seriously, "I want you to be careful with this girl. She's dangerous. Do you understand?"

I frowned. "Dangerous? It seemed like you liked her."

"I do. I've always had a fondness for people with fire in them. This little Bean of yours certainly has that. But it is advisable, always, to be careful around fire. You don't want to get burned and, equally important, you don't want to be the reason it gets put out."

I nodded. I had a history with fire. I knew the scars it could leave. "I think I understand."

Nana grimaced as he got to his feet. "Good. One worries, you know, when one's children start venturing close to a flame for the first time."

"Did you have this talk with Mom too?" I asked as he started to make his way to the door.

"Yes," Nana said with a tired sigh. "But she reached into the inferno anyway. I suppose she didn't know what a devil your father would turn out to be. Take heed, be cautious, and you will be safe. It's what I have taught you."

He started to leave.

On any other night, I would have let him go. Just then, however, I needed...something. I didn't even know what it was, but I called out to him anyway. "Nana?"

He turned to face me.

I tried to figure out what to say. I'd been alone most of my life. But the loneliness you feel when you've grown unaccustomed to it is...it's a deeper, more profound ache than usual.

I couldn't ask him to stay with me to talk, of course. He would think that was juvenile. Besides, Nana had never really been a good listener. Who I really needed with me—and couldn't have—was Muneera Nizami.

My eyes fell on my grandfather's model of an atom and on Rayyan Uncle's guitar that hadn't been used in ages. Maybe I could at least feel connected to Mom if some of her things were here, inside this house, like her brother's and father's belongings. Maybe it would make her seem closer than she was.

"In the garage," I said finally, "I know you said not to open the boxes, but I was wondering where Mom's things are? Her name wasn't on any of them."

"That doesn't matter," Nana said sternly, "unless you intend to disobey me. Do you intend to disobey me, Arsalan?"

I sighed. I knew that tone. There was no reasoning with it. I shook my head.

"Good," he said, closing the door behind him. "Let it be ever so."

Chapter Nine

When I got up the next morning, Beenish Siraj's note was sitting on my side table. I'd thought about crumpling it up and throwing it away, but my mind was still whirling with questions about Diamond, about Ms. Siraj's involvement, and about what Beans had even been trying to do.

I needed clarity. I needed these last few days—which had been great days—to make sense. I'd thought there was something worth liking about Beenish. I'd thought I'd seen something in her, some kind of spark, which I ought to get to know. It seemed important to understand how and why I'd been wrong.

So I decided to go to the mall like she had asked. It was the only way to get answers.

I put on Rayyan Uncle's uniform—the khaki pants and white shirt along with the yellow tie and green blazer that I'd routinely worn until recently. I picked up my briefcase. There was no reason to carry it, but I wanted to show Beenish I was unaffected by what she had done.

At the Arden Mall food court, I waited for her. She was late, which, given the circumstances, was inexcusable. I tried to get myself to stop bouncing my leg under the table—Mom had always said that was rude—but couldn't.

Around me, the air was heavy with the slightly oily smell of food prepared faster than ought to be possible. Chattering crowds of happy, animated people either drifted by or sank down in chairs around me. It was starting to get busy.

"Your fashion sense has regressed a little, Arsalan."

I looked up at the sound of the familiar voice and found myself confronted by a bright smile.

I stood up. "Ms. Siraj?"

She smiled. "You can call me Qirat if you want. Outside of class, of course."

"Okay," I said, not certain how else to respond to that. "Are you here with Beenish?"

"No," she said, "I'm meeting her here, actually."

I frowned. "I am as well."

"There must be some kind of misunderstanding," she said, reaching into her purse and drawing out her phone. "Let me see where she is so she can explain." After waiting for a few minutes, she said, "Salaam. I'm at the mall. Where are you? Arsalan is here too. Did you double-book yourself? Call me."

Looking at me, Ms. Siraj—Qirat—offered an apologetic shrug. "She'll call back soon, I'm sure."

I gestured for her to take a seat. When she did, I sat down as well.

"You didn't have to get up for me. I might be a teacher, but I'm not an aunty yet."

"You are still a lady, though," I said.

"Right. I forgot. You're a gentleman, not a typical high school student."

I wasn't sure exactly how to respond to that either. I settled for trying to explain my behavior. "I read a lot of books."

"That must be it." She sounded amused. "Why are you meeting Beans here? Another shopping trip?"

I made a face. "I should hope not. Beenish has some strong opinions when it comes to clothes."

"Not just clothes," Qirat told me. "But you can't argue with results."

That was a disappointing thing for a physics teacher to say. You *could* argue with results. The entire history of science—even the scientific method itself—was just people arguing with results. I would have definitely pointed that out to Nana. I didn't right now. It was the kind of know-it-all comment my mom had said might make me seem insufferable to others.

When I didn't say anything, Qirat asked, "So, have you figured out why the world is round yet?"

I shook my head. "I haven't had a chance to think about it."

"The answer," she said, "has to be something universal, doesn't it? The Earth isn't the only planet that's round."

I shrugged. "I'm not really allowed to discuss it with you. That's the rule."

"And you always follow rules?"

"I do what I am told without fail."

She raised her eyebrows. "Really? How unlike Beans. But she does like telling people what to do, so it makes sense she likes you. Speaking of which, where is that girl?"

As she began messaging Beenish on her phone, a man marching in our direction caught my attention. He was tall, in his thirties, with thick, full hair. The amount of gel in it was astounding. As soon as his eyes met mine, his lips pressed together so tight they seemed to disappear. He reminded me, in that moment, of my father.

Maybe that is why I rose to my feet and stepped back, even though he was still a few tables away from us. Qirat looked at me and smiled. "Let me guess. Be—Sham! What are you doing here?"

The man—Sham—grabbed Ms. Siraj by the forearm in what was obviously a painful grip and yanked her to her feet. His voice was soft but artificially so, with a hint of nasty, fake cheeriness, like unpleasantly shimmery satin in a garish color. "Who is this?"

"Hey!" I managed to say. "Let...You—you should let her go."

He looked up at me, smirking. He did not release Qirat, and she did not try to pull away. "He doesn't sound very brave, does he?" With a disapproving click of his tongue, he added, "Unsurprising. He's just a boy. Didn't realize that was your taste, Qirat."

"Sham, please. I didn't come here to meet him. I swear. This is one of my students. Arsalan Nizami. He's waiting for Beans. He's a friend of hers. I was supposed to meet her here too. It's a little confusion. That's all."

"Oh." A sudden, swift smile from Sham, like the strike of a serpent. "Well, that's reasonable." He released Qirat and held out the hand that had been hurting her a moment ago. "Doctor Shamshir Inteha. Her fiancé."

I hesitated and glanced at my teacher. She nodded encouragingly at the offered handshake.

Your father doesn't get angry for no reason, Arsalan. You must have been doing something wrong. If you'd just listen, jaan, he wouldn't hurt you. Just listen and obey, okay?

I took the offered hand. It was warm and a little damp, but the grip was strong and mean. "My apologies for the misunderstanding," Sham said, friendly now. "Qirat isn't allowed to meet other men without me around. It is improper, you see. But you, Mr. Arsalan, are not a man, are you?"

I wasn't sure what to say to that, but I couldn't just be quiet. My life would have been easier, I think, if I'd been better at being quiet.

"It's Mr. Nizami," I told him.

For a brief moment, I saw irritation on Sham's face. Then he chuckled and looked at Qirat. "What a weird kid."

"He's Beenish's friend," Ms. Siraj said again. "She told us both to meet her here. She got confused, I think, or just forgot, so we were waiting for her."

Sham gave me a sly grin. "You're after Beanie Baby? Can't say you've got much taste in clothes, but in women one has to give it up, haan? She isn't as pretty as this one"—he waved in his fiancée's direction—"but she'll have a better body when she's a little older. I can tell."

Qirat made a strangled sound, either an expression of disgust or distress, I couldn't tell. Her head was bowed a little, her face a mask.

"It isn't like that at all. You're—"

He ignored me completely. "That girl will be difficult to control. She's headstrong. And she doesn't understand how much shame her mother's past still brings her. She's not like Qirat here, who knows how lucky she is to have a *doctor* agree to marry her, don't you?"

"Yes," Qirat said quietly.

"Beenish has more of their mother in her, I think. You might even manage to get what you want from her without—"

"Shamshir, please!"

Ms. Siraj's fiancé looked at her for a moment, then appeared to relent. "Like I was saying, I didn't know who you were, and I got a little upset. Sorry about that."

"You don't need to apologize to *me*," I said, with all the civility of an ice pick.

Sham seemed to take it as absolution. "I thought, 'Why would Qirat invite me to lunch—for the first time ever—only to show me she's chatting up someone else?' It didn't make any sense but, you know, brazen mother, brazen daughters, so..."

Qirat seemed baffled. "I didn't call you."

"You texted me."

"I didn't."

"Is this some kind of joke?" Sham demanded. He pulled out his phone and shoved it at her. "Is that not a message from you?"

"I—yes, but—I didn't send that."

"Beenish," I said out loud, realizing what the only possible explanation was. She had wanted me to see this, to meet Sham. This wasn't a mistake. It was deliberate.

Both of them turned to look at me.

"All of this might be her idea of a prank," I suggested after a moment of hesitation.

Qirat shook her head. "That doesn't seem like her."

"It does," Sham said. "Immature, childish, and disrespectful. It's just like that girl, isn't it, Arsalan? You know, when my family first came for tea to see Qirat, to evaluate her as a potential match, Beenish switched the salt and the sugar? She's an unpleasant little thing."

No one seemed to have anything to say to that. After a moment, Sham exhaled and went on. "Well, now that I'm here, we might as well make the best of it. I'll buy you lunch, Qirat. I can do better than a food court." Looking at me, he added, "It was nice to meet you."

It would have been polite, of course, to say the same thing to him.

Instead of doing so, I simply nodded, bowed slightly to Ms. Siraj, and made my escape.

"That was an awful thing to do," I told Beenish as soon as she picked up her phone. I tried to keep my voice low, controlled, because I was back home, and it was possible Nana was sleeping. Also, as I'm sure he would point out, it is best to be well-mannered whenever possible.

It'd be nice if Beenish didn't make it so hard, though.

"I know," she said softly. "I'm sorry."

I wanted to drive home how horrible her actions had been, but the obvious remorse and sadness in her voice gave me pause.

"Was Sham really mean to Qirat?"

I nodded, though she couldn't see that. "He is not a gentleman."

There was no response for a minute, then Beenish said, "I needed you to meet Sham. I needed you to see for yourself that he's basically cat poo."

"Why? None of this makes sense."

"That's because you think I'm also a shitty person. Like him."

"I don't think that," I protested.

"Yeah. You do. You really do. But I can explain. Can I come over so we can talk?"

I hesitated.

"Really?" Beans asked, some of her usual energy back in her voice. "You don't even want to see me anymore? Even after I apologized? Even when I'm telling you I can explain? What the—"

"No," I said quickly. "It isn't that I don't want to see you. I just don't want to see your eyes."

"What?"

"Your eyes, they're . . ." I stopped myself from saying what I was about to say—that her eyes were distracting and made it impossible for me to trust my own judgment. Beenish Siraj didn't deserve compliments right now. "They're like tar."

"Ew. Gross. What does that even mean?"

They're dark and hot and dangerous and, at least in this situation, possibly toxic.

"I'm not sure," I said, deciding it was best not to explain that particular metaphor. "But I just think that—"

The doorbell rang.

I let out a deep breath. "You're already here."

"Yeah. Sorry. I can put on sunglasses if you want."

I hung up on her and went to get the door.

"Wow," she said when she saw what I was wearing. "You're so mad at me that you transformed back into Dorkimus Prime."

"We've got more important things to talk about right now."

"Fine," she said, walking past me. "But this isn't going to go how you think it will."

"Not much ever does."

117

"So," I said slowly, pacing the length of Nana's garage—at least the part that we'd cleared out—as I tried to make sense of the mad rush of words that Beenish had thrown at me. "Your sister is being forced to marry this Sham Inteha person?"

Beenish, who was sitting on a large box full of my grandfather's stuff, shook her head. "First of all, he's not really a person. He's more of a turd. Also, she isn't being *forced* to marry him. People can't force someone to marry anyone. Imams are supposed to make sure of that."

"But it happens."

"Crimes happen. This isn't one. I mean, my dad and stepmom aren't going to drag Qirat to the wedding and make her marry Sham. They've just convinced her that he is her best option. Her only option."

I nodded. "Right. Because your mother—your biological mother—was a..." I struggled to find a polite way to put it. I couldn't remember exactly how Beenish had said it. "Harlot?"

"Arsalan!"

I knew that hadn't sounded right. Still, I held up my hands to defend myself. "You were the one who told me."

"I *said* she was a dancer in movies in Pakistan. I *said* that there was a huge scandal because she did a shitty movie where some of her work was criticized for being a little slutty." She paused, then added reluctantly, "Maybe more than a little."

"I may have gotten the term wrong."

"You think? She danced under some waterfall and her saree got a little... Okay, it got super revealing and some religious clerics had a coronary. But calling her a harlot is totally overboard. Who even talks like that anymore?"

I inclined my head to concede the point. "Sorry. But I'm still not following. What difference does it make what her profession was? Everyone is entitled to be treated with respect no matter what they choose to do."

"That's not the way the world works."

I was about to point out that the more time I spent away from Nana's house, the less convinced I became that the world worked at all. Humanity often seemed to fall dramatically short of its own basic standards. It wasn't until I'd spent time around other people that I'd come to realize how rare a person my great-grandfather was.

I didn't say any of that. It was too much of a tangent. I was still trying to make sense of Beenish's explanation as to what she'd been thinking.

"Anyway, your mother was publicly shamed over a decade ago and shunned. Because of that, some kind of dishonor attaches to you and Qirat in the arranged marriage process?"

"Right," she said. "Basically, not a lot of people want to be associated with my family because of who my mom is.

Which didn't really matter until my father left Mama and married Roshni."

"Because Roshni Aunty wanted you and your sister out of the house, so she started looking for matches for both of you."

"Exactly. She was the one who found Sham for Qirat and then, along with my dad, pressured her to agree to the marriage."

"Then," I went on, "to disrupt the plans your father and Roshni Aunty have made, you came up with a plot to ruin the wedding. You decided to dance at it and made up a contest so no one would know what you were planning to do."

"See? Simple?"

"'Ridiculous,'" I told her, "is the word you're looking for."

Beenish crossed her arms. "What's ridiculous about it?"

"Doesn't dancing improve weddings? I thought desis were famous for it."

"We are not all the same. My father's social circle is very religiously conservative. And Sham's parents...they're beyond that. They're weird, Arsalan. What part of this are you not getting? You know what? I can show you." She pulled her phone out of her pocket and pulled up something for me to read. "Check it out."

I found myself looking at a document titled "Ironclad Rules for the Marriage of Shamshir 'Sham' Inteha and Qirat Siraj."

"'Wheretofore heretofore,'" I read, "'it is herein and hereby so agreed upon to and by the parties...' Is this supposed to make sense?"

"Keep going."

I did. The "rules" were incredible in the worst way possible. Sham and his family were demanding that Qirat's parents pay him $50,000 in cash "prior to acceptance of delivery of the bride" along with a few other "minor" items, including a home theater system and at least seven suits belonging to some guy called Tom Ford.

"You see the problem?"

I nodded. "Asking for a dowry is illegal."

"And fucking awful!" Beenish said so loudly that it echoed off the concrete of the garage.

I winced, wondering if Nana had heard.

"This isn't the Stone Age and this isn't the Old World. I mean, seriously? My family has to pay these fools to take Qirat? That is messed up."

I agreed. I'm not sure where the concept of dowries had come from, but I did know that it had been a cultural problem in the subcontinent for a long time. Years ago, I'd heard my mom talking to her friends about parents who had gone broke or taken on massive debt just so they could pay a groom's family to move forward with a wedding.

The list of rules didn't end there, though.

"'Due to the importance of modesty in our religion, women will be absolutely forbidden from performing dances or other exhibitions of impropriety so as to not inflame the men.'" I looked up at Beenish.

She grinned. "But I'm going to inflame them so hard. Wait. That sounded different in my head. Out loud, it just sounds gross."

Ignoring her, I turned my attention back to her phone. "'The biological mother of Qirat, Aiza Ex-Siraj, will have nothing whatever to do with the ceremonies and will not be permitted to attend the wedding.'"

"Yeah."

"That's just cruel." I couldn't imagine graduating from high school without my mother being there, despite knowing it was something I'd have to do soon. The thought of not having her at my wedding...Well, I guess I might have to do that too, if I ever got married.

"These aren't good people, Arsalan. I need to...This is something I need to do, it's the only thing I *can* do, and I need your help. You promised."

"Because you lied to me."

"Actually," she said, "not that it really matters, but I didn't lie to you. I never told you we were going to enter a dance contest."

I started to protest, then stopped and thought back. "You lied to Qirat and she told me," I remembered. "But when it came up after that you never corrected me. It was a lie of omission."

"It's just that I didn't know you," she explained. "I couldn't share my secret plan with some random guy. What

if you'd told Qirat? I had to make sure you were cool."
She looked me up and down. Then put up air quotes and
repeated, " 'Cool.' Anyway, what difference does it make to
you where you dance as long as I set you up with someone
like I promised?"

That was close to being a valid point, but... "Making a
fool out of myself in front of strangers I'll never see again
is different than making a fool out of myself in front of desi
uncles and aunties."

"Who are also strangers," she reasoned.

"It isn't the same. I don't know why but it doesn't feel the
same."

Beenish grimaced. "Yeah. I get that. It's like the time I got
kicked out of the mosque, you know? When I was kicked out
of a movie theater, it didn't bother me at all."

I raised my eyebrows. "You were kicked out of a
mosque?"

"Can we focus and get my apology out of the way, so that
we get to your apology, and move past this?"

Wait. Beenish Siraj actually thought I'd done something
wrong? Unbelievable. "What are you talking about?"

"You are sorry, right?"

I shook my head. "You mean generally speaking?"

"No. For very specifically being a jerk in this particular
situation."

"I've done nothing wrong."

"Really?" Her disbelief was, for a brief moment, the
hardest substance on the Earth, surpassing diamond and

graphene and everything else by a mile. "You didn't come up with a messed-up theory about how I was playing a twisted prank on you? A theory based on absolutely no evidence and the idea that I'm basically a Sith Lord?"

"What's a Sith Lord?"

"How are you so bad at being a nerd? Whatever. It doesn't matter. What matters is that you think I'm capable of some truly evil shit. I mean, we've spent some time together. Didn't you ever think to yourself, 'Hey, Beans seems like a nice person. She wouldn't do something this terrible to me or anyone.'"

I found myself staring at the ground as she spoke. The floor was worn and cracked in places, not broken, exactly, but damaged in sometimes significant ways that seemed entirely random.

"Wow," she said. "You never came close to having that thought, did you?"

I shook my head.

"That's fucked up, Arsalan."

I nodded. There was perhaps some excuse to offer here. Beenish's "plan" and her reasons for acting the way she had were so convoluted and ill-conceived that I couldn't possibly have been expected to guess them. I had, however, entirely failed to give her the benefit of the doubt. I hadn't paused to consider that she wouldn't wound me like that.

That was effed up. I was effed up.

"I am sorry," I told her. "Truly."

"How can we be friends if you think so little of me?"

Her voice was soft now, softer than silk and soapstone. "It's impossible."

"I don't know. I've never really had a friend."

"Well, I guess that streak of yours is in no danger of being broken. Let's just do what we promised to do and get out of each other's lives."

Chapter Ten

I highly recommend gyms for people looking to punish themselves. They are spaces full of instruments of torture. Treadmills, for example, were designed in the eighteen hundreds to torment prisoners. Also, the experience of lifting weights, over and over for no reason, just to put them down again, is definitely something Sisyphus would relate to. After my last conversation with Beenish, I was in the mood for a little self-flagellation, and so calling Diamond Khan and subjecting myself to this hell seemed like the thing to do.

It wasn't long before he had me sitting on a contraption with a bar dangling overhead, which was connected to a pulley system and a massive set of numbered weights. "This will work your shoulders, pecs, and back. How much do you think you can manage?"

I eyed the mechanism uncertainly. "Sixty or seventy pounds?"

Diamond laughed, then leaned over and set the weight to ten.

"That's insulting," I told him.

"Physics doesn't care about your feelings, Niz."

That was an impossible statement to argue with, so I reached up, grabbed the black rubber handles on the bar, and easily pulled it down. "I'm not feeling very challenged."

"Five sets of ten," Diamond said, sitting down on a machine designed to strengthen his legs. "You okay? You seem down."

"This is how I always am."

Two. Three. Four.

He seemed unconvinced. "It's okay, bro. We don't have to talk about it."

I didn't bother replying, focusing instead on the exercise I'd been prescribed.

Five. Six. Seven.

"Everything okay with Beans?" Diamond asked a moment later. "She texted Friday after school, wondering if you'd said anything about a conspiracy. She didn't explain, but then she doesn't like to talk to me much anymore."

He said the last part with the air of a person who had lost something important.

Eight. Nine. Ten. My shoulders and back were protesting

a little now, tightening up, and making it difficult to both listen to Diamond and keep count.

"What kind of conspiracy stuff are you into? Is it like Illuminati shit? I definitely want to know about them."

"No," I said. "It isn't like that."

Eleven. Twelve. Thirteen. Or was I supposed to start over at one?

"But you wouldn't tell Diamond if it were, would you?"

Fourteen. Fifteen.

"I guess not."

"I'm telling you, bro, if you know how to join those guys, you better tell me. Diamond wants in."

"Sacramento...not exciting enough...for you?" I asked, trying not to let on how much I was having to exert myself. Sixteen. Seventeen.

He shrugged. "It's fine. I mean, I want to leave and see the world, you know? For now, it isn't so bad. Beans keeps things from getting boring. At least, she used to."

My shoulders and arms were on fire now, and the muscles around my neck felt stiff. I glared at the weights accusingly. Maybe they were labeled wrong. There was no way I was working with just ten pounds.

"You okay, Niz?"

"Fine," I snapped. I let my hands drop to my sides. I had to. I couldn't go on. Diamond, thankfully, didn't say anything, which made me like him a bit more than I had before.

"So," he said after a few seconds, "we were talking about Beans. You and Beans."

128

"What about us?"

"How's it going?" he asked.

"How is what going?"

"You know. Arsalan and Beenish, sitting in a tree..."

I stared at him. "Why would I be in a tree? Why would anyone?"

He didn't answer. He was an odd one, this Diamond. Of course, I was odd too, but we were completely different. He was Byron and I was Aurelius. He was in color and I was in black-and-white. Then again, I suppose our strangeness was something we had in common. I recognized it in him and could appreciate it.

Nana once told me that the Prophet had said that God is odd, and so he loves that which is odd. Of course, I'd done enough reading to know that Nana had not only been paraphrasing but also taking significant liberties with the meaning of the Prophet's words to make me feel better about myself. The actual saying was about odd numbers, not odd people.

All that is to say that, despite Diamond's extravagant mannerisms, I didn't mind being around him. I wasn't sure why he felt that he knew me well enough to ask me personal questions, though.

"If you are insinuating that there is anything untoward going on between Beenish Siraj and myself, I assure you that is not the case."

"Chill out, bro. I was just asking."

"Why?" I demanded.

"Beans and I are friends."

"It didn't look like you were friends at the MSA bake sale."

He deflated a little at that. "We are, bro. It's just...it got a little messy. We're working through it. She did ask me to help you with this." He extended his impressive arms out as if to encompass the entire gym.

I nodded. Then another thought occurred to me. "Were you inquiring because you want to court Beans?"

Diamond snorted. "Court? You're hilarious, Niz. And, no, man. It just...it seems like she likes you. I want her to like you. I think if she finds someone, maybe she'll move past what happened, and things between Diamond and her will get better."

I wasn't really sure what to make of that. I could have informed him that Beans most definitely did not like me right now, in any sense of the word, but I didn't want to talk about it.

Besides, Diamond wasn't done speaking. "Everything got weird because Roshni Aunty—that's Beenish's stepmom— tried to set me up with her for the whole arranged marriage thing, and my family said no."

I frowned. "Really? Your family said no?"

"Don't sound so surprised. Diamond is a catch. Also, there's the whole thing with her biological mom and her... lewdness. Have you seen Aiza Aunty's dances on You-Tube? You should look them up, especially the waterfall one. Actually, you shouldn't, because Allah is watching and

130

astaghfirullah and everything...but it is super hot. It got Diamond to realize he's a man."

I made a face. That was information I had not needed.

"Anyway, it's not like Aiza Aunty is an angel now, but that wasn't the only reason. Beans isn't like Qirat Api. She gets in trouble, she talks back, she's reckless. She isn't exactly daughter-in-law material in my family's opinion. There's too much...something about her."

"Fire," I told him. "It's fire."

"Actually, she's a whole fireworks show. She's the Fourth of July. Anyway, Beans found out my parents had turned her down because, of course, Roshni Aunty rubbed it in her face. Next thing you know, we're talking about it at school and Beans is pissed."

"At Roshni Aunty?"

"And my family. I mean, we were always just friends, so it isn't like we had feelings for each other, but Beans was upset my parents had brought Aiza Aunty into it. She thought my family could have been more...diplomatic. She was pretty rude about it. Called them assholes."

He stopped talking for a while, looking like he'd rather not go on.

I gave him time.

"So Diamond may have said that Aiza Aunty could have tried being a little less of a whore..."

I winced. "You should not have said that."

"Beans thought so too, because that's when she broke Diamond's nose."

"Well...you had said something unfortunate."

"In the extreme," Diamond agreed. "But she was saying all this stuff about my family and it just...it came out in the heat of the moment. I didn't mean it like—" He shook his head and gave up trying to explain himself. "I made a mistake."

Making mistakes, I could understand.

"So," I said, "you're the guy she punched in the face. That makes a lot of sense."

He frowned. "What's that supposed to mean?"

"Nothing," I said quickly.

"Uh-huh," Diamond said. "By the way, is something wrong with your arms?"

"No."

"Then..." He looked pointedly up at the machine I was supposed to be working on. I sighed, but I'd recovered enough to try again.

One. Two. Wait...Hadn't I been at around thirty before? I was pretty sure I had.

So, thirty-three. Thirty-four.

"After that," Diamond said, picking up his tale, "she got suspended. I went to the principal and explained what had happened. Asked that they let her come back, but there's a zero-tolerance policy against violence for some reason."

Thirty-five. Thirty-six.

I couldn't hold back a groan as I let the weights go. I'd reached my limit.

Mercifully, Diamond didn't call me out.

"Did you apologize?"

"Many times. Then I went and told Qirat Api what had happened and said I was sorry. Even went Diamond Standard, you know, and visited Aiza Aunty to explain, so she wouldn't get mad at Beenish for getting suspended...not that Aiza Aunty and Beans talk much. They haven't seen each other in ages."

I couldn't imagine not seeing my mom for any significant period of time. I mean, I could, obviously, but...Anyway, this conversation was about Diamond, so I kept my focus on him. "Sounds like a difficult thing to do."

"It wasn't great. Bro, I did everything I could to make things normal. I even made Beans a bouquet of flowers from the yellow ones that grow around the school."

"The dandelions?"

"Diamond doesn't know."

"Those are weeds."

He frowned, confused. "But they're so pretty. The point is that she doesn't forgive, that girl."

"'My good opinion once lost is lost forever,'" I mused. "That's a quote from—"

"Batman," he said, nodding sagely.

"What? No! It's—"

"It doesn't even matter, bro," Diamond said, and though it mattered a great deal, I decided to let it go. "The reason I'm telling you all this is because maybe you could put in a good word for me with Beenish? I just want things to go back to the way they were. I want a fresh start."

I didn't point out that those were contradictory desires. I was being very restrained today. Mom would've been proud.

I also didn't tell him I wasn't in any position to put in a good word with Beenish just then.

"It's not fair," Diamond declared. "You get to start over in everything that's fun. Football season is new every year. You can restart in a video game whenever you want. If you're painting something or baking something or creating burner accounts on social media to tell your friends how you really feel about things, there's always the chance of a new beginning. It's not like that in life. It's almost like life isn't meant to be fun."

"It isn't."

"Diamond doesn't like that. You know what else Diamond doesn't like? Lack of effort. Let's go, Niz. We're here to work, not to talk. Did you get in fifty reps?"

"I got...closer to fifty than zero."

He didn't seem to know what to make of that. Finally, he just shook his head. "Whatever. Let's move on. We can come back to this machine."

I sighed. "Wonderful."

There was another letter from my father waiting for me when I got home. Nana, who was solving old chess problems from a stack of newspapers next to him, was too absorbed to mention it. That was just fine with me. I didn't feel like going round and round with him on whether or not I ought to read

Zeeshan Nizami's correspondence. He didn't understand why I did it, and I couldn't explain it to him, not without telling him that the house he loved, and in which he lived, was no longer his own.

I picked up the letter and went to my room. I'd planned on taking a shower, because gyms are disgusting and smell like the graves of all the sweaty socks of humankind. However, there are some tasks that rob us of our free will when they call. That is to say that, despite how much we wish to resist, eventually we have to submit to them. Like death and defecation, for example.

Ms. Siraj's extra credit assignment was lying on my desk. I'd meant to give it some thought today. I probably wasn't going to figure out the reason behind the shape of the world now, though. It seemed like an impossibly tall task for a boy who couldn't even figure out the shape of his own life.

Instead, I read what I'd been sent:

Arsalan,

Send a report card, if possible. If not possible, send a test or assignment. Anything I can use to make sure you are still going to real school. I know you said you are, but you were always too clever for your own good.
Didn't get any wishes or card for my birthday from you. Don't think you would've forgotten your mothers. When I complained, the imam here asked

135

what I had sent you for yours, and I had to admit I'd forgotten too. Like father like son. When is your birthday? Sometime in January?

Still sober and doing well. Not that you asked. Feels good. Feels like a fresh start. I was thinking of changing my name maybe. It'd be like a symbol, like someone converting to Islam. I was thinking Nuayman, after Nuayman ibn Amr. If you don't know who that is, ask the old man. He thinks he knows everything.

Hope you are praying all five times a day. Remember the Fire. I'm sure you haven't forgotten the lesson I taught you, though maybe it was a little strict. Will send for you soon, as promised. You won't have to be alone for long.

—Zeeshan

I dropped the letter in the bottom drawer with all the others, leaned back in my chair, and closed my eyes. I'd never managed to forget my father's lesson about the importance of prayer. I'd just turned seven, so it had been January, and praying had become an obligation. I don't recall if Zeeshan Nizami had been drunk or not. Probably not. He only got wildly righteous during his brief periods of sobriety, like he was trying to make up for his habit of drinking alcohol, a grave sin in Islam.

He'd asked me to pray, and I'd said I didn't want to. So he'd lit a match and threatened to burn me like God would burn me in hell. He'd come at me, chasing me around our apartment, stopping to light a new match every time one burned out.

I remembered what it felt like when I'd tripped over my own feet, what it'd felt like when my father had pinned me against the floor, his knee on my back. I could still feel the weight there. I could hear my own frantic begging and then whimpering as the match, put out an instant before it was pressed against the side of my neck, fell beside my face, discarded, as he'd simply gotten up and walked away, not bothering to look back.

A toxic little laugh bubbled in my chest.

The Prophet said: "Mercy will not be shown to those who do not show mercy."

So when men like my father stood before God, hearts proud, arms folded, heads bowed, weren't they just wasting their time? Because even though they were sure that they understood Him, I don't really believe that He, if He is as loving as He claims, understands them.

Chapter Eleven

"All right," Beenish Siraj said. "Let's see what you can do."

Her voice was cool. I hadn't realized there had been warmth there before, but now that it was gone, I missed it. All that was left in its wake was the business we had between us.

This business required me to dance. The song Beenish had put on, "Twist Kamariya," had a suggestion of what to do built into it. However, twisting my back seemed like a bad idea, despite what the upbeat number suggested.

"Let's go," she urged, clapping her hands to spur me on.

I took a deep breath, then started to move. I put my right foot in, then took my right foot out and shook it all about.

I looked at Beenish, who seemed stunned, but not in a good way, so I decided to switch things up.

I bounced on the heel of my left foot, then shifted my weight to the right side, moving my arms like a T. rex as I did so.

She cut the music.

"What are you doing?" Beenish demanded. "You can't do that. It's offensive."

"Offensive?"

"That's the white man's shuffle. It's not okay for us to use that. It's cultural appropriation."

"Oh," I said. "Sorry."

A small smile flitted across her lips.

"The world is more complicated than I thought it'd be," I explained. "I think that's why I make so many mistakes in it."

If Beans understood that I was talking about misjudging her, she didn't let on.

"Look," she said, with more patience than my performance probably warranted, "dance is like . . . It's your body's vocabulary. If you let your heart speak in the way you move, you'll be good at it. Does that make sense?"

I wasn't sure I liked the idea of letting my heart speak. It didn't have a lot to say that was cheerful.

"It'll make sense once we're actually doing it," she assured me. Then she folded her arms behind her back, stood on the toes of her right foot. Moving slowly, she extended her left leg forward before folding it back at the knee, until her heel hit her thigh. It was simple, and it was a version of what I'd done, but the way she moved was different. Beenish had made it all seem like one motion. Plus, she was graceful and confident, like the wind gliding between raindrops.

"Why does it look different when you do it?"

"When I do the Hokey Pokey, I just do it. You think about how to do it, then while you're doing it, you're worried about what to do next or how you might make a mistake or what people watching will think. You're using your brain too much."

"You keep accusing me of that."

"Because you keep doing it. Look, if you want to get all cerebral about it, remember that Simonides said that 'dancing is silent poetry.' You can teach someone syllables and forms and stuff, like haikus and rubaiyat, but you can't teach them how to be a great poet. Only life can do that. I can teach you how to dance, but only your heart can make you a dancer."

I stared at her.

"What?" Beans demanded.

"That was pretty deep."

"Fuck you," she said, not entirely unkindly.

"It's just... you're so... effervescent that it's easy to forget you're more than just bubbles. I think maybe we simplify people to understand them."

"Yeah, well, 'in the depth of my soul there is a wordless song.' "

That was a line from Khalil Gibran.

"Okay," I said. "You can stop showing off now. That's really kind of my thing."

"All right," Beenish agreed. "Let's shut up and dance."

"You look like you're in pain," Nana said as I limped around the kitchen a week later, getting dinner together. Tonight we were having saffron rice—which was just rice with a little bit of butter that I'd put saffron in—and yogurt sprinkled with sumac. The name made it sound difficult to make, but it couldn't have been easier. It was the opposite of dancing, is what I'm saying.

"I am in pain," I confirmed. "I've found myself a harsh mistress."

"Don't complain, Arsalan," he said mildly. "There are people who pay good money for that kind of thing."

"Gross, Nana. Can you please not?"

"The truth is that you do look a little worse for wear. You can borrow my cane, if you like."

"Very funny," I grumbled. I had to admit, however, that between the continuing sessions with Diamond and Beenish, I'd started to have a little less trouble imagining what it must feel like to be a hundred years old. Every muscle in my body was sore, though some hurt a lot more than others. If this was how I felt just seven days after I'd shown Beans my version of the Hokey Pokey, it seemed unlikely that I'd survive the months until Christmas Eve.

Despite that, I wasn't entirely unhappy. Going to the gym

wasn't as unpleasant as I'd expected it to be. As for Beenish, things had started off awkwardly, but the more we talked about dance, the warmer she got. Maybe the damage I'd done to our young friendship was less than entirely fatal.

"So, Nana," I asked, trying to sound casual, "have you ever heard of Nuayman ibn Amr?"

He frowned. "Who?"

"That's what I said."

Nana slouched forward, his face scrunched up with intense focus. "I have heard the name. I just can't remember where."

"It's not important. I can google it at school."

He harrumphed. "That is how the world ends, you know. Not with a bang, but with the pitter-patter of a computer keyboard."

"I'm pretty sure that the Prophet said it'd be a lot more dramatic."

My great-grandfather's eyes narrowed, then widened, and he smiled in triumph. "Yes. The Prophet. That's where I've heard the name. Nuayman ibn Amr was one of Muhammad's Companions."

I frowned. For someone who had been made to read as many history books as I had, I'd never heard of him. The people who had lived their lives around Muhammad were famously great. Islamic texts portrayed them all as either incredibly wise or charitable or brave. Almost entirely without exception, they were also said to be unwaveringly pious and beyond reproach.

142

Throughout our studies, however, Nana had suggested that the truth was more complicated. He thought the Companions had been human, with flaws and failings of their own. It was important to focus on their virtues, he claimed, because Islam's teachings derived from stories these people had related about Muhammad. Arabia had been an oral culture then, and the story of the Prophet's life, the things he had done and said, had not been written until much later.

If you did not have faith in Muhammad's friends, you could have no faith that you knew anything about him. Nana thought that was one reason why imams everywhere spent a lot of time telling you about the wonderful qualities of these men and women.

"Why are you asking about him?" Nana demanded. "Is this about your father?"

"How did you know?"

"Nuayman was an alcoholic."

"Really?" I sat down, then got up again, realizing I'd forgotten to give Nana his food. This was the first time I'd heard that one of the Companions had defied Islam's teachings and committed a significant sin.

"I don't know much about him," Nana admitted. "But he was apparently a funny, well-liked man who was close to Muhammad, but who couldn't stop drinking. He was punished for it more than once." He paused, then added, "Please tell me that Zeeshan Nizami did not have the gall to compare himself to Nuayman ibn Amr."

"He's thinking of changing his name to Nuayman," I told him.

Nana's laugh was the coldest thing in California.

"I think it's meant to be symbolic," I said. "He's apparently been sober for a while."

"Nuayman was a good man with an addiction. Your father is a cruel man with one," Nana said. "They are not the same."

It was probably best to change the topic. Discussions about Zeeshan Nizami messed with Nana's blood pressure. "Doesn't matter," I told him. "After all, what's in a name?"

"Apparently," Nana grumbled, "a stunning lack of self-awareness."

"Speaking of which," I said, "did you know that my name means 'lion'? I'd forgotten, but someone at school brought it up recently."

"It also means 'fearless,'" Nana said, "and 'brave.'"

I snorted.

"What?" Nana teased. "You don't think that's an accurate description of you?"

I thought about the plastic hangers that had been used to beat me until they broke upon my back, of what it had felt like to be locked in a dark closet for not behaving, and I shook my head.

"Perhaps you'll grow into it," he suggested.

"No," I said. "I don't think there is much chance of that."

I went to visit Mom the next day after school. I couldn't remember the last time I'd managed to wait more than a day after receiving an upsetting message from my father before going to see her. It helped to speak with her anytime I had to deal with him, to remind myself that there had once been light in the world. But practice with Beans took up a great deal of time, and homework was an unceasing and implacable foe. It hadn't been possible to make the long drive out to the cemetery on Eagles Nest.

Still, as always, I was glad I had come. I got to tell Mom about what had happened with Beans, about how I'd screwed up the chance to make a friend.

"Why did you tell me to do the one thing I've never been good at? Why force me to deal with people?" I demanded with a little bit of exasperation. "You could have said, 'Look up the origins of words and you'll find the world beautiful.' That would've been both true and easy to do."

She didn't have anything to say for herself. I suspected, however, that she was confused. Muneera Nizami had suggested I search for love, not friendship. But she hadn't absorbed nearly as much Old English from Nana as I had, and I'd just made a connection that hadn't occurred to me before.

"They are the same thing, love and friendship. Or, at least, they're related. 'Friend' comes from 'frēon,' which means 'to love.' Not that I've got any talent for either one of those things."

Mom waited for me to go on.

145

"Given that is true, doesn't it follow that just becoming friends with Beenish—or anyone—would complete your mission in a way?"

I wasn't sure my mother would agree. I was pretty certain, in fact, that as she lay dying, my mother had been hoping I would one day find someone to take a romantic interest in me, someone who would want to spend a lifetime with me. In her last moments, the discipline of etymology had probably not been on her mind.

I had often tried not to wonder why that had been one of her last thoughts in the world. Surely, her relationship with my father had made her life horrid. It hadn't been a source of beauty, but of pain. How was it possible that after everything her husband had done and everything he had failed to do, my mother had still valued romantic love?

Somehow at the end of her life, even when he'd failed to show up, she hadn't been free of thoughts of him. I hadn't understood then—I still didn't understand—the power my father had over her. I couldn't figure out what had kept her, and by extension me, with him when we should have left.

"I suppose," I noted quietly in the face of her silence, "love and friendship aren't the same thing at all. 'Frēo,' another root that 'friend' comes from, means 'to be free.' Maybe the difference between the two relationships is that the bonds of friendship can be broken, as I've just discovered with Beenish. But there can be no freedom from love."

When I got home, I found that Nana was not alone. Beenish was with him, and they were poring over his chessboard, locked in what looked like an intense game.

"Arsalan," Nana greeted, "your friend came by and found me playing with myself—"

Beans snickered.

"—so she offered to join me." He gestured at the plastic pieces before him. "She has a fascinating mind. I have quite the game on my hands."

I raised my eyebrows. Nana was tremendously experienced and made me help keep him in constant practice. "I wouldn't have guessed you played," I told Beenish.

"Well," she replied, her tone slightly gentler than a cactus, "it's already been made clear that you know absolutely nothing about me, hasn't it?"

I winced at her prickliness. So did Nana, though he would never be so gauche as to stick his nose into a personal dispute.

"I said I was sorry," I reminded her quietly, though I'm not sure why I bothered lowering my voice. Nana's hearing was bad, but not bad enough that he wouldn't hear what I said while sitting right in front of us.

"I know," she said. "Let's not worry about it, okay? We've got to practice. Just let me finish up here—"

Nana, who had been fiddling with his last remaining bishop, swept it across the board in an uncharacteristically aggressive move and said, "Check."

Beans didn't bother to think her move through. It was

147

clear she had predicted he would do this, which meant that Nana had fallen into a trap. We both saw it a moment before she executed it, bringing in a rook and plucking his bishop away.

"Checkmate," she countered.

Nana stared at the board. "Remarkable. Well played, young lady. That was brilliant." He reached out and tipped over his king. "I daresay, Arsalan, that she's better than you are."

"I doubt very much that is true." I really didn't like how uncertain I sounded.

Beenish, for her part, stuck her queen on her most offensive finger and held it up to me.

"Nice," I muttered.

"I hope we get the chance to play again," Nana told Beans. "I've gotten bored playing against my grandson. He's hopelessly predictable."

"Hey!"

"You, on the other hand, are brutal and reckless, my dear. I enjoy that."

Beenish shrugged. "Sure. We can play again. Honestly, though, I don't really like chess. I mean, why does it end when the king dies? That's the patriarchy in action right there. The queen does all the work."

"That's because she is the most powerful piece on the board. She can go almost anywhere she chooses. But if it helps you, we could change the rules," Nana suggested. "Switch the roles of the king and the queen entirely."

"I guess," she said. "But then she'd be as useless as the king. Why can't she stay powerful and keep the game going after the king falls?"

"Because you can't have everything you want in this world," he told her.

Beans grinned. "Yeah. People have said that to me before. I didn't believe them and, no offense, I don't believe you either."

After three weeks of practicing together, I was pretty certain that I cared about nothing as much as Beenish Siraj cared about dance. It seemed to be part of her, as much as her skin and bones. She made it seem effortless. She wasn't just as good as some of the heroines in Bollywood movies—she was better. And sometimes it wasn't close.

What I'm saying is that we were not the same.

When I tripped over my own feet for the second time in one session, Beenish cut the K-pop song she'd been blasting. She did not bother to help me up.

"You, sir, disgrace the name of Blackpink."

I didn't tell her I had no idea what she was talking about. She knew.

"Maybe it's the music?" I suggested.

"It's not the music."

"But it isn't anything like what we'll be using at Ms. Siraj's wedding, right? So why—"

"Just call her Qirat. And, yeah, I'm trying to get you to

learn how to move, to loosen up. You're still like a robot executing commands or something. Have some fun. You know what fun is, right? No, of course you don't. I'm going to be stuck with Mr. Spock trying to do the bhangra."

I didn't say anything. What was there to say, really?

"You can't just memorize steps and then repeat them," she said, reaching for some water. "You have to put yourself into it. Stop using your—"

I was pretty sure she was going to say "head" because that was the direction in which she tossed a plastic water bottle.

"Ow," I yelped as it struck me in the face.

Beenish gasped and rushed toward me. "Ohmygod. Are you okay? I'm so sorry. Didn't you see it coming? I thought you'd catch it."

"Why would you think that?" I demanded, rubbing the top of my left eyebrow. "I'm not a linebacker."

"That's . . . not how linebackers work."

I grimaced.

"Right. Sorry. Not important right now." Beans grabbed my arm and pulled me to the center of the garage so she could look at me in better light. She tilted my head around, touched my forehead gingerly, and seemed satisfied.

"You're fine," she said.

"Yes," I agreed. "You didn't do any lasting damage."

She smiled at me properly for the first time in forever. "I'm working on it."

Then something strange happened. Well . . . nothing happened, actually, but it felt like something had. Whatever it

150

was, it made us both realize we were standing very close. There was a moment, a very definite moment, in which I was suddenly hyperaware of my surroundings, of her, and then she cleared her throat, ran a hand through her dark hair, and stepped back.

"Thanks," I said before I realized that was a stupid thing to say. She had, after all, nearly injured me. I just wasn't used to catching things. It wasn't a skill I'd ever had a reason to develop.

"I'm glad you're not hurt."

"I didn't think you'd care, given that we aren't friends anymore." It was supposed to be a joke. It didn't come out as one.

"Don't make me throw something else at you," she warned me.

"I just meant—"

"Seriously, Arsalan, I don't want to talk about it, okay? We're doing this thing together, so let's do that. Everything else will sort itself out."

I wondered if I should say what I was thinking out loud. That was usually a sign I was about to say something I shouldn't. "Like things sorted themselves out with Diamond?"

She crossed her arms and glared at me. "What's that supposed to mean?"

"He told me what happened between you two. He doesn't think you've really forgiven him. I think he's starting to wonder if you even can."

There was a pause. Then Beenish asked, "Did I do something to make you believe I like opening up and talking about feelings?"

Well, there had been that day when she let it slip that her relationship with her biological mom was complicated. However, that had been an accident. Anyway, it was clear the answer Beenish wanted was "no," so I shook my head.

"Good. Can we get back to work now? You can judge me for not being over what happened with Diamond some other time."

I probably should have done as she asked, but she'd misunderstood me. "I wasn't judging you. I—"

"Doesn't matter."

"It does," I explained, speaking quickly before she could interrupt again. "I'm not in the position to expect anyone to forgive me or anyone else. When my father used to lose control, Mom would always remind me that forgiveness is next to godliness. But I'm not very godly so I never really managed it myself. I just meant that it'd be nice if you did accept my apology because...well, I don't know that many people and of the people I do know, you're...not the worst."

Beans stepped forward, concern on her face. "What do you mean 'when your father lost control'? Did he hurt you?"

I hadn't meant to mention that.

We never mentioned that.

Mom told me that the government would take me away from her if I ever told anyone that her husband hurt me.

I suppose that no longer mattered, but when you are seven

years old and in pain and your mother is kneeling before you, tears in her eyes, begging for a promise, and you give her your word, you keep it.

"It's...not important. He's not here anymore," I said quickly. Finding a smile, I pointed at the water bottle and tried to be funny. "Right now the only person I'm worried about hurting me is you."

My attempt at humor fell flat. She didn't say anything.

"Can we call it a day?" I asked. "I don't much feel like dancing now."

"Sure," she said. "We can pick this up later."

Chapter Twelve

The lazy sun was crawling its way up the horizon. It seemed as reluctant as I felt at the thought of cardio early on a weekend morning. Diamond Khan, however, had said that this was part of his routine. It was what he did after Fajr prayers on Saturdays, and he'd insisted I join him. He didn't appear to be the kind of person who took things seriously, but he seemed very committed to helping me get in shape.

It is human nature to be accommodating toward a person who is doing something nice for you, even if you haven't asked for it. That's probably a significant reason evangelists of every religious stripe have any success.

While I had asked Diamond for help, I was certain that it

was Beenish's request, not mine, that was behind his determination to improve my fitness level. He wanted to win back his friendship with her.

I now knew a little bit about how that felt.

He was on the basketball court when I arrived at Northgate Park. It was clear that this sport was something he practiced. His success rate was impressive.

When Diamond noticed me, he waved me over.

"Salaam, bro. You ready to play?"

"Not at all."

"Come on, Niz. You'll be great at this." He walked over and handed me the ball. "You're tall and you're good at math."

I looked at him uncertainly. "What does math have to do with basketball?"

"This whole game is basically a trigonometry problem, right?"

I frowned. I hadn't thought about that. You could, in theory, use trig to calculate the angles needed to make various shots, figure out how the ball should be released, and so on. However, I doubted very much that this could be applied in practice. I did not follow sports, but I knew that mathletes are not highly sought after by professional leagues for their in-game prowess.

I was standing just behind the semicircle that exists on the court for some reason. I tried to guess the distance to the basket—I'd never been very good at that—and after determining how far the ball had to travel, and at what velocity, I heaved it up into the air with both hands.

It did not get anywhere close to the basket.

Diamond stared at me.

I looked down and cleared my throat. "Trigonometry isn't my favorite."

It took him another few seconds to fully recover from having seen my shot attempt. Finally, he said, "Maybe we should just go for a jog?"

I nodded eagerly, and that was how we spent the morning.

Actually, that was how we spent the next twenty minutes, after which I was lying on the cool, dewy grass, gasping for air. Diamond stood over me, shaking his head.

"Your stamina is improving, at least. You couldn't manage this long at this speed on the treadmill when we started."

"Nothing wrong with my stamina," I protested. It wasn't entirely true, but I could have gone on for at least a little while longer. "My leg cramped."

"That's because you skipped stretching. It's important, bro. Doesn't Beans make you do that before you guys dance?"

She did, always, insist upon it. I'd thought it was an unnecessary—if visually arresting—exercise, despite Diamond's claims to the contrary. Apparently, I had been mistaken.

Maybe the exertion had made me light-headed, because I spoke more of the truth than I usually would have. "Warming up with her is fun."

He chuckled. "I bet."

I felt more embarrassed than I had on the basketball court. "I meant—"

"Diamond knows what you meant, bro. That girl...she's a choice piece."

That didn't seem like the kind of thing Beans would appreciate hearing. It seemed like something Sham, Qirat's awful fiancé, would say.

"Objectively, I mean," he went on. "I know you think Beans is hot. But she doesn't really do it for Diamond. Diamond likes girls with bigger—"

"I don't want to talk about her," I said quickly, forcing myself to sit up. It didn't matter if this was the usual manner in which men conversed, though I couldn't be sure. Diamond was the first "dude" I had been around for an extended period of time. His words still seemed ungentlemanly to me. "Not like this. She wouldn't like it."

Diamond shrugged. "She's not here."

"It doesn't matter. It feels...disrespectful. I am sorry if that offends you."

He stared at me, but in an entirely different way than he had after I'd missed my basketball shot earlier. This time I was able to meet his gaze. Finally, he whistled and said, "You've got it bad, bro. You're fucked." He paused, winced, then muttered astaghfirullah. "You wouldn't mind talk like that if you weren't totally into her."

"I hope that is not true."

Diamond got to his feet and held out a hand. I took it,

and he yanked me up with so much force that my shoulder screamed in its socket. He wasn't trying to be mean, though. It was clear that he simply didn't know his own strength.

"Diamond likes you, Niz. You're classy. Reminds me of my dad."

"Oh. Well, thank you. Um…is your dad…is he still with us?"

"Huh?" Diamond seemed confused for a moment, then snorted. "Yeah, yeah. He's great. He's just busy, that's all. Travels a lot for work. You know how it is."

I nodded. I did, in a way, know what that was like. Mom had basically worked all the time to make ends meet after my father left. I wished I'd had more time with her while she was alive.

"Are you going to tell Beans?"

I frowned. "That your father travels for work?"

"No, Niz. That you like her." He smirked and added, "Or that you'd like to—"

"Can you stop, please?" I interrupted. "I don't like her. I mean, you know, I think she is…pleasant to be around. However—"

"I get it," he said. "You're still in Egypt—"

God save me from people who think they're witty. "Please tell me you aren't about to make a 'denial' joke."

Diamond deflated. "Nah," he lied. "What makes you think that?"

How dance practice was going with Beenish was a matter of perspective. Over the next few sessions I made some progress, halting though it was. Unfortunately, despite these meager gains in my performance, every session left me feeling awful. Emotionally, that is, not physically—though that also remained a challenge, despite Diamond's efforts.

Beans was still rather distant and cool. Things were a little better than they had been, but...I missed her, which was ridiculous, because she was with me so much of the time, and yet she might as well have been light-years away. All I could do was keep hoping that one day, she would forgive me.

Actually, that wasn't all I could do. Nana had a couple of old Bollywood movies in his collection of videotapes, so I tried watching those, hoping that if I could impress Beans with some dance moves from them, she'd feel a little more kindly disposed toward me.

It wasn't much use. Bollywood had changed a lot in the fifty-odd years since Nana had last bought one of their productions. The men, especially, lacked the kind of skill that dancers now exhibited and seemed to only be putting in a tepid effort.

I was in the middle of one of these films when Diamond called, asking me to meet him at the mosque. Apparently someone in the congregation had had a kid a few months ago, and the new parents feeding everyone in the community was part of their newborn's aqeeqah. As nice as the idea of a good meal sounded, I think I agreed mostly because, for the first time since the night Mom had died, I had something to ask of God.

I felt awkward as I pulled into the parking lot and awkward as I walked into the building. It didn't help that some uncle had left his sandals out in the foyer for me to trip over, instead of putting them away on the shelves provided for that purpose. One didn't wear shoes inside a mosque, which made perfect sense when you thought about the fact that people would be putting their foreheads on the ground there.

Thankfully, no one saw me stumble or, at least, if they did, they were nice enough not to say anything. It helped that Diamond was clearly looking for me, because he spotted me immediately.

"Wasn't sure you'd make it, bro," he said, giving me a hug for some reason.

Not sure how to react, I patted him tentatively on his back. "And miss having food that I haven't had to make myself? Unthinkable."

He pulled back, clearly surprised, "You cook?"

"Yes."

"Are you good at it?"

I shook my head. "Dinner at our place is pretty abysmal."

He started to say something but was interrupted by a man carrying a...well, I am not sure what it is called, actually, but it is one of those contraptions that allows a person to lug a small child around. It would be fair to describe it as an unwieldy, open-air suitcase, I suppose, with rather precious cargo.

160

This, it turned out, was the host with the baby who was being honored. It seemed uninterested in the proceedings. The middle-aged uncle greeted Diamond enthusiastically, calling him Heera, then turned his attention to me.

"This is my friend," Diamond told him, "Arsalan Nizami."

Instead of responding with some version of *Who the hell are you and what are you doing at my party?*, the uncle—I'd missed his name—shook my hand warmly and thanked me for coming.

I wasn't sure how to answer. There was a long, unnatural pause. Then I pointed to the tiny human, which was staring at me with impossibly big eyes, and said, "Cute."

"His name is Ghalib."

"Like the poet? I asked.

The new father nodded, his face shining with pride. Suddenly, I felt like I knew something important and personal about this man I'd just met. I knew that he, like myself and Nana, valued the beauty found in words.

"Hi," Diamond chirped at the baby from beside me.

Ghalib continued staring at me, though, unblinking. Obviously, he expected something from me. Feeling a little ridiculous, I raised my hand and waved.

For a moment, there was no reaction. Then Ghalib gurgled happily and gave me a huge, toothless smile. I couldn't help but grin back.

As the uncle wandered away to mingle with his other guests, I wondered who that child would grow up to be and what shape his world would take. I had been new like him once, as had Diamond and Beans and Nana and my parents too. But then life had happened and we had reacted to it. We'd become who we were because of the things that happened to us, or didn't happen to us, and because of who was around us, or who was absent.

I sighed.

"You okay?" Diamond asked.

"Yeah…it's just…" I waved my hand in the air, as if trying to grab hold of the threads of destiny and fate that sew us all to what our lives become. "I hope the universe is kind to him. I hope he finds the world beautiful."

I was sitting outside in the dark, leaning against one of the mosque's walls, when Diamond came to find me. He was carrying a Styrofoam cup full of steaming chai in each hand and offered me one. I took it with a quick "Thank you," even though I was not much of a tea person.

"Why are you out here?"

I shrugged and blew on my drink before taking a hesitant sip. It was a bit too sweet and entirely too milky for my taste. "It just felt a little uncomfortable in there."

He sat down beside me. "Okay. Guess this is better than going to hide in the bathroom."

I shot him a sideways glance. So he had realized that I'd been desperate to flee the Muslim Students' Association bake sale a while back.

"That's right. Diamond's no one's fool, bro."

"So it would seem," I agreed.

"Can I ask—Niz, man, how come you're so uncomfortable around your own people? You are one of us, right? When people ask what you believe, you say—"

"I am a Muslim."

"Right," he said. "Even though you add you're a 'nominal' one, you still identify with the religion. So, how come you don't like being around it? It's part of you."

I took another sip of my tea and looked up at the sky. The full moon was magnificent. It would start to diminish soon and would then disappear entirely. I wondered how it felt when its glory began to fade at the end of each month. Did it start to feel small and dull and useless?

"Yes, being Muslim is a part of me," I attempted to joke, "but I don't like myself very much."

I winced as soon as I said it. There had been too much truth in that jest.

What was wrong with me? First I'd let it slip to Beans that my father used to hurt me, and now this....

Diamond seemed to be searching for something to say in response. I sighed. I'd put him in an awkward position. To make the conversation easier, I asked, "Why are you religious?"

"I was raised that way."

"Right. And I wasn't."

"Okay, but you've like read about it and stuff, haven't you?"

My drink was cool enough to sip easily now. "It isn't the same. Nana taught me to approach religion with my mind, critically, analytically, but you know what Allama Iqbal said, right?"

Diamond shook his head.

"He said you can't reason your way to faith or to love. Your heart has to take you there."

Diamond thought about that for a long while. It was the longest silence we'd ever shared. It was nice—serene and contemplative. "Okay, but that doesn't answer the question. Why do we—other Muslims—make you uncomfortable?"

I closed my eyes. I saw my father in one of his fits of repentance and piety, when he used to be consumed with shame and rage and disappointment. It was when he was at his worst. I used to prefer it when my father drank. I knew that when religiosity seized him, he would use it as an excuse to hurt me more.

Logically, I knew that this didn't mean something was broken in Islam. Something was broken in my father. But a part of me that was still a child, still trying to find a place to hide from his dad, that part of me didn't like being around religious people. I could rationalize it as not wanting to be a hypocrite, or however else I wanted, but that was the real truth.

I exhaled, then opened my eyes.

I appreciated my nana's faith, or lack of faith, more than I'd appreciated the violent bursts of zeal that enraptured Zeeshan Nizami. My great-grandfather was Muslim—I was

Muslim—because, despite our distance from it, Islam had shaped the lens through which we saw the world.

If that wasn't enough for Diamond, he could go eff himself.

"It gets to be a lot for me after a while," I lied, "when there is a big crowd of people, that is. I'm not really used to it."

"Oh," he said, relaxing now that my discomfort was reframed as not being about him, his friends, or people like them. "That makes sense. Diamond is the opposite. He doesn't like being alone."

"I find that it helps me think."

"Exactly, bro. Diamond doesn't like thinking."

I couldn't help but smile at that. "Why not?"

"I don't know. Mostly my brain likes to think about hot chicks and sweet kicks and cars and movies and stuff, but then…always…Diamond starts wondering—I start wondering—if I should change it up." He caught me looking at him oddly and hurried to add, "I mean, I love being Diamond. He's a sexy beast, but not everyone thinks that. Like my dad, you know, he thinks I should focus more on school and spend less time at the gym and not worry about clothes and jewelry and hair and shit. He wants me to be Heera Khan."

The admission that he saw Diamond and Heera as different people was surprising, but I nodded. I could, in part, relate. I'd never been the son my father wanted either.

"It isn't that I don't love my dad or that he doesn't love me. It's just—"

"Sometimes it feels like who you are isn't enough," I said quietly.

"Yeah. I swear, bro, my dad would like it if I were more like you."

I laughed. "I am sure my father would feel the same way about you."

"We should switch places."

I shook my head. "I'm...pretty certain you wouldn't like that."

After a moment, he said, "Speaking of people who are disappointed in me, has Beans said anything about me at all?"

I hesitated, wondering if I should lie to make him feel better, then shook my head. "Sorry."

He made a face. "Maybe Diamond wasn't as important to her as she was to him."

"I'm actually surprised the bouquet of weeds didn't work." I wasn't being sarcastic. The fact that the gesture was flawed made it, in my opinion, all the more endearing. "Have you tried apologizing again?"

"It's useless. Told her 'sorry' a hundred times. Diamond isn't sure what else to do. It isn't like she ever apologizes. She didn't say she was sorry for calling my family names or even for damaging this perfect nose."

"I don't know what to tell you. Maybe she'll come around."

He gestured up vaguely to the dark heavens above us. "If Allah wills it. Honestly, though, that girl...she's so

166

stubborn, bro, maybe it won't ever happen. She's been pissed at her own mother for years. She barely talks to Aiza Aunty. If she can't forgive her own mom, what chance does Diamond have?"

That was a depressing thought.

"I'm really hoping that she'll start to like you as much as you like her," he added.

I exhaled forcefully. "I already told you, I don't—"

"Are you really going to lie to Diamond in a mosque, Niz?"

I scowled at him. "We are *outside* a mosque."

"You'd be good for her. She's like an open flame and you're like...you're like water, you know? You're low-key and calm. You guys would balance each other out."

"You know what I don't like to think about?" I asked. Then, without waiting for him to guess, went on. "Impossibilities. It's a waste of time. Beenish will never think of me that way. You know that, right? So stop bringing it up. Please."

"What makes you so sure?"

"I'm clearly not her type."

He chuckled. "Man, Diamond has been friends with her for ages, and he doesn't know her type. She's never actually liked anyone. Now if Diamond doesn't know what her type is, you definitely don't."

"I know she's never going to be interested in some loser," I snapped.

There was another silence. It wasn't like the one before.

It felt uncomfortable and constricted, like a viper trying to shed its old skin.

"Arsalan," he finally said, very gently, "you're not a loser, man."

I kept my gaze fixed on the moon above. I wasn't sure what to say next. I didn't know how to get out of this conversation.

Then God saved me.

Inside the mosque, the adhan began to sound.

"Come on," Diamond said, getting to his feet. "We're being called to pray."

Chapter Thirteen

A week later, when Ms. Siraj requested I stay behind after class, I worried that she'd ask me again if I'd finished the extra credit assignment about the shape of the world. I hadn't had time to ponder it, which was odd, because I'd always had time for extra schoolwork before.

Beenish Siraj and Diamond Khan were not good for my grades. There was no longer any chance that I would challenge Annika Bryzgalova's position as the top student at Tennyson. I was ahead enough of everyone else, thanks to the arts education that Nana had given me, that I could comfortably skip most readings. Material in classes like language and composition or world literature wasn't at all challenging. The sciences, however, demanded more work.

It turned out that Qirat didn't want to talk about school. Instead, she asked, "Dance practice still isn't going well, is it?"

"Did Beenish tell you?"

"How come you never call her Beans?"

Didn't I? I suppose I had only ever used Beenish's nickname around Nana, with whom I could be myself. Around everyone else, I'd always been formal, which was only appropriate. To her sister's question, I answered, "That is an intimacy I haven't been granted."

Qirat chuckled. "How many Victorian romance novels have you read in your life? All of them?"

"This isn't a romance novel and we aren't Victorians— well, we are a little Victorian, with our arranged marriages and socially enforced norms of modesty and propriety—"

"Arsalan."

I cleared my throat. "I don't like to take liberties with people. Especially not Beenish. Not right now." At Qirat's quizzical expression, I added, "I...did something stupid, and now she doesn't want anything to do with me."

"You didn't try to kiss her or something, did you?"

"I would *never*! Well, actually, never is overstating the matter a little, but—"

Qirat held up a hand. "Relax. It was a joke."

"Oh. I'm still getting used to those."

She smiled. "So my little sister doesn't want anything to do with you, hmm?"

"Yes. She's made that very clear."

"Right. She's made that very clear by going to your house and hanging out with you every day."

I frowned. "That's different. It's for dance practice."

"If you say so. Anyway, I'm sorry that isn't going well. And no, to answer your question, Beans didn't tell me. I guessed." Ms. Siraj held out a piece of paper. "She's asking for a favor on your behalf from someone she doesn't even like to talk to much. Things must be desperate."

It was a note written by Beans. I recognized her sweeping, poorly restrained handwriting. It was an address, followed by a command to show up there at three o'clock.

"What is this?" I asked.

"That," Qirat replied, "is the glass you break in case of emergency."

Diamond was standing by the Eldorado when I got to it after school, looking at it the way people examine dinosaur bones.

"Cool whip," Diamond said, then immediately realizing who he was talking to, was kind enough to clarify. "It's a nice car."

That was an unexpected reaction. "Really?"

"Yeah," he said, as if it were completely obvious.

"You don't think it's old?"

"It suits you. You're a classic man."

I had to chuckle. Diamond had been trying to squeeze self-esteem-building compliments into all our conversations since our talk at the mosque last week. This one was a reach. "It's actually my nana's."

"He's a badass."

I raised an eyebrow at that. I wasn't sure how Nana would react to being called an ass of any sort.

"You ready to go?" Diamond asked.

"You're coming with me?"

"You don't even know where Aiza Aunty lives." He raised his arms to keep me from objecting. "Beans told Qirat Api you had a map and a compass or something, but Qirat thinks it'll be easier if Diamond is with you."

"Aiza Aunty? Beenish is sending me to meet her mom?"

"Yup," Diamond chirped. "We both get to bask in the glory of the world's hottest aunty." As I pulled out keys, he asked, "Hey, can I drive?"

"No. Is Beenish coming with us?"

"Oh, Beans doesn't visit her mother," he said, gesturing for me to unlock the passenger-side door. He was blocking it, however, so I had to push past him. He probably didn't realize that the car didn't have remote-controlled locks. "There a lot of bad history there."

Almost all history, in my experience, was either bad or was about to become bad. The world is a bowl of milk destined to go sour.

"Beans said to tell you to mind your own business if you ask questions about their relationship," Diamond volunteered preemptively. "You're a dancer, not a therapist."

"I'm not a dancer."

172

"But you will be once Aiza Aunty is done with you."

The thought of having to spend any significant amount of time with a desi aunty was not appealing. The most I'd interacted with aunties was in the days after Mom had passed, when droves of them stopped by, wearing white, to cluck over me.

I didn't like the way they had looked at me. It wasn't their pity that bothered me—it was the knowingness in their eyes. It was as if they thought they understood me somehow and knew that my life would be better if I lived it exactly how they wanted. There was a sense of heavy-handed, overconfident wisdom about them.

"What's Aiza Aunty like?"

"Man, she's super pretty. She could still be in movies now, I think."

That was not helpful information. I ought to have been more specific. "I see. But is she unpleasant or nice or..."

"Oh. Well, she's not the worst."

I glanced over at Diamond.

He held out his hands in a helpless gesture. "She's not mean. Exactly. Well, she's a little mean, but you're okay with that, right? After all, you get along with Beans, and since that's your jam, you shouldn't have a problem with Aiza Aunty."

"Mean is not my jam," I protested.

"Whatever powers your tower is fine with me."

I shook my head. "You're a poet, Heera Khan."

He grinned happily at the compliment, missing my

173

sarcasm entirely. "Just…be prepared, okay? She's super into the Mughlai decor. You know what I'm talking about, right? The Mughals were like kings and stuff?"

"I may have heard of them," I said dryly.

Nana had always taken my education seriously, but he was particularly uncompromising about history. I didn't always know what was happening in the world now, but I definitely knew what had happened before, sometimes in minute, unnecessary detail.

For example, in ancient Rome, they used to punish those who killed their own fathers by sewing them into leather sacks with a rooster, a dog, a viper, and a monkey. Then they used to throw the sack into a river.

Did I need to know that? No.

But I did know it, so Diamond could be certain that I knew about the Mughal Empire.

"You got quiet," he noted. "What are you thinking about?"

"Murder," I told him.

He sat up in his seat a bit. "Um…okay, then."

"Not regular murder," I reassured him. "Patricide specifically."

"That's…good?"

"Actually, I should be thinking about fratricide. Brothers killing brothers. That was more the Mughal jam."

Diamond rubbed the middle of his forehead with the base of his palm. "You know what, bro? I think you're going to get along with Aiza Aunty just fine."

As soon as I saw Aiza Aunty, I knew that she was grand. She was beautiful, yes, and you could spot some of Beenish and some of Qirat in her face. However, she was still very different from both her daughters.

The movie star in her was more than skin deep. She was a performer in the way she sauntered, in the way she spoke, and in the way her hands moved while she was talking, every gesture large and expansive.

She didn't just open the door to her apartment when Diamond knocked. She *flung* it open and followed the gesture up with an imperious toss of her brown hair.

"Heera Khan," Aiza Siraj said by way of greeting. "Many suns have set, many moons have risen, since last I saw your face."

"Sorry, Aunty," he said. "It's just that—"

"There is no need to apologize," she told him dismissively. "It isn't as if I missed you." Then she turned her attention to me with an intensity I'd only ever seen her youngest daughter exhibit before. "And you must be Arsalan Nizami."

I bowed in greeting and Aiza Aunty took the opportunity to grab my face in one hand, pulling me down closer to her.

"Hi?" I managed the best I could with her thumb and index finger exerting a pincer grip on my cheeks.

In response, she only muttered, as if to herself, "Tall. Beans is not tall."

I started to pull away and, thankfully, she let me go. "Is that a problem?"

"I've always thought that couples should look like they are a fit for each other." She adjusted the fancy, steel-gray saree she was wearing.

I raised my eyebrow. "You mean dance partners?"

"The height difference in this case is acceptable," she said, which was not an answer to my question. Instead of elaborating, she whirled around to glide back into her apartment. Diamond looked at me and pretended to wipe sweat off his brow in mock relief.

"Time has not made you funnier, Heera," Aiza Aunty called over her shoulder.

"How did she see that?" Diamond whispered.

I started to shrug but then stopped. Aiza Aunty's place was...a lot. It was overdecorated in the lavish style of the kings of bygone days, with elaborate patterns and bright colors everywhere. There was a lot of gold and deep maroon. It felt like a museum more than a place to live, which actually made me feel a little at home.

"So you are called Nizami, yes?"

"Actually," I told her, "everyone who knows me calls me Arsalan."

"But I do not know you, Nizami." Aiza Aunty pointed me to a wood chair upholstered in red with white elephants all over it. "Tell me, what makes you special?"

"He's not special," Diamond said.

"I'm really not," I admitted.

"Your name is special. My forefathers were emperors, you know, and yours, I imagine, given your last name, were poets in their courts. It could be that our blood is connected through time."

Nana had never taught me much about our ancestry, which was fine. It was not a subject I had any desire to study. The impulse people had to be proud of their forefathers was understandable, but if you took pride in the triumphs of other people, did you not also take on shame for the blood they had shed and the lives they had destroyed?

Kings and those who served them were especially problematic. I had scars enough from my own personal history. I didn't have any desire to deal with the legacies others had left behind.

"I've never really cared about that," I told Aiza Aunty.

"Why not? There is power in blood, you know. It is the first thing you inherit. Of course, it also carries congenital conditions." She nodded to Diamond. "Like disgrace, as my children have found out."

Diamond turned a distressing shade of purple. "I'm sorry, Aunty," he said. Almost everything he'd said so far had been an apology. "Like I've explained to you before, it's just…my family, they're good Muslims. They don't want to be associated with a family where…I personally don't think there is anything wrong with what you did. But you know how people talk."

Good Muslims. I couldn't help but shake my head. It was incredible how little the righteous applied scripture to their

177

own lives. " 'No bearer of burdens will be made to carry the burden of another,' " I quoted.

Aiza Aunty barked a harsh laugh. I could tell I'd risen in her estimation.

Diamond, for his part, scowled, "You said you were a nominal Muslim."

"I never said I was an uninformed one."

"In Istanbul," Aiza Aunty volunteered, "I once heard someone say that one never knows who has money or who has the faith."

Heera sighed. "Well...anyway, I'm just...I am sorry for how my family acted."

She looked at him for a long moment, then shrugged. "I do believe Nizami was saying something about people being held responsible only for the things they themselves have done."

Diamond seemed surprised that the verse I'd cited could apply to him as well as it had applied to Beans.

"I would like to speak to Nizami a moment," Aiza Aunty told him. "Be a dear and make us some tea. You'll find everything you need easily enough. While you're doing that, I'll see what I can do about turning Pinocchio into a real boy."

As Diamond wandered toward the kitchen, I said, "That isn't a very good analogy. Pinocchio was famous for lying. I never lie."

"Truly?"

"Not if I can help it," I amended.

Aiza Aunty chuckled. "That is a very large, very vague

exception. But it's good if you don't lie. Honesty is important in dance. It shows. Beans, however, seemed concerned that your movements are awkward and stiff."

"She keeps telling me to stop overthinking things."

"Which is both good and useless advice at the same time, hmm?"

I nodded. "I mean, I wouldn't say that to Beenish, but yeah, exactly."

"Does my younger daughter scare you?"

"Yes."

She smiled. "Excellent. Now, Beans is probably right. I will judge for myself, of course, when we begin, but the idea is indeed for your movements to look natural. The artifice in the art should be veiled from your audience."

"But if you tell someone not to overthink something," I countered, "that just makes them think more. They worry about overthinking."

"I understand," Aiza Aunty said. "Being relaxed, however, is still key. It also helps, if you can manage it, to have fun."

"I don't really know how to have fun. Not outside of books, anyway."

She leaned back in her seat and looked at me like I was a curious thing. "Interesting. Do you know why Beenish sent you to me?"

"What do you mean?"

Aiza Aunty responded with a question of her own. "Has my daughter said anything to you about how she feels?"

"I think she feels like she needs a dance partner for her . . . uh, contest."

"I am a professional . . . well, was one, anyway, and I still have many connections. Beenish could have asked me to introduce her to any number of boys who can already dance. But that's not what she asked. Clearly, she wants to dance with you. A boy who struggles with fun. It might be worth considering why."

I stared at Aiza Aunty. She was right, of course. Holding an audition and trying to find a partner on her own made sense if Beenish was determined not to contact her estranged mother. Now that she had decided to, though, continuing on with me dragging her down was completely illogical. As Aiza Aunty said, there were professional dancers they could hire or ask favors of to replace me.

"Anyway, I can teach you the craft. But then, so can Beans. What you're missing is the magic of it all. That you have to experience for yourself in order to understand it."

"Magic?" My skepticism was so profound that it almost made my question sound disrespectful.

"Yes. I'll write a spell that might help. All you have to do is give it to Beenish. You believe in magic, don't you?"

"No."

"You will, Nizami. You will."

I gave Beans her mother's "spell" when she came by Nana's house the next day, as usual, for our dance practice. She was

180

wearing a large hoodie over her tights, and on it was printed, in a giant font, PROTAGONIST.

She read the note wordlessly, then looked at me. "Did you read it?"

I shook my head. "Aiza Aunty said it was for you."

"You can," she said, handing it back to me.

I frowned and started following her as she marched to the garage. The note from Aiza Aunty was just two lines. The first simply said, "Dance with him."

The second was a sequence of musical symbols that meant nothing to me. I started to ask Beenish what they represented but was distracted by the sight of her peeling off her hoodie. No matter how many times she did that, it remained...sorcerous.

She glanced at me and I looked down, crossing my ankles and feeling my face turn as pink as her leotard—no, wait, she'd corrected me about that before. It was a camisole unitard, I think.

Beans held out a hand. "Come dance."

"Shouldn't we warm up? You always—"

"Now, please," she said.

As I took her hand, she stepped close and guided my fingers to her waist. It occurred to me instantly that I'd never been this close to a girl before. I hadn't even really touched a girl before. Suddenly my heart was panicking, hammering away at my chest as if to make sure that I knew this was a moment of considerable importance in its rather inert existence.

It was like a mountain remembering that it was, in fact, a volcano.

"You're okay," Beans said softly.

I licked my lips, because I was suddenly parched, but nodded.

I think I said I was fine.

From the little bit of mischief in her smile, I think she knew I was lying, that she suspected her entirely platonic actions were making everything seem a lot more complicated than they had been just seconds ago.

With one hand resting on my arm, she held up her other one. When our fingers touched, she interlaced them.

"Ready?" Beans asked.

"There's no music."

"Right. Let's pick something old...something you'll be comfortable with." She called out, "Hey, Siri? Play Dean Martin's 'Sway with Me' on repeat."

"Now playing," a disembodied female voice intoned, "Dean Martin's 'Sway (Quien Sera)' on repeat."

I couldn't help but grin at the first few notes of the familiar song. It wasn't often I heard music that I knew well, but Dino—as Nana called him—featured heavily in my great-grandfather's collection of records.

Then a distressing thought occurred to me. "Wait. Is it really okay that your phone—this Siri AI—is constantly listening to us?"

"Don't worry about it," Beenish commanded. "Now, you're going to feel me move, and then you're going to follow. That's all I need you to think about. Don't look at your feet. Focus on my eyes. Focus on being here with me."

"What if I step on your toes?"

"I'm a big girl. I can take it. Besides, we'll go slow. It's your first time."

"So no acrobatics?"

"Not today. Ready? You're not looking at me, Arsalan."

"It's…embarrassing. I'm not used to being this close to someone."

"Are you blushing?" Beans asked. "Wow. You're such a gaon ki gori."

I frowned. "Did you just call me a village girl?"

"You totally are, though. This is like a Bollywood movie. I'm the dude from the big city who corrupts you, takes your honor, and ruins your life."

"You have weird fantasies."

"Shut up," she said. "Come on, Rapunzel. Let down your hair. Let's have some fun."

Beans stepped closer to me. Just a little. Just enough that her chest was almost touching mine. I was very aware of the warmth of her fingers, of the soft skin of her bare arms. All levity fled the room.

She touched the side of my face gently, forcing me to meet her gaze. Then she began to move. I felt the muscles in her left hip shift as she stepped back once, then again, and I followed.

Dino was still singing, but the music seemed distant. My attention was captured entirely by Beenish's eyes. They were

the color of space, of the universe. I could spend an eternity staring down at them and barely begin to chart the play
of dark upon dark. I'd never solve the mystery of where the
spark in them came from.

We slowly made our way over the cool concrete floor of
the garage. Her playfulness vanished, replaced by amusement, followed by...fondness, I think, chased by...some-
thing else. I realized, as I let myself study her other features,
that color had rushed to her cheeks too, and that her smile
was gone, but her lips were parted just a little, as if she were
considering saying something but didn't know where to
begin.

I was drawn to them. There was a sudden, almost irresistible need to touch her lips with mine, more urgent and
desperate than anything I'd ever felt before.

My God.

I resisted the impulse to kiss her, of course. She'd said
we weren't going to be friends. People don't kiss their non-
friends. Well, I suppose they don't kiss their friends either,
exactly, but...it didn't matter. She didn't want me to kiss
her.

In fact, Beenish would probably slap me if I tried. More
than once.

She touched the side of my face again. There was no need
to this time. She already had all my attention. "Where are
you wandering off to, Arsalan? You're here with me. Right?"

"I am."

"Don't you want to stay in this moment?"

"I do."

She smiled. "Then stay."

"I will."

I hadn't realized before how intimate simply looking at someone could feel. I don't know how long we danced together, but it was long enough for me to lose my breath, for a hint of sweat to build up on Beenish's top lip and forehead. It was long enough that when we stopped and stepped back from each other, it was unnatural, like how the movement of your arms through the air feels after you've been swimming for a while.

My first thought—once I was capable of thought again—was that things would be awkward now. I'd felt so connected to her. How do you share that and then just move on? What do you say? What do you do?

You wiggle your toes, apparently, as you fiddle with your phone, freeing it from an endless loop of a classic song. That's what Beans did, with a grin on her face. "Look at that. Every toe survived. That wasn't so bad, was it?"

"It was...not bad at all."

She shook her head. "You were amazing. Holy shit. That was..."

"A little magical?" I suggested. Aiza Aunty had said that she was writing me a spell. She had not been joking, apparently.

"Yes! How the hell did Amma figure that out after meeting you one time? You just needed to slow dance."

185

"That's what the musical notes she drew were? A slow dance?"

Beans shook her head. "Not really. It's just 'You Are My Sunshine.' When I little, Amma would make me stand on her feet and we'd dance to it. She just...Well, she was right. She fixed you. You weren't thinking and you were having fun. That woman is as amazing as she is infuriating. There is no one like her."

You are, I wanted to say, but it wasn't clear to me that Beans would see it as a compliment. It was true, however. Beans was amazing. All the wizardry had come from her, even if the instructions had come from Aiza Aunty.

"This is great. You've had a breakthrough, but there's still a ton of work to do. You have to learn how to stay in that zone you just discovered—"

There was a sharp knock on the garage door that made her jump. It had come from Nana's cane.

"We're in here," I called out.

Nana let himself in. He was holding mail in his hand.

"It's from your father."

The news made my heart sink a little, but successfully dancing with Beans had it soaring so high that it didn't really matter that much.

"Thank you. But I can read it later."

"It's not a letter, Arsalan. It's a postcard. From San Diego. Your father is coming home."

Chapter Fourteen

"I know I should have handled it better," I told Mom, sitting in front of her headstone. The cemetery was cold and nearly pitch-black. There was no moon and the lighting in this place hadn't been designed for people to wander around in after dusk. Much like the Earth itself, cemeteries rely on the sun to make them habitable.

I wished, for the hundredth time, that I had a phone. I could have called Nana and Beans. I could have told them I was fine and apologized for freaking out and running away from the house. I hadn't been thinking. I'd just needed to go.

Zeeshan Nizami was coming back to Sacramento.

Fuck.

I ran a hand over my face, then through my hair, willing myself to breathe. I'd just calmed down. Getting worked up again was pointless.

Somehow I'd let myself hope that he'd stay in Arizona forever, comfortable with the world's largest solar telescope and the original London Bridge. It seemed like a place my father might belong. It did get really hot there, after all.

"What am I supposed to do now?"

My mom didn't respond. She was no help.

But why would she be? She's always protected him more than she protected you.

I shook my head. I didn't want to think that.

I wouldn't think it.

I never thought it.

But it was true. It was fucking true.

I got to my feet and began pacing. I had to find my center again.

"Deep breaths. Deep breaths. Everything's going to be okay, Arsalan. You'll be fine."

That was a lie, just like it had been when Muneera Nizami had said it right before she died. Just like it had been every time she'd said it after her husband had hurt us.

"I don't want to think these things!"

My voice echoed in the emptiness around me.

No, not emptiness. Lifelessness.

I was usually so good at keeping these thoughts out. I was so careful to dam them up. What was happening? My emotional control had been slipping. I'd been telling secrets to Beans, confiding in Diamond. I'd gotten careless.

Today was terrible. My thoughts were relentless. I'd kept them at bay forever, but they'd found a path into my conscious mind and they would not stop.

Was this because of Beans? Because I'd actually been happy, had actually been open, when the news that my father was returning had struck? Had there just been too far to fall? Or was it the dancing?

Because it felt like my mind was moving with its own rhythm now, each thought chased by another one, unable to resist the gravity of its logic like I'd been unable to resist the gravity of Beenish Siraj, of the next step and the next inevitable step after that. Inexorably, I was being drawn into the heart of darkness.

"How do I make it stop, Mom?"

Why are you asking her?

Why would she help you now?

She never has before.

"Please. I just want to . . ."

What? Go back to Nana's place and hide from time and the world?

There is no protection to be had there anymore, Arsalan. He's coming home. It's his home. He owns it.

You can't hide. And Nana will have to face reality too. It's what he is scared of. That's why he lives in the past, so he can pretend things are safe, and all you do is pretend with him.

But there is no pretending anymore. Zeeshan Nizami will make sure of that.

His coming is at hand.

I dropped to my knees next to Mom.

"Help me," I demanded.

There was no answer.

As expected.

I looked up at the immense, unending dark of the sky. It was either cloudy and I hadn't noticed, or the smog in the city was worse than usual, because the heavens looked empty.

"Help me," I whispered.

Again, there was silence.

Of course there was.

I was alone.

And you always will be.

I bowed my head in submission to this truth.

Then a bright light shattered the horizon, blinding me.

I tried to focus, but it was useless. My eyes were still fighting to adjust to how suddenly the night had broken.

I saw a shape. Someone, I realized, was running toward me.

"Beans?" I asked.

I hoped.

I prayed.

Beenish Siraj threw her arms around me, and suddenly my existence was warmth and softness and the smell of bitter oranges, and I began to cry.

It took a while for me to gather myself. Beenish didn't say anything. She didn't ask me why I was weeping, or say that I should stop, or lie and assure me that everything would be okay. She just held me. If she hadn't, it would have taken me longer to pull myself together. She kept me from scattering into too many pieces.

"Sorry," I said as I finally pulled away from her. "I just... Thank you."

Beans smiled a little and swiped at her own eyes quickly, before clearing her throat and looking at everyone who was with us and yet not with us at all. "You're not nearly goth enough to be here right now, Arsalan."

"Neither are you," I countered.

"I so am."

I considered pointing out that she was still wearing her pink unitard, but I didn't. "Nana told you where to find me?"

She nodded.

"And he told you... everything?"

"Yes," Beans said softly. "And I don't know what to say really."

After a moment, I said, "Anyway, like I said, I'm sorry about..." I waved at my face. "My father taught me real men don't cry in front of people."

"I think that's pretty fucking stupid."

"Speaking of stupid things, and while I'm apologizing—"

"Don't," she said. "You don't have to."

"I shouldn't have misjudged you, Beenish. I am sorry. It's just…" I gestured around us, and my voice threatened to break again. "I'm all messed up inside and sometimes, most of the time, everything makes sense and I can get along fine, but other times the cracks show. I'm so used to people hurting me, I just assumed that's what you were trying to do as well."

"I'll forgive you if you never talk about it again."

"That sounds more than fair," I said.

She held out her hand. "Friends?"

I took it gently and held it for a moment before letting her go. "Yes please."

"We should hang out, then."

"Now? Here?"

"Yes now," she said. "But not here, obviously. Let's get something to drink. It'll make you feel better."

"Oh." I got to my feet and helped her up. "I…Well, I know I talk about not being all that Muslim, Beenish, but I actually don't drink."

"And we're underage," she reminded me. "I was saying we should go get some coffee."

"Right. Of course."

"And you should keep calling me Beans."

Beans first suggested that we go to The Naked Lounge. Once

192

I stopped blushing, she explained that it was just a café and you weren't required to take your clothes off. That this was, in fact, probably discouraged.

"The name is very misleading, then," I pointed out.

"You know what? Let's just go to Temple. It's more your speed."

Beenish's order at this second coffee shop was frightening. She got a latte with three extra shots of espresso, even though she was told it already came with two. For my part, I decided to go with milk.

"Just milk?"

"Warm milk," I clarified, wondering why I was getting such odd looks from everyone else in line. No one said anything, though Beans did step away from me as if to disassociate herself from my company. "I don't want to have trouble sleeping tonight."

"You're such a wimp," she said.

I shrugged. That was a fact undisputed.

"Are you cold?" I asked her as we waited for our drinks.

"What? Oh, because I put the hoodie back on? It's CYA. I mean, it's literally to cover my butt. Tights or anything that looks like them," she said, gesturing down to the legs of her unitard, "don't exactly meet Muslim modesty standards otherwise."

"I hadn't noticed," I lied.

"Uh-huh. Well, my dad and Roshni would flip out if they heard a word about it from any aunty, which you know they eventually would. Hell, even Qirat would be upset."

"Really?" I asked. "She seems...cool."

"She still lives by a code." Beenish looked at me out of the corner of her eye. "Someone can be religious and still cool, you know."

"That has not been my experience."

"Okay, but you've basically only been around shitty people your entire life." She winced when she realized she was talking about my family—my father, I suspected, in particular. "No offense."

"Didn't religious people kick you out of a mosque once?"

"Yeah," Beans said as our names were called. "But that was like one time."

"Are you going to tell me about it?"

"And deepen your prejudice that Muslims can't be fun?" she demanded. "Nope. Not going to do it." As we found seats, she asked, "Anyway, your dad isn't religious, right? I mean, because of the drinking—"

"He's gotten more pious, actually," I told her. "Strange fits of religion he's always known..." I paused to see if the unusual syntax would tip her off to the Wordsworth reference. It apparently didn't. "But whenever that's happened before, he's always lapsed. Now he's apparently with some group of preachers in Arizona, and they've helped him stay sober, so maybe it'll stick this time."

Except he's not in Arizona.

I shoved the thought away and focused on Beans.

"What about your mom?"

"Islam was a part of her life," I said, "but she was more

spiritual than anything else. She wouldn't have been one of the aunties commenting on your . . . hindquarters."

Beenish, who was in the middle of taking a sip of her coffee, started laughing, choked, coughed, grabbed a napkin to cover her face, and generally dissolved into disarray.

"What?" I asked.

"The world won't end," she gasped after she'd recovered a little, "if you say 'ass,' Arsalan."

"I know," I snapped. "Just so you're aware, I said the F-word earlier."

She was the soul of skepticism. "Did you really?"

"Well . . . okay, I didn't say it. But I thought it."

Beans gasped dramatically.

"I get it. I'm—"

"Sweet," she said. "I think it's sweet. Like you opening the car door for me the first time we drove together."

"You told me no one does that anymore."

"I know. Both those things can be true at the same time, can't they?"

That was impossible to argue against, so I drank my milk.

"You remind me of my mom," she said a moment later.

"Aiza Aunty wouldn't like that comparison at all."

"And that's a plus," Beans said with a grin. "But seriously, you both talk a little weird. You don't dress like anyone else—at least, you didn't until I got my hands on you—and there's just something about you two—"

"An old-school gentility?" I suggested.

She scoffed. "No. It's like . . . a broken wing. What you

195

went through, what you're going through, is way worse, but Amma went through a lot of crap too. It changed her. You know about her past, right?"

I nodded.

"It wasn't like she did just one absurdly daring thing. She kept pushing and breaking social and religious boundaries of what was acceptable over and over. I don't really know what she was thinking. She grew up like I did. I mean, you know, except the fact that she was in Pakistan. But she grew up in a household where that kind of thing shouldn't have been an option for her. Her family was worried it would bring them shame."

"But she did it anyway?"

Beans nodded. "Meeting my father helped. He was totally in love with her, I think, and she made him promise he'd let her dance after they got married. I don't think he imagined she'd be that...bold, that reckless, when she got what she wanted."

"She wasn't wearing a CYA hoodie, in other words," I said.

"Amma was wearing...a lot less than that. I'm not sure you understand what a huge deal this was. Have you heard of Qandeel Baloch?"

I shook my head.

"Qandeel got famous a few years back for being Pakistan's Kim Kardashian."

I sighed. "That's not a helpful reference for me."

Beans huffed, possibly trying to think of another parallel,

then gave up. "She got famous for posting provocative pictures of herself online."

"Okay," I said. "Why are we talking about this person?"

"Qandeel Baloch was strangled to death by her brother because her actions 'dishonored' their family."

I sat back in my chair. "That's...horrible."

"Yeah. It's also a good way to gauge the kind of consequences social shaming can have for women who step out of line."

"What line?"

Beans shrugged. "We're always either wearing too many clothes or not enough clothes, and no one wants to mind their own fucking business." Taking a deep breath, she went on. "Anyway, Amma became notorious after her appearances in those movies. Her family basically disowned her. Her in-laws were freaking out. It was a mess."

"Have you asked her why she did it?"

Beans shook her head.

"Why not?"

"Because I'm not sure Amma owes anyone an answer to that question." She hesitated and then added, "At the very least, I'm not sure she owes one to me. My father felt differently, I guess. He moved us here, to get away from it all, but her fame followed our family. The world is a small place now. There's nowhere to hide."

"So your parents got a divorce."

"Right. Dad got way into Islam, almost like he was trying to distance himself, as much as possible, from Amma. He

197

married Roshni, who is like her exact opposite. I mean, the woman sets up arranged marriages, Arsalan. I'm not sure you could get Aiza Siraj to attend an arranged marriage, much less actually be the cause of it."

"And all this reminded you of me?"

Beenish sighed. "It's hard to explain."

"Evidently."

"Do you really want me to flip you off? Because I will."

I held up my arms in surrender.

"But yes. You guys are similar, in a way. Something changed in Amma after all that. She became colder, more withdrawn. I mean, she was never like...she wasn't affectionate or cuddly or anything, but later she was...It was like she forgot how to be in the world. You're like that a little."

It didn't seem like she was done speaking, so I stayed silent.

"Roshni pretty clearly didn't really want Qirat and me around and said we should go live with our mother. Dad said no, because he thought Amma would be a bad influence. And Amma said no too."

"Why?"

Beenish shook her head. "Some bullshit about how she didn't want us associated with her disgrace. But that didn't make any sense. We were always going to get tagged with that. Aiza Siraj just didn't want us around. She wanted to be free. She's always wanted to be free. Her daughters were obstacles to that."

"I can see why that upset you."

Beans shrugged. "I guess. Sometimes I think I'm unreasonable. I mean, Qirat got over it. I...couldn't. I can't."

It was time to try out a quote I'd tried on Diamond before, one which he had tragically misattributed. " 'My good opinion once lost is lost forever.' That was said by—"

"Crown Prince Mohammed bin Salman of Saudi," she said. "I know."

I buried my face in my hands.

"Anyway," she said, "that's all of my baggage. Well, that's the heaviest of it. Go ahead. Psychoanalyze me."

"I really have no interest in doing that."

Beenish raised an eyebrow. "Really? What are you interested in, then?"

I found myself smiling. Given how crushed I'd felt tonight, it was a remarkable thing. And it was because of Beans.

"Well, Ms. Siraj," I said, "if it's all the same to you, I think I'd just like to dance."

I got home late and found Nana waiting for me in my room. That was surprising. It was significantly past his bedtime. There was a slender book in his lap—he'd apparently decided to reread *The Prophet* by Khalil Gibran—but he was looking at my desk. Specifically, he was looking at an unopened letter lying on it. He'd clearly placed it there.

"More charming correspondence," he said, without bothering to greet me or ask how I was or even where Beenish had gone. "From your father, I think."

"I thought you already got the mail."

"That was yesterday's mail. I went back to the mailbox after five, just to see if anything else had come."

"Those are long journeys for you, Nana," I said. "You went all the way to the end of the driveway twice. You must be exhausted."

He exhaled. "I see that your wits, such as they are, have returned at least. Dramatic of you to storm off like that. You're spending too much time around teenagers, I think. This is why school is a bad idea, just like prisons are. Melons catch their color from observing other melons."

I had no idea what he meant by that. When this happened with other people, it meant that I'd stumbled upon a pop culture reference I didn't understand. When it happened with Nana, it was usually because he was translating something that made sense in Urdu that didn't really cross over into English well.

I held out my hand for Zeeshan Nizami's letter. Nana, who was seated at my desk, picked it up and gave it to me. I didn't feel scared or alarmed for some reason by his new correspondence. The day I'd had so far had left me drained of all emotion. I was exhausted. Besides, it wasn't as if things could get worse.

Arsalan,

Did you get my postcard? I am sure you are glad I am on my way back to Sacramento. If not glad, best learn to be.

Heading to Los Angeles soon. Am traveling with a group of imams and scholars. They appreciate me and use me sometimes in their sermons as an example of redemption. They call me "The New Nuayman." I like that. Have looked into changing name. Have decided to do it. Maybe I'll change your name too. Arsalan ibn Nuayman. You'll get used to it.

From LA, we are going to Mecca for the small pilgrimage. At the House of Allah, I will pray for you to become a blessing instead of a burden for the people in your life. I've been taught that miracles do happen.

When we return, our plan is to visit and preach in as many mosques in California as we can. By mid-December we will be in Sacramento. I will see you then.

—Zeeshan

I gave the letter to Nana, who seemed surprised by the gesture. It was the first time I'd invited him to read something Zeeshan Nizami had written, but the thought of explaining what my father had said seemed unbearably tiring.

As I wandered over to my bed and collapsed on it, Nana fumbled around in his jacket pockets for his reading glasses, didn't find them, so held the paper far away from his face.

"This is a reprieve," Nana announced once he'd managed to get through the entire thing. "I thought he was going to be here any day now. Wasn't that what you thought as well? At least you have until December before you have to deal with him."

"What difference does it make?" I asked. "He'll be here eventually."

"The difference time makes depends on what you do with it. We could use these months to seek legal counsel. We could tell the police how he treated you. We could perhaps even get a restraining order to keep him away from you and away from my house."

Except this isn't your house, I didn't say.

"Mom could have done that. She chose not to. You think she would like it if I reported him now?"

"I think Muneera," Nana said quietly, "is rather past having opinions."

That was true.

"I realized something about Mom when I went to see her today. Actually, no. I've always known this, on some level, but I finally accepted it."

"And what was this epiphany that you had in that grave-yard you're so unnaturally fond of?"

"Mom loved Dad more than she loved me."

"Arsalan—"

I closed my eyes. "She would have left him otherwise. She would have taken the steps you're suggesting now. But she didn't. And sometimes, when he'd start beating me and she begged him to stop, if he wouldn't listen, she'd say, 'At least don't hit him in the face. Not in the face, Zeeshan.' It

202

was a small mercy, but it wasn't meant to protect me, was it? It was to protect him."

Nana bowed his head and, for once in his very long life, didn't seem to have anything clever to offer.

"Life would have been different," I said, "if there were just one person in it who loved me more than they loved anything else."

Nana looked back up suddenly, grabbed his cane, and struggled to his feet.

"Think about what I've said," he told me gruffly. "About what you want to do with this time you've been given. Don't they make you read any Tennyson at your so-called Tennyson High? ''Tis not too late to seek a newer world.' You are at the beginning of your odyssey, my son. At such times, it is best to do as the Mevlana said: 'Love those who are clear joy and wander not into the neighborhoods of despair.'"

Chapter Fifteen

There was a man once who went before a sultan. Accused of a crime, he begged the sultan for forgiveness. Though evidence against the man was strong, the ruler, moved by his pleas, showed the man mercy. The sultan told him that he would be executed, but that the sultan would give him a year to live before the punishment was carried out. The man, overjoyed, laughed, which confused the sultan.

As Nana tells it, the sultan asked, "Why are you so happy? Did you not hear we will take your life? All you won from us is a year."

"A year contains within it the possibility of eternity," the convict replied. "My innocence may become clear before then, or I might die. You might perish. Your empire might fall. The world might end. I fear not tomorrow. I am satisfied with today."

That story hadn't seemed like a big deal when Nana had read it to me years ago from his endless supply of worn books. Now I was glad that he had. It was suddenly very important to me. That's the thing with stories. You never know when you'll need them.

"Niz! You have to pay attention," Diamond admonished. "You're the spotter. Diamond's life depends on you."

I rolled my eyes.

We were at the gym, where Diamond was bench-pressing a ridiculous number of pounds. My job, apparently, was to stand there and catch the bar in case he pushed himself too hard and couldn't lift the weight off himself. The problem, of course, was I'd be of no real help if Diamond got himself into trouble. I wasn't nearly strong enough to actually assist him. My role, therefore, was purely ceremonial.

"What's going on with you?"

I sighed. "Nothing."

"Nah. You're definitely distracted. What is it?"

I cast about for something safe to say and finally decided upon a subject Diamond might actually be able to help me with. "Have you heard of Nuayman ibn Amr?"

I'm not sure what Diamond was expecting, but he was clearly surprised by that question. "Yeah? He was one of the Prophet's Companions, right?"

I nodded. "Yes. It's just...his name keeps coming up,

and I keep forgetting to run a computer search when I'm at school. What is he famous for? I know he had a problem with alcohol."

"Which he got punished for," Diamond recalled. "But even though he sinned, and kept sinning, the Prophet still liked him. They were friends."

"How can a prophet care for someone who won't stop defying divine law?"

"Bro," Diamond countered, as if he were saying something obvious, "if a prophet doesn't, who will? After all, mercy is the point of religion."

I wanted to ask him, if that was true, how he could justify the existence and threat of Hell, but I held my peace. Nana always advised me not to argue with Believers. They would not appreciate my questions, he warned, and it was likely I wouldn't appreciate their answers.

Anyway, if Diamond was right, then there was another, more immediate question I wanted to pose to him. If religion was all about love and grace, then why had Zeeshan Nizami shown none to me, even as he'd become more zealous?

My experience was that the more God there was in my father's life, the more pain there was in mine.

"Did Nuayman hurt people?" I asked after a moment.

"No." Diamond shoved his bar back into place and sat up to look at me. "Why would you even ask that?"

I let out a deep breath. Beans already knew. There was no harm in telling Diamond my history with Zeeshan Nizami. I just wasn't used to sharing these deep truths about myself with people. Perhaps this kind of naked honesty was the cost of making friends.

Or perhaps it was also one of the blessings of having friends. I suspected it'd be nice to have someone know you, really know you, and still accept you despite the damage you had suffered and the damage you had caused.

Like the Prophet had done for Nuayman ibn Amr, apparently.

It was strange that I hadn't figured that out before. Then again, I had been alone most of my life. I suspected now that the grim woods I had walked through would have been less terrifying if Diamond or Beans had been walking with me.

You were alone all the time because your mother isolated you. Because she was trying to protect her husband.

I shook my head. I wouldn't think like that.

I would not let darkness cover every memory I had of my mom.

"Arsalan?" Diamond prompted.

"There's... someone I know. My father. He gets drunk—used to get drunk—and he'd hit... people."

I couldn't exactly read the way Heera looked at me. Probing? Perhaps, but in a nice way. He wasn't just being curious. He was actually concerned. "Does he hit you?"

"No," I said. I cleared my throat. "Not anymore. He lives in Arizona now, but his last letter... He said he feels like Nuayman ibn Amr."

"That's... some claim, bro."

I shrugged. "We're not a very modest bunch, my family."

"From what I remember, Nuayman was known for being a jokester. He'd prank people, even the Prophet. The Prophet thought he was funny."

"Really? I haven't read much about the Prophet's sense of humor."

"The world would be closer to Diamond Standard if more people did. Anyway, I'll look into Nuayman for you."

"That's fine," I told him. "I can do it."

"Niz, you can't just look this stuff up online. Google is a bad imam. Not everything on it is true and even if it were, it's just information. It's not wisdom. You need wisdom. So I'll talk to my sheikh and report back. Just promise me you won't trust your soul to the internet. That's the danger zone, bro."

"All right. Thank you. That's very kind, Diamond. You don't have to go through the trouble."

"Relax. It's cool. After all, what are friends for?"

Practices with Beans were going better than they ever had before. Since our breakthrough, I had found a groove. I understood the importance of being in the moment, of relaxing and focusing on the now. Beenish was clearly happy with how much I'd improved, though I'm pretty sure she thought all the credit belonged to Aiza Aunty.

I suppose the lion's share of it did. However, Aiza Aunty wasn't the one who was practicing in front of a mirror after Beans went home. She wasn't the one digging through Nana's old records for upbeat songs to practice with. That was all me.

Yes, Beenish's mother had unlocked the door for me, but I was the one walking through it and into a mental space where there was nothing but the dance...and Beans. The pride I felt in myself was therefore, I thought, justified.

Still, there was room for improvement. So when Beans suggested—well, demanded—I go back to her mother for additional tips, I agreed.

I could tell, however, when I showed up at Aiza Aunty's door a few weeks after our introduction, that this meeting would be a different experience than the first. Instead of being full of fire, she was subdued. She still had an affected grace about her, but her regal mannerisms seemed half-hearted. She seemed less like a royal at the height of imperial power, and more like the last Queen of the Mughals, bankrupt and beaten, with little hope of a better tomorrow.

"Nizami," she said by way of greeting, "did your mother never teach you that it is rude to be on time?"

"I try to be early, actually, if I can."

"How horrible," Aiza Aunty joked. At least, I think she was joking. It was difficult to tell because she remained completely straight-faced. "Well, come in, then. You will have to excuse the mess."

As I stepped inside, I saw that her apartment was pristine. I gave her a puzzled look, and she gestured to herself.

"I am the mess, dear."

I looked at her more closely. Her saree was less elaborate than the one she had worn last time, and her hair was not as immaculate as it had been before. There was something else that was wrong, though. Something more. There was a frailty in her voice that seemed new.

"Are you all right?"

"Of course. Birthdays are difficult, but if you'd had the common courtesy to be half an hour late like a proper desi child, I would have gathered myself."

"Oh," I said. "Happy birthday, Aunty."

She snorted and brushed off my wishes. "Why would my birthday be difficult? That is always a party. Today is Beenish's birthday. Didn't you know?"

I shook my head.

"So you didn't get her anything?"

"Obviously," I said, feeling a little embarrassed, though that was hardly logical given the circumstances.

Aiza Aunty clucked her disapproval. "It seems that the quality of boyfriends has really dropped over time. In my day—"

"Beans and I aren't—"

"Yes, I know, you have no formal agreement but…" She trailed off, vaguely waving her hands in the air as if trying to express something ineffable. "Surely not every veil has to be lifted, Nizami, for you to see the shape of things."

"No. Really. Aunty, I'm not sure if you heard, but she has actually promised to help set me up with someone in exchange for dancing with her. That's all that's going on."

"Has she actually gotten you a date?"

I shook my head.

"Has she discussed other girls with you?"

"No, but—"

With the gleeful intensity of a chess player about to bring down an opponent's king, Aiza Aunty pressed on. "Has she even asked you what kind of girls you like?"

I sighed. "Can we start practicing? This conversation is pointless. As I've told my great-grandfather and Diamond Khan, our relationship isn't like that. It can't be. She's amazing. And I'm..." I gestured up at my awkward frame and height, which Beenish had once called unnecessary.

"I see. You know, Arsalan, one of the things I've learned in my life is that we tend to become trapped by the way other people see us. People say you're shameless, and you start to think you really are shameless. They say you've dishonored yourself and you start to think they're right."

" 'Hell is other people,' " I quoted. "That's Sartre."

"Hmm. I like that very much. Because we can't escape the way the world sees us, and we end up tormenting ourselves with their opinions."

"That's what he meant," I agreed.

"Do you think he ever considered the possibility that heaven, also, is other people?"

"I...don't know."

Aiza Aunty smiled. "Well, then I've given you something to think about. All right, let's get some work in. Afterward, I strongly suggest you buy my youngest a birthday present." She picked up a remote and turned on her television, which was thinner, larger, and more colorful than what we had at home. She picked a song to play called "Shakar Wandaan" from the Pakistani movie *Ho Mann Jahaan*.

"That isn't the song that Beenish picked. She wants to dance to—"

"I know. She's wrong. Tell her I said so."

I gave her a wary look.

"Despite what that girl may pretend, she isn't infallible."

"I really don't want to upset her."

"Too bad," Aiza Aunty said with a shrug. "Part of being a good 'friend' is giving warnings when a person is about to do something they'll regret. Beans wants to do an item number. Do you know what that is, or are you too much of an ABCD?"

"What?"

"American-Born Confused Desi," she explained.

"Ah. No, Beenish explained it to me."

"So you know that I'm something of an expert in item numbers. I don't want the kind of attention that comes with it to attach to Beans. If she wants to dance, she can do it with dignity and grace. I don't want her to become me."

"Why can't you tell her yourself?"

Aiza Aunty sighed. "Beenish and I... we don't talk a lot. In fact, she called me for the first time in two years after she met you. It was... a shock."

"Two years?"

"She wanted pointers on how to quickly teach someone with no experience how to dance. We've been speaking more since, but I'm not in the position to lecture her on how to behave, which is how she'll see my advice." She allowed herself a bitter smile. "That happens sometimes with mothers and daughters."

212

"This is why you said her birthdays are difficult."

"That started when I left her and Qirat with their father and that Roshni woman, when I refused to take custody of them. It's something I would do differently if I could."

"She did call you for help. She does send me here. That's something."

"Yes," she agreed. "It is something."

Heera Khan looked around the mall and shrugged help-lessly, apparently as bewildered by the task before us as I was. "What do you get a girl for her birthday, bro?"

"I don't know. That's why I asked you to come here with me."

"Diamond is out of his league, Niz. He doesn't buy women presents. Well…okay, except for my mom, but I always just get her a gift card for a spa. Oh, and my sister is like twelve, so I just give her cash. Can't you do that?"

I was pretty sure Aiza Aunty would be disappointed with that choice. "Seems impersonal. Also, I only have about fourteen dollars."

"Oh," Diamond said. "Yeah. We should definitely think of something else, then. Let's walk around and figure it out."

I sighed. This was not how I had envisioned my day going. It was, in fact, not how I'd envisioned any day in my life going. I always knew what I wanted before going into a store. That way you went in and you came out without wast-ing any time or money.

Well...that was true with the exception of bookstores. But one does not buy books. One befriends them.

"Hey," I said, realizing that there was a solution I'd actually enjoy, "isn't there a bookst—"

"No," Diamond said. "No way."

"But I know exactly what—"

"No."

I groaned. "Why?"

"It has to be something romantic."

"It really doesn't," I told him.

"When you called Diamond, you told him Aiza Aunty said she thinks that Beenish likes you."

"Which is ridiculous."

"Brother, the only way anything that Beans has done makes sense is if she thinks you're spicy, okay? Does this contest she's entering even require her to have a partner?"

Diamond didn't know there was no actual contest, that Beenish was just trying to disrupt Qirat's wedding. But... he was right that she could do that without having a partner. I agreed with her that the rules for Qirat's wedding were ridiculous, and the guy she was marrying was "the rankest compound of villainous smell that ever offended nostril," but breaking the rule about dancing wouldn't cause the wedding to be called off. It would just cause a scene, and dancing with a boy would cause a bigger one.

Was making a scene the point?

"All Beans really wants is to be a dancer like her mom," Diamond went on. "Maybe you should get her a tutu. What is a tutu anyway? Like I know it's an outfit, but is it only for like little girls or—"

I held up a hand for him to be quiet. There was something important about what he'd just said.

All Beans really wants is to be a dancer like her mom.

And what had Aiza Aunty said to me earlier today?

I'm something of an expert in item numbers.

I don't want her to become me.

And when Beans had first explained why she couldn't pursue her dream of a career in dancing, she'd said, *My mom doesn't want me to end up being just another version of her.*

The rules for Qirat's wedding didn't just prohibit dancing. They prohibited the presence of Aiza Aunty at her eldest daughter's wedding.

I was thinking of doing something that'll really catch people's attention. I'm thinking it has to be an item number.

I hadn't gotten what Beenish was trying to do. Yes, she was breaking the rule about no dancing at Qirat's wedding, but that was a side effect, not her actual goal.

What she really wanted was to have her mother there, and since Aiza Aunty would not be invited, Beenish Siraj would make sure everyone knew that her spirit was with them, and that it was still proud and unbroken.

"The internet says girls like candles," Diamond informed me, looking up from his phone. "What do they need candles for?"

I was the perfect partner, not because Beenish was attracted to me, but because my ineptitude in dancing gave

215

her an excuse to get back in touch with Aiza Aunty and learn exactly how her mother would have danced at Qirat's wedding, if she could be there.

"I'm not olive oil. I'm an olive *branch*," I said aloud.

"What are you talking about?" Diamond asked. "Why are you smiling? Maybe you should get her something funny? Bro. Bro. *Bro*." Diamond grabbed my arm to point at a store we were walking past. I looked up at the sign that read VICTORIA'S SECRET.

He pulled me back so that we weren't standing close to the entrance and said softly, "Don't look directly at it. People will think we're weird."

"Um...okay."

"You should get something from there. It's perfect," he said. "Lingerie is totally romantic. Besides, how much can a bra cost? Like five dollars?"

I was still a few mental steps behind him. "Underwear is romantic?"

"Of course. Niz, don't you know anything about women?"

"I know that if I gave Beenish undergarments, she'd murder me."

"Which would also be hilarious. It'll be fun either way."

I shook my head, and as I was doing so, a brighter, less seductive sign caught my eye. "There," I said, pointing to the right. "That's perfect."

Chapter Sixteen

"What are you wearing?" Nana demanded when I came down- stairs a few hours later. Before we'd left the mall, Diamond had insisted that if you were going to give someone a gift for their birthday, you had to do it on the day itself. Apparently, it was a Cinderella situation. After midnight, your gift might as well be a pumpkin.

I'd used his phone to see if Beans could stop by Nana's house. Apparently, she was doing something with her family but could sneak out later at night. My present was not important enough to warrant that kind of risk, but she'd hung up on my protests, so she clearly disagreed.

In response to Nana's question about my outfit, I said, "It's a polo shirt."

"Hmm," he said, obviously unimpressed. "I don't like the collar. It's floppy and spineless. It lacks character."

"It's what people wear," I told him.

Predictably, he started muttering something about all true gentlemen being gone from the world.

"It's Beenish's birthday," I continued. "It seemed like I should dress up."

If Nana had an opinion about that, he chose not to share it. "Well, wish her well for me. I hope you got her something."

"I did."

"What is it?"

"A toy."

He sighed. "Arsalan. You two aren't children anymore."

"It isn't like that," I protested. "It's a toy adults can enjoy."

Nana raised his eyebrows. "That seems inappropriate and forward."

"*No!* It's not a—listen, please? That's just part of her gift. For the rest of it, I'm going to need your help."

He still seemed unconvinced but nodded. "Very well. Tell me what you need."

It was around ten o'clock before Beans made it over. She was, for the first time since I'd known her, not wearing a

T-shirt with something printed on it. Instead, she was wearing a simple black shalwar kameez, with a proper dupatta and everything.

I may have stared a little.

"Shut up," Beans said preemptively before sticking out a hand, "and give me my present."

"It's upstairs," I said, "in my room. It's really more of an experience than a thing, so you have to come with me."

"Smooth, Nizami," she teased.

"If you're not comfortable," I added quickly, "you can wait here and I can bring it down. I just—"

"It's fine," Beans said. "I trust you."

I bowed my thanks.

She shook her head, which made me think that other boys may not have reacted that way. But she also smiled, which made me not care what anyone else might have done.

The experience of letting Beenish into my room was very much the same as letting her into the house. I instantly saw a place I knew well through new eyes. The room was immaculate, I had made sure of that, but she was obviously surprised to see Rayyan Uncle's old guitar standing against the far wall.

"You play?"

"My uncle—this was his room before—did, I guess. The cassette player is his too."

My contributions to the setting were pretty nominal. There were textbooks, of course, and the clothes I had gotten with Beans, along with a picture of Nana and Mom, standing together, when she had been my age.

Tonight I had added, after some pleading with Nana, two cardboard boxes with the name "Muneera" scrawled over them in Nana's careful, shaky handwriting. I'd also brought up a chair from the dining table for Beenish to sit on.

She ignored it completely, however, and instead flopped onto my bed as if it were no big deal. "Sorry it got late. My dad and Roshni insisted on going out to celebrate my 'big day' and I couldn't get... Why are you looking at me like I'm a ghost?"

"You're on my bed."

"Yeah?"

I stepped a little farther away from her. "I'm pretty sure that isn't okay."

She propped herself on her elbows, attempted unsuccessfully to blow a dark strand of hair out of her face, then asked, "What? You're worried you're going to get cooties?"

"Aren't *you* worried what people would say?"

"There's no one here."

"Yes. But doesn't that make it worse?"

She sat up and patted a spot next to her, obviously meaning for me to sit there. I hesitated.

"There are no desi aunty spies around. My reputation will be fine. Also, I promise I'll keep myself from jumping you," she said, "I mean, how would I? I don't even have the key to your chastity belt."

"Hilarious," I muttered, but I did as I was told.

"See?" Beans asked when I was sitting by her. "Neither one of us got pregnant. It's a miracle. Anyway, like I was saying, I'm sorry I'm late."

"I didn't mind waiting for you."

She seemed pleased to hear that but didn't say so. "You found your mother's things?"

"Nana had them hidden in the attic."

"Why?"

"To spare me grief, he said. Nana thinks there is nothing in there but sorrow, and that it takes time for the wounds of the soul to scab over. He says it doesn't help to keep picking at them. He was protecting me."

"He does that a lot," Beans observed in a way that made it clear she didn't think it was a good thing.

"He's...become familiar with pain over the years. He's just trying to keep heartache away from me."

"How has he managed so far?"

I couldn't think of an answer.

Mercifully, Beenish didn't wait for one. "So are we opening these boxes? Is that my present?"

I got to my feet. "No. Um, I mean, yes, I do want to open them with you, but that isn't all of your present." I went over to the nearest bookshelf, picked up a plastic bag, and pulled out what looked like a ball of wrapping paper.

I held it out to her. "My presentation needs some work."

She grinned, took the offering, and began unwrapping it. "Thanks."

"It's not anything special. It's just—"

Beans laughed and pulled out a tiny stuffed animal, about the size of her palm. "You got me a porcupine. I love it. Thank you."

"Really?"

She nodded, her shining black eyes darker than the Kaaba in Mecca. "Yeah. It's perfect."

I put my right hand on my heart. It was something I'd seen Nana do when accepting a gift. I'm not sure why I copied the gesture just then, but it felt right.

"Now," I said, walking over to my desk and grabbing a pair of scissors, "for the boxes."

"Wait. Can you tell me why we're doing this?"

"For one," I admitted, "I don't want to do it alone, and there is no one else I can do it with."

"But that isn't the only reason."

"Yes. That's why I said 'for one,' implying, of course—"

Beans let out a sigh.

I hesitated, then went over to sit beside her again. "I'm going to say something. Please don't get mad."

"It doesn't sound like there's much chance of that."

"Will you listen?" I asked her softly.

"Yeah," she relented.

"I went to see Aiza Aunty today, remember? And—"

"Arsalan." Her tone contained more than a hint of warning. It was all warning. "Don't."

"You just said you would listen."

She glowered at me in an expression so similar to the stuffed animal that I'd just given her that I almost laughed.

"Look, Beans. I was with your mother today, and she misses you. She's hurting. I think you're hurting too. I think this whole 'dancing at Qirat's wedding' plan...I think, maybe, it's a way for you to connect with her, consciously or not."

She crossed her arms. "I thought you said you weren't interested in psychoanalyzing me."

"That was before I figured out that you were using me to make Aiza Aunty a part of Qirat's wedding, symbolically speaking, that is."

"I wasn't *using* you," she protested. "I—"

I waved her concern away. "I don't mind. But I think maybe you should move past having me act as a proxy. Maybe you want to talk to Aiza Aunty about what we're doing yourself."

"You're asking me to forgive her?"

"I can't ask you that. I can't forgive my father. But, the thing is, my father wasn't the only one who messed me up. I tried not to think about it for the longest time, but..." I closed my eyes. I took a breath. These were words I did not want to utter. But they were part of my gift to Beans.

Besides, I'd already decided tonight was the night for opening boxes.

I looked at her again and quietly added, "My mother hurt me too."

Beenish laid a hand on mine. "She hit you too?"

I shook my head. "She didn't make me safe when she could have. I realized that on the night you came and found me at the cemetery. Mom knew my father wouldn't stop, but she stayed with him, which meant I stayed with him."

"I understand."

"Until I met you, I'd managed to ignore what Mom did. I'd managed to pretend she was basically an angel."

"I never told you any different," she protested.

"You told me I was effed up when I just assumed you were playing a prank on me. You asked me why I never considered the possibility that you might not be trying to hurt me. It's because everyone has hurt me, Beans. Even Mom. That day, what happened with you, made me see that."

"I'm sorry," Beenish whispered. "I didn't mean for that to happen."

"It's okay. Truly. I'm telling you because...I can't forgive Zeeshan Nizami, but I will forgive my mom. Not for her sake. For my sake. It's what I need."

Beans was quiet for a minute, then said, "So while we're unpacking Muneera Aunty's things, you want me to think about whether I need to forgive my mother?" She shook her head. "You know I'm not good at letting things go. I haven't even gotten over what happened with Diamond. My mother hurt me way more than he did."

"You don't have to forgive anyone you don't want to forgive. I just wanted to tell you what I know and you don't."

"What's that?" Beans asked.

"That sometimes the world stops and there are no tomorrows."

The first thing I saw were Mom's clothes. There was the long dress she had worn at my father's last birthday, and right below it was a heavy, green shalwar kameez that she'd put on for the wedding of...actually, I couldn't remember whose it had been. A coworker's child, maybe.

These nicer outfits gave way to simpler, more mundane ones. Her ASSIST THE CHEF apron, her favorite T-shirt, a splotchy pink pair of formerly white joggers that I'd put into the wash with a red shirt in an attempt to help with the laundry.

Like every aunty, there were glass bangles and a collection of sarees she owned but never really wore, her prayer rug, a few old watches, half-empty bottles of perfume, an almost unused winter coat because this was, after all, California.

"Are those her diaries?" Beans asked.

I nodded and left them where they were.

"Wait. You're not going to read them?"

"Do you keep a diary?" I asked her.

"I have Instagram. It's this social media app where you post pictures of yourself or your food or outfit or stuff you're reading. Anything you want. And then people look at your pictures and like them and stuff."

"Why do you use it?"

She had to think about that for a minute. "It's a way to share your life with people."

It seemed more like a way to get judged, but I didn't say that. I'd never really cared to elicit the opinions of strangers. I could imagine the awful things people were thinking about me perfectly well. I didn't need confirmation from them, thank you very much.

I understood this was a flaw of mine. Nana always said that

you were balanced if the praise and the censure of other peo-ple meant the same to you. A forum like the one Beenish was describing didn't seem designed to lead to such balance.

That was, however, beside the point right now. "Shar-ing implies choice. You want other people to see what you put on the internet. I don't know if Mom wrote these diaries thinking they'd ever be read. It's private."

Beans shook her head.

"You think I'm wrong?"

"No," she said. "You're right. But we are very different people."

That much was true. I smiled. "Qirat says that opposites—"

"Attract?"

"Balance each other out."

Beans actually blushed. I'd never seen that happen before.

While I gave her a moment to recover, I looked over her shoulder and noticed my grandfather's model of an atom. It was a depiction of the simplest element in the universe. Hydrogen. Just one proton with one electron caught in its orbit, opposites that had found a relationship—a balance—with each other. And because of this, life was possible. It was the stuff stars were made of.

Beenish turned to follow my gaze and frowned. "What?"

"Nothing. I was just thinking about fusion."

"Is that like a nerdy euphemism for sex?"

I must have turned as red as the sun. "What? *No!* I meant—"

She giggled. "Relax. I know what you meant. It's just

a little surprising that right now, when you've got a girl in your room for the first time in your life"—she paused long enough for me to nod my confirmation that her assumption was correct—"you're thinking about science."

"Biology is a science."

"Shut up."

I did. I started putting Mom's things back carefully, like Nana had packed them. Beans helped. We worked in silence until the boxes were ready to be sealed again. I rose to my feet and helped Beans up. Instead of stepping away from me, she stayed close.

"Hey," she said.

"Uh...hi?"

She looked up at me, that remarkable intensity I'd never gotten used to—that I didn't think I'd ever get used to—bright in her eyes. "Thank you for my present. I know this wasn't easy for you."

I shrugged. "It wasn't that difficult. It was only ten dollars."

Beans grinned. Then she got on her tiptoes and kissed me gently on my cheek. "I didn't mean the porcupine."

"So?" Nana asked as soon as I came down for breakfast the next morning. "How did it go?" I gave him a reproachful look, but he was clearly too curious to leave off prying. "Beenish didn't depart until pretty late last night. A good sign, I presume."

"It took a while to get through Mom's stuff."

"And you're okay?"

I nodded. "You didn't need to worry that some of her old things would hurt me."

"Didn't I? I wonder," he said, "if you would have gotten through the experience so well a month ago. Or even now if you'd been by yourself."

I wasn't sure, truth be told. But it had been nice to have Beans with me for the task.

"Well," Nana huffed, "I see that you're useless for details, as always. I will get my information from Beenish when she comes over to play chess."

"When is she coming over?"

He shrugged. "She drops by whenever she wants. Not much for routine or planning, that girl. However, I suppose no one is perfect."

"She drops by? When I'm not here?"

"It is when you're at school."

"She's supposed to be as well," I protested. "She's been skipping class to hang out with you? Why?"

"I assume because she has excellent taste," he said.

"What do you two even talk about?" I asked. "You have nothing in common."

"Mostly," Nana admitted, "we talk about you."

I didn't like that at all.

Nana frowned, as if reading my mind. "I don't see what difference it should make to you. You know, Arsalan, you are not the only one who needs friends."

"You hate people," I reminded him.

"I wasn't talking about me. You know that Beenish has no real relationship with either one of her parents or her stepmother. I think she enjoys my wisdom."

"And your humility, I'm sure," I muttered.

"Well," Nana said, "I've never made any claim to that. Anyway, I am not at all interested in your indignation. We have both been keeping things from each other, yes? You never told me you were going to sabotage a wedding."

I stared at him.

"Oh yes. I have that nugget of information. Really, I would have expected you to try to talk her out of it."

"I've been dealing with a lot," I said. "Besides, I don't think talking Beenish out of anything is possible."

Nana took a sip of his tea and sighed. "I've always had a fondness for people with minds of their own. I wonder if that is the reason my life has, generally, been rather miserable."

I thought about what to say next. It wasn't strange to me that anyone would want to spend time around Nana. I actually enjoyed spending time with him myself, at least when he wasn't being insufferable. If he were more inclined to put himself out there, I was certain he'd actually be popular.

"What does she say about me?" I finally asked.

Nana smirked. "Why? Are you hoping she's confessed her undying affection for you?"

That would have been nice, I had to admit, though I didn't have to admit it out loud. "If you've been talking to Beenish, you know that we are just friends."

229

"That is because you are both exceedingly stupid," Nana said. "And, despite everything you have lived through, you do not realize how dark the world is and how rare it is for two bright lights to find each other within it."

"Are you going to answer my question?"

He considered for a moment, then nodded. "Ms. Siraj thinks that I have failed entirely to prepare you for the world. She thinks I have kept you here"—he gestured expansively at his entire home—"in this little bubble of time, hoping you would never have to fall. As a result, if ever if you do fall, you will not know how to get back up."

"That doesn't sound like Beans."

He inclined his head. "True. She is too kind to say any of that out loud and not yet articulate enough to say it as well as I did."

I sighed. Nana was certainly "feeling himself" today, so to speak.

"I hope..." He paused to clear his throat. "I hope you realize, young man, that if I have failed you, such failure was born not of neglect or apathy but came from a place of caring."

"I love you too, Nana."

"Well," he said primly, straightening his jacket and squaring his shoulders, "there is no need to get sentimental, I'm sure."

"We," Beenish announced when she came over a few hours later, "are going with 'Shakar Wandaan.'"

For a moment, I had no idea what she was talking about. In my defense, she was wearing a shirt that read AVERT YOUR GAZE, which, ironically, was difficult to look away from. It clicked a second later. That was the song from the Lolly-wood movie *Ho Mann Jahaan* that Aiza Aunty had picked out, then had me practice to. I'd already heard it a million and a half times.

Beans grabbed me by the elbow and pulled me toward the living room, where she sat down on a sofa and pulled out her phone. "Come check out the video."

"I've seen it," I reminded her, "at your mother's place. We're going with her recommendation?"

"Yes. Why so surprised?"

I couldn't very well say *Because I thought you were too petty to take a good suggestion from someone you are upset with*, so I kept my mouth shut.

"Anyway," she continued, "even if you've seen it, you still have to pay attention. We're going to copy some of the steps, but from what you've said Amma had you practice, she obviously has a few variations of her own too." Her finger hovered over the screen, ready to play the song. "If you see a move you think is cool, let me know."

As music filled the house, I watched as an actor whose name I didn't know—I never actually knew any of their names—began to lip-sync.

"His shirt is very orange."

"Maybe focus on the dancers instead of their outfits."

I did and was quickly alarmed that there was more

jumping in the opening sequence than I was entirely comfortable with. As the backup dancers really got involved, I also noticed that they were on a marble surface. The fact that they weren't slipping and sliding all over the place was impressive.

"How are they doing that in dress shoes?" I asked Beans. "That should be impossible."

"They're pros," she said simply.

I watched as everyone twirled around one another with apparently effortless precision. The coordination that they'd achieved, like electrons whizzing past one another in perfect synchronicity, was quite something. The colors, the music, the decor all added to the spectacle.

An actress—the heroine, presumably—made an appearance. She too was wearing orange, and I realized then that the outfits of each couple, and what the background dancers were wearing, had all matched. A lot of attention to detail had gone into the few minutes we were watching. As the beat picked up and the movements on-screen got faster and faster, a controlled frenzy, Beans turned to look at me. "What do you think?"

"That looks like a lot of work for two people."

She nodded. "Yeah. We're going to need help. At the very least we'll need someone to work the sound system and stuff."

"We could ask Diamond," I suggested.

Beans bit her lip. "Like I told you, his family is friends with Roshni. He might tell them what we're doing and they might tell her. It'd ruin everything."

232

"I don't think he'd do that to you."

"What makes you so sure?"

"He loves you."

"Pfft. He doesn't."

"He does," I insisted. "He said you guys had been friends all your life."

"Then I broke his nose, remember? That isn't the kind of thing someone gets over."

I smiled. It was fascinating how, when human beings found something difficult to do ourselves, we assumed it was challenging for everybody. "I think you're wrong. Besides, he's religious. Isn't forgiveness one of their things?"

She thought about it, then sighed. "Okay. Fine. I'll talk to him. Ugh. This is going to suck. You know I despise heart-to-hearts, right?"

"You'll manage," I said. "But if you want us to look anything like these people"—I pointed to the actors frozen on her screen—"we're going to need costumes and—"

"They aren't 'costumes.' They're lehengas and cholis and ghararas and shararas and—"

"Clothes," I corrected. "We'll need clothes. Maybe a set. Ideally, even backup dancers because these performances really don't look as good without them."

"Arsalan," she warned, clearly figuring out where I was going. "I already said I'd talk to Diamond. Don't go for two here."

"What?" I asked innocently. "I'm just saying—"

"You're saying we should ask my mother for help. I'm

233

not there yet, okay? What you did last night was very sweet, but I haven't... I'm just not there yet. So can you drop it, please?"

I nodded. "Absolutely. I won't bring it up again."

"Good," she said. "Now let's dance."

Chapter Seventeen

To celebrate his reconciliation with Beenish Siraj, and to thank me for my role in it, Diamond Khan gave me a gift I would rather not have received. It was a skintight neon-yellow T-shirt with a huge picture of Diamond giving the thumbs-up sign, a goofy grin on his face.

"Wow, right?" he prompted, as I wondered how to dispose of this horrid thing without hurting Heera's feelings. The kindness of other people could, I was learning, be a difficult thing to bear.

I figured that my best bet was to "forget" the shirt at Northgate Park, where we then were, and claim someone had taken it. Of course, this would require that Diamond actually believe that someone would steal this present. I doubted he, or anyone for that matter, was that credulous.

I realized that Diamond was still waiting for a response. I managed to say, "Um...yes. Definitely 'wow.'"

"Bro! You're speechless! Diamond didn't even know that was possible."

"I. Am. Speechless," I agreed.

"Since we're all friends now, I figured we should look like a squad. The Diamond Squad? Catchy, right?"

I frowned. "What do you mean 'we'?"

"I had matching ones made for me and Beans. We should all wear them to school on Monday."

I let out a sigh of relief. There was my out. Beenish would join a nunnery before she'd wear this shirt.

Now that I thought about it, I hadn't actually come across the word "nunnery" outside of *Hamlet*. It was entirely possible they did not still exist.

"Where do nuns live?" I asked Diamond.

He seemed completely blindsided by the question. "I don't know," he said. "In a church?"

I shook my head. Unhelpful.

"Honestly, Niz, Diamond does not get how your mind works." When I started to explain, he cut me off. "And, no offense, Diamond doesn't even want to know. You're in, right? For Monday? It'll only look cool if we all do it."

I nodded slowly. This was a risky gambit, but one that was probably going to succeed. "I'll wear it if you can convince Beans to wear it."

"She'll definitely be in. You've seen how much she loves custom tees."

"Sure," I said. "Anyway, we should warm up if we're going to run."

As we began stretching, Diamond asked, "How'd you do it? How'd you convince *Beenish Siraj* to accept that I was sorry? When that girl cancels you, it is eternal."

I smiled, thinking back to a dark cemetery. To the light that had cut through the night and the image of Beans running through it. I hadn't done anything. She'd forgiven me. It had been her choice. I wasn't sure why she had made it, but I was grateful she had.

"I mean, even though it's been three years, she still refuses to go to the mosque." Seeing that I was confused, he started to add, "There was a small...issue with her and—"

"Is this the story of how she got thrown out of a mosque?" I asked. "I *have* to hear it. I heard it happened, but I'm not sure why."

"No one threw her out," Diamond protested. "The imam...strongly suggested that if she couldn't respect his rules, she should leave."

When he stopped talking, I gestured for him to go on, though it was clear that this wasn't a story Diamond wanted to tell.

Reluctantly, he continued. "Okay, so like every year there is a super big deal of an event called 'The Noble Mawlid.' You've heard of mawlids?" When I shook my head, he added, "They're like these big celebrations of the Prophet

Muhammad, Peace Be Upon Him. Imams give speeches and there are singers who recite poetry to honor him and stuff."

"And Beans feels like she got kicked out of one of these things?"

"When they were picking what singers would be invited for the mawlid, one of the uncles on the Board of Directors went on a power trip and decided to show everyone how pious he was by saying that no women would be allowed to sing. He said a woman's beautiful voice is a lure for the hearts of men."

"They were at the mosque," I pointed out. "He could have had the men pray for more resolute hearts."

Diamond made a face. "I hate that judgey tone, Niz."

"I'm not judging anyone...much."

"It was one out-of-control uncle. You can't blame the whole mosque for that. He had the power, and he made the rules."

"Until Beans," I guessed.

"Yeah," Diamond said tiredly. "Before the performers who'd been hired could start, Beans ran into the men's section of the mosque, grabbed the mic, and started yelling a song into it."

"That sounds incredible."

"It wasn't," Heera assured me. "Have you ever heard Beenish sing?"

I shook my head.

"Then, bro, your head should forever be bowed in thanks to Allah for that mercy. It was awful. But she wouldn't give

238

the mic up and they couldn't like wrestle it away from her because—"

"They couldn't touch her."

"Right. By the time Roshni Aunty and Qirat came over from the women's section to take her away, we'd all been tortured for a long time." He shuddered.

"There's nothing wrong with a little rebellion once in a while. I think it's great."

Diamond gave me an odd look.

"What?"

"Have you ever broken a single rule in your life?"

"No," I admitted.

"Then how come you like that she did?"

I shrugged. "I guess opposites attract...and balance each other out."

"Well, Diamond is definitely glad you rubbed off on each other." After a moment, a silly grin spread across his face. "Just not literally, I hope."

"Unnecessary and uncouth."

"That's my brand. Come on. It's time to run."

I sank into the tub of hot water and exhaled. The stiff muscles in my arms and shoulders, thighs and calves relaxed a little. Two weeks had passed since Beenish's birthday, and they had been brutal.

Ever since she had decided on "Shakar Wandaan" as the song we were going to dance to, Beans had seriously upped the intensity and length of our practices. We were working, over and over again, on the same steps, not only trying to perfect our execution but also our synchronicity.

It had taken a while for my brain to process that I didn't have to try to make sure her movements and mine were the same. I just had to listen to the music, to the change of its rhythm, and react to that instead of reacting to Beenish. In a way, it wasn't accurate to say we were dancing together. We were actually dancing with the music and trusting each other to do the same.

That said, Beans was a frustrating teacher. Her rare compliments were always followed by minor, unending criticisms. *That was awesome, but you need to move your leg farther right before you spin, and your wrist needs turn this way so that your palm opens toward the crowd, and* etcetera, etcetera. The phrase "Let's take it from the top" had become the bane of my existence.

I complained a little, but mostly about how sore I was all the time. Between Diamond's workouts and dance practice, my body was getting significantly more activity than it ever had before. It did not seem to like it. Nevertheless, Beans had recorded some of our sessions, and there was definite, even marked improvement in my performance.

Anyway, my whining about how everything hurt when I moved is what had made me end up in the bath. I'd never been a bath person. A quick daily shower had always seemed both efficient and sufficient. Beenish, however, had gotten me a eucalyptus-and-spearmint candle and insisted that I try soaking for relief.

It was surprisingly nice. Lying in the pleasant warmth, I let my mind wander. The last month and a half had been very strange, and since I'd met Beans, my world had completely changed. She could be all the things I'd heard she was—prickly and stabby and sharp—but she was also gentle and kind and funny and passionate and soft and bright and...

I groaned and slid farther into the water so that it was tickling my chin. Thinking about Beenish was useless, even though it was something I did more and more of. Even if the impossible were to happen, even if she could like me in a romantic way, the truth was that my father was coming to get me. Developing feelings for her was, in these circumstances, idiotic.

"Then you are an idiot," I told myself, giving voice to a part of me I consistently tried to ignore. Because the truth was that I did like Beenish Siraj. I'd known that for a while. I'd suspected that she might be dangerous for my heart since we'd first met up at the mall.

When she had stepped into my arms and we had danced slowly together, I'd known for certain then.

When she had found me in the cemetery that night, when she had held me in the dark...I shook my head.

"Stupid. You can't do anything about this. You can't. It'll ruin everything."

There it was. The more sensible part of me, the part Nana had taught me to always let prevail whenever a conflict broke out in my soul.

I decided to listen to it. I always had. The only difference was that ever since I'd met Beans, I'd started to wonder if following my mind instead of my heart would really make me happy.

Not that it mattered. Because there was still Zeeshan Nizami, and as long as he was in my life, happiness was impossible.

I sighed, got to my feet, and began to dry off. That was enough moping. Marcus Aurelius would not approve and neither would Nana.

I was fortunate Nana didn't care about my grades. He wouldn't have approved of them either. They'd been slipping because of all the time I was spending on things other than school. Most of the material I was still ahead on because of my rather unconventional schooling, but areas where Nana was weak—like trigonometry—I needed to keep up with the class. Beenish wasn't coming over to practice tonight, so it was an opportunity to get some work in.

Wrapping a towel around my waist, I made my way back into my room, where Qirat's extra credit assignment, thumb-tacked to the wall, seemed to be staring at me with reproach.

"Fine," I told it. "I'll get to you."

Its expression, obviously, did not change.

I was walking over to pick up clothes off the bed when I caught sight of myself in my uncle's full-length mirror. I looked different. I stepped toward my reflection. I moved differently too, like I was more sure of myself.

Was that some definition in my previously untoned

stomach? I ran my hand over it. Yes. Well...probably. It was nothing compared to the actors in the music videos, but it was something. Hadn't Beans said, at one point, that she liked abs?

I'd have to talk to Diamond about putting more work in on my core. He liked to focus on arms. People could see arms, he told me, if one wore the right kinds of shirts.

I flexed both arms simultaneously. The response from my biceps was muted, but again, it was present. This was progress. Anyway, it didn't really matter how I looked without a shirt on. What mattered was that I looked good while dancing.

I hummed the words from "Shakar Wandaan"—which translated to "Give Away Sweets." It was a celebration by a poet whose beloved had come home at last. I wasn't great at carrying a tune, but still I threw my arms up in the air, palms open, and began to rock my shoulders up and down. It wasn't something Beenish had taught me, but I was pretty sure this was a classic move. I looked a little stiff when executing it, but I always looked a little stiff when dancing.

One thing that I didn't have, that Beans seemed to possess naturally, was what she called "lachak." There was a sharpness to my movements, like I was cutting through the air instead of flowing through it like Beenish did. I just wasn't as flexible, as pliable, as she was. This seemed to bother her a lot less than it bothered me.

It's how you dance, she always said. *Don't worry about it.*

But the way you dance is better, I'd point out.

She never disagreed. She could be nice, but never that nice.

Someone—it took only a second for me to realize it was Beans—cleared her throat behind me, and I yelped in a much higher pitch than I'd known I could manage. Then I looked down at my bare torso, grabbed *The History of Civilizations* off my desk, and held it against my chest.

"Sexy," Beenish said wryly.

"How long have you been standing there?"

She smirked. "Wouldn't you like to know."

"I'm not decent."

"Yeah," Beans agreed, "but that's the fun part. Hey, don't get pissed at me. You left the door open."

"Because no one ever comes up here. What are you doing here anyway?"

"Diamond and I thought it'd be cool to hang out."

I frowned. "And do what?"

Beans chuckled. "Nothing, dude. Just...have fun."

"How does one manage that, exactly?"

She sighed. "Jesus Christ. Just come with us, all right?"

"Fine," I said. Studying could wait another day. "Go downstairs so I can change, please."

Beenish raised an eyebrow in a way that made her seem ridiculously mischievous.

"Downstairs." I pointed with one hand. "And close the door behind you."

"Okay. Don't spend too much time making yourself look

pretty, though. You look almost as nice as I do when I've got nothing on. It's totally unfair how boys get to just walk out of the shower and go about their day."

"I imagine you look stunning with nothing on," I said before I could think to stop myself.

This time Beans raised both her eyebrows.

"I—I mean...," I stammered, "I don't *imagine*—"

"I was talking about makeup," she said, her expression completely neutral. "I meant when I've got no makeup on."

Hi, God. It's me, Arsalan. I know we don't talk much, but if you would be so kind as to kill me now, I would truly appreciate it.

I waited for lightning to strike me or something. Nothing happened.

"Right," I said a moment too late. "Yeah. I knew that."

When I made it downstairs, I found Beans trying to perch Nana's brown felt cowboy hat on her head in the foyer, while in the living room, Diamond and my great-grandfather were discussing something so intently that I assumed it had to be religion or politics. Nana didn't follow any world events, though, so it was probably the former.

"Like mixing matter with antimatter," I muttered.

Beenish looked up and the hat flopped over her eyes. It was entirely the wrong size. I raised the brim with an index finger and smiled at her.

"Hi," I said.

She gave me a sheepish little wave. "It's not staying put. But it looks good, right? It'd have been a cool idea for a costume."

"You celebrate Halloween?"

"No," Beans grumbled. "My dad has this whole theory about it being the devil's holiday and not okay for Muslims to celebrate. How come Satan gets to have all the fun?"

"An excellent question," I conceded.

"It doesn't matter. We have to spend all our free time practicing anyway."

"Except for now."

"Heera wants to go to Old Sac. Have you ever been?"

I shook my head.

"It's a part of the city they've preserved from like the eighteen hundreds. You'll fit right in."

"Why are we going there?"

Beans shrugged. "They've got these old trains that he loves to look at. I don't really get it, but whatever. Makes him happy and we haven't gone in a while because...well, you know, I did break his nose. That was a little...less than nice."

"It may have been a tad bit excessive," I agreed.

"Not by much. He *was* a jerk."

I nodded. "So he has told me."

Beans smiled, took off the hat, stretched to her full height, and placed it on my head. "You were right, though. He really was sorry, and I feel better after giving him a second chance. Thank you for that."

This might have been a good time to argue that I was likely also right about Aiza Aunty, but I'd promised not to.

"Maybe being good at making lemonade isn't a bad thing."

I frowned. "What? I swear, Beans, you're the queen of non sequiturs."

"I just mean...lemonade is compromise, right? Just like forgiveness. It's accepting that things are the way they are and learning to be okay with it. And that's your thing. When life hands you lemons, you go with it. You never fight back. You make lemonade."

"It's not my thing," I protested. "And I wouldn't say I never fight back. I...There was the time...Okay, but what you don't get, Beans, is that we can't change the hand we're dealt." When your mother gets into a car accident and dies, there isn't much you can do about that. "We have to accept the world as we find it and live in it as best we can."

"That's crap. If life tries to give me lemons, I throw them back. Pelt the world with them until it gives you what you want, I say. No surrender, no compromise."

"Except with Diamond."

"Yeah," she agreed. "Like I was saying, seems like a little lemonade can be a good thing. But if you compromise too much, you end up like Qirat. Marrying a walking cat turd like Sham."

"I have no intentions of marrying a turd of any variety."

"Then you have to learn to throw some punches," she

said. More seriously, she added, "You don't just get handed the life you want, Arsalan. You have to fight for it."

Was she talking about my father coming here? What could she possibly expect me to do about that? Before I could ask, however, Nana made his way over to us with Diamond.

"I return to your care," Nana said, "this most credulous and earnest young man. He is a True Believer, this one."

Diamond, for his part, looked like he was trying to figure out if he'd been complimented or insulted.

So, they had been discussing religion like I'd thought. I wondered what the specific topic of their discussion had been, but I didn't ask. It would just get Nana going again.

"You shouldn't judge True Believers. Not everyone thinks skepticism is a virtue," I reminded my great-grandfather, which was my hint that he should be nice.

Nana did not pick up on it. "Then not everyone is wrong."

"Your great-grandfather is super knowledgeable, bro. Diamond wasn't expecting that."

"Because I am not religious I must be ignorant? Isn't it marvelous that people who practice religion assume that anyone who does not believe as they do has simply not made an informed choice?"

Diamond floundered. "Uh..."

"He didn't mean anything by it, Nana," I said.

"I am not offended," he assured us. "It was simply an observation." He clapped a hand on Diamond's shoulder. "No hard feelings, young man. I hope your beliefs bring you both peace and happiness."

"Yeah," Diamond said. "Totally. You too."

"Thank you." Nana looked at me out of the corner of his eye and winked. "I fear, however, that there is not much chance of that."

Old Sacramento was quaint but trying. I would have liked it more if Beenish and I had gone there on our own. The creaking of the wooden boards under our feet, the cobbled roads, the horse-drawn carriages, and the tiny shops by the river were all perfectly lovely. The problem was that Diamond apparently had some kind of obsession with trains and wouldn't stop talking about them. He didn't seem to realize that neither Beans nor I really cared about them.

"I wish Nana could see this," I told her when Diamond went to find a bathroom and we got a moment alone. "He'd love that there is an actual record store. And you better believe he'd go to that place that makes pictures look old."

"Don't all his pictures already look like that?" Beans asked.

I frowned. "Actually, I haven't seen a lot of pictures of him. They're probably in one of his boxes."

She shook her head. "He's adorable, but he's—"

"Eccentric?"

"Sure. That's a nice way to put it." She bit into some bright blue cotton candy she'd bought and then offered me some. I shook my head. "Have you guys talked yet?"

"About what?"

Beenish frowned. "Nana has been saying for a while that he wants to talk to you about what will happen when your father gets back in town. He said you've been avoiding the subject. He's worried."

"Oh. Well, there isn't much to say. My father is going to get here eventually, but so will death. We don't go around worrying about that all the time, do we?"

"That's the spirit," she said with obviously fake cheerfulness.

"Beenish," I said, "I'm serious. You don't know Zeeshan Nizami. You don't know what he is capable of. There is nothing Nana or I can do that will stop him from getting what he wants."

"What are you talking about? Arsalan, he'll get here in December, right? You just have to hold him off till the middle of January, when you're eighteen. Then he won't be able to make you do anything. You'll be free."

"No," I said quietly, "I won't."

"Yeah. You will. You can't just let him run your life forever. This is what I was saying earlier. You can't just roll over, dude. You have to—"

"He owns the house, Beans!"

She stared at me, processing what I'd just told her. After a moment, she asked, "Really?"

"Yes."

"Shit. Nana never said anything about that."

I sighed. "Nana signed the house over to Mom when he was sick a while back. I don't think he thought about it after she died. I don't know much, but I guess my parents did their wills together. Everything of hers was to go to my father and vice versa."

"People challenge those, right? Did you ask a lawyer?"

"My father did. He says he'd win any court case. And that if I don't listen to everything he says—"

"What a fucking asshole! Oh, sorry." This apology was directed to a five-year-old and his mother who happened to be walking by. "Anyway, I shouldn't talk about him like that. He is your dad, after all."

"I try to never be offended by the truth."

"So what's your plan? You're going to let your father boss you around until Nana dies and you don't have to worry about how he'll deal with losing his house?"

"It sounds stupid when you say it like that," I told her. "If you can think of a better plan, though, I'm open to suggestions."

"You should talk to Nana. He should know. Maybe he has a solution. Like maybe he's secretly rich or something."

I shook my head. "He's really not. And I don't want to worry him. I'll deal with it." When she rolled her eyes at me, I added, "He loves his place, Beans. He has spent sixty-nine years there...." That wasn't entirely true, but I wanted her to giggle, as she always did when that particular number came up. She was, however, not amused this time.

"He loves you too, Arsalan."

"And he'll end up resenting me if I cost him his home."

"No way," Diamond said, coming up behind me and

251

joining the conversation. "We aren't going home yet. We haven't even been to the train souvenir shop. You've got to see it, Niz. It's really cool. This way."

"Is it really cool?" I asked Beans.

She shrugged. "It's cool to him. What else matters?"

"Nothing," I said. "Nothing matters at all."

Beans and Diamond both kept halal, so they took me to a restaurant in Natomas called Chicken-n-Waffles. They had a Hot Chicken Challenge going on, where you could choose between sliders ranging from "No Heat" to "Reaper." The latter sandwich was apparently so dangerous that you were to eat it at your own risk.

Beans, who was the only one brave enough to order it, was completely unaffected by the deep red spices that coated her food. Diamond, who had ordered "Mild," was sweating, gasping for breath, and wondering if he ought to order milk.

I'd gotten a Caesar salad. Beenish actually booed me when the waiter delivered it. Explaining that it was, obviously, the king of all salads did not make it any better in her opinion.

"So I was thinking," said Diamond, setting his sandwich aside, apparently giving up on it entirely, "about this whole 'dancing at Qirat Api's wedding' plan Beans told me about. Do you really think it'll go well?"

"What do you mean?" she demanded. "It'll go perfectly."

Diamond and I exchanged a glance.

Beenish caught it. "It will. You'll see. It's genius. And you guys? You're like the people who told da Vinci he'd never get a flying machine to work."

"And he didn't," I pointed out. "He drew some, but he wasn't reckless enough to actually try one out."

"Well...my point still stands. All great minds are told they aren't going to succeed. Everyone told Edison things wouldn't work out before he came up with the light bulb."

"He famously failed around a thousand times."

Beenish scowled. "Fine. I can't think of any other inventors right now, but how about when people told Columbus that he wouldn't find India. The dude was unbelievably awful, but—"

"He ended up not finding India?"

She glared at me. "Why can't you let me have this?"

"I'm just telling you the truth."

"Guys," Diamond interrupted, "maybe you should get a room."

Beans scowled.

"Why do we need a room?" I asked.

Diamond looked at me a moment, then laughed. "Niz, you're really something, you know that?"

"Focus," Beans said, pulling us back on track. "So you both think it isn't going to work? And you're telling me now? After months of planning and practice?"

Diamond held up a conciliatory hand. "Your problem is that the plan isn't grand enough, Beans. Most of these dances people do at weddings kinda suck. They're..."

"Amateurish," I suggested as he searched for the right

253

word. I'd seen enough of those videos by now to know what he was saying was true.

"Right. If you're going to make a statement, make a Diamond Standard statement. You should have backup dancers and proper lighting and sound and outfits. Of course, most people can't get all that stuff. Most. People."

Beenish closed her eyes and exhaled. Diamond was talking about her mother.

He looked at me. "You should ask Aiza Aunty for help."

"I can't."

"Fine." He pointed at Beans. "Then convince her."

"I can't."

"What? Are you scared of her?" Diamond asked.

"Yes," I admitted. "But also, I promised her I wouldn't bring up Aiza Aunty again."

I felt Beenish's fingers brush gently against mine under the table. I looked at her beside me, but her gaze was fixed on Diamond. Then it happened again. And again. I could suddenly think of nothing to do but take her hand. A moment later, she interlaced our fingers.

I reached for my water, my hand trembling a little as I took a sip.

Our friend was oblivious to my state. "You're not bringing it up, are you? Diamond already did that. You're just giving your opinion. Beenish may not care what you think, but Diamond does."

"I care," she said firmly. "Don't be a jerk, Heera." Beans squeezed my hand. "Do you agree with him?"

I exhaled. This seemed like a good moment to lie, if only so that Beenish Siraj would keep holding my hand.

But I decided to tell the truth. After all, Mom had told me on her deathbed that I should not lie, so I avoided speaking falsely whenever I could.

"No. I don't agree with him. But only because I don't think dancers or the stage or anything really matter. That isn't what this is about. This is about you and Aiza Aunty. It always has been."

Diamond started to interrupt, but I held up a hand.

"We've talked about this, Beans. You're the only one who gets to decide how badly you are hurt. Only you know if you're willing to let your pain go, to trust again, to start over, to build a new history with your mom. You should do what you need to do. But do it for yourself, not to make this dance look better."

I turned to look at her and the infinity in her eyes.

"Just know that I'll be there, dancing with you, no matter what you choose."

She did not pull her hand away from mine.

Thank God.

Chapter Eighteen

"Today is a good day to do this," Beans said. "Qirat will be there. She goes to see Amma every Saturday. She'll be there in case this goes south."

I wasn't sure if she was talking to me or to herself. She had shared this information with me already. I glanced over at Beenish sitting in the Eldorado's passenger seat, staring out the window, biting at her bottom lip every so often and cracking her knuckles.

"It'll be fine," I said, not because I hadn't previously said the same thing in a hundred different ways, apparently to no avail, but because it seemed like she still needed to hear it.

"I hope so," she said. "Because if it doesn't, I will murder you."

I laughed.

"I haven't decided how yet, though. I'll let you know when I figure that part out."

"I wouldn't mind being surprised," I said. After a moment, I added, "You're not really going to be mad at me, though, right, if things don't go well? I mean, I didn't actually convince you to do this. You came to this decision on your own."

"You said it will be fine," Beans pointed out.

"It will."

"Then you have nothing to worry about, do you?"

"That's not really reassuring."

"Tell me about it," she said, then stopped talking while her phone told me which way to go. "We should have just taken my car. I know the way there."

"You do? I thought you hadn't seen your mother for a couple of years."

Beenish nodded. "When I first got my license, I'd go out to Amma's place and just sit in the parking lot. I'd think about going in, but...well, I never did. I guess that sounds stupid."

"I go to a cemetery and talk to a headstone," I reminded her. "So, no, I don't think it sounds stupid."

"You're not talking to a headstone when you're there," she said.

I nodded because it was true.

At least, I thought it was, which was the next best thing.

I pulled into Aiza Aunty's apartment complex and found a parking spot.

"You're sure you want me to come with you?" I asked.

"Um, yes, definitely. I need you to hold my hand."

She meant that literally. Our fingers were locked together when she rang the bell to her mother's apartment.

"Arsalan!" Qirat greeted me before she'd even finished opening the door. "What a surpr—"

My physics teacher stopped speaking when she saw I was not alone. Her hands flew to her lips.

"Oh. My. God. How did you…Ohmygod."

I glanced at Beans. "I think she's happy to see you."

Beenish started to reply, then tensed suddenly as her mother's voice called out, "Who is it, Qirat? If there is someone selling something—"

Aiza Aunty walked into sight, carrying a red silk dupatta that slipped from her hands as she saw who had come to visit.

She stood there, staring at Beans, her breath coming faster and faster until tears started falling from her eyes. She didn't bother to wipe them. I wasn't sure she could move.

Trembling a little, Beenish took an uncertain step forward. "Amma?"

I think Aiza Aunty tried to respond, but the sound that came out was a low, wounded cry, which was all meaning but had no meaning. It was not an apology like Beans had wanted. But as Aiza Aunty reached out with a shaking hand, Beenish, suddenly weeping, broke away from me and threw herself into her mother's arms.

Qirat, her eyes shining, shook her head in amazement. "You know, Arsalan, you don't have to study physics if you're already an alchemist."

"I didn't do anything," I said.

"Really?" she asked.

"I swear. I was just myself."

"Well…then I guess your mere presence has completely altered the shape of our world."

I think Beenish heard Qirat, because she pulled away from her mother and rushed back to me, stood on tiptoe, and pulled me into an embrace. Suddenly everything smelled of bitter oranges again.

"Thank you," Beans whispered.

Before I could respond, her lips—accidentally I am sure—grazed the crook of my neck. Their touch was soft and impossibly delicate against the spot where my father had once pressed a match and threatened to burn me.

Diamond Khan crouched before me, peering up as I stood gasping, hands on my knees. I kept sucking in air, but there didn't seem to be enough of it. My legs burned and the cramp in my left calf had only just subsided.

"You okay, bro? You look like you're dying."

"We're all dying," I managed to spit out.

"I guess," he said, sounding doubtful. "But not right at this second. Maybe you should sit down."

I waved off his concern and ran a towel over my face, wiping away the sweat on my forehead. I was in the best shape of my life, but an hour of fairly intense cardio still wasn't a joke. Matters of the heart seldom are.

Diamond handed me a bottle of some kind of energy drink. It was an unnatural, toxic-looking, bright green liquid. I eyed it with some apprehension.

"It'll make you feel better."

I drank. It was unpleasant. Salty and sugary with flavors that didn't taste like anything except chemicals that had been mixed together.

"People actually drink this?"

"For electrolytes," he explained.

"Not worth it," I decided.

"Seriously," he said, "let's sit, Niz. You're going super hard for a guy who never cared about this stuff before."

"If you're going to do something, you might as well do it properly. That's what Nana always says."

Diamond chuckled. "Actually, the Prophet said that. Or something like it anyway. Your nana just repeated it."

I shrugged. "If you say so."

"Speaking of which, I found out some more stuff about Nuayman ibn Amr."

"What? Oh. Can we talk about that later? My heart is beating so hard, I can't really think."

260

"Sure, bro. No worries," Diamond assured me. "By the way, if you see Aiza Aunty before I do, tell her I've found a few guys to help with security for the dance you and Beans are doing." When I looked at him blankly, he added, "She doesn't want any interruptions or anyone trying to cut the music."

I nodded. That made sense. Once Aiza Aunty had heard what Beans and I were actually up to, she'd embraced the idea with glee. She'd also seemed to know how to plan something like this properly, unlike her youngest daughter. I think she saw that it was a way to connect with Beans, maybe even that it had been Beenish's way of reaching out to her.

Her only condition had been that Qirat be told what her sister was planning.

"I feel a lot better now that Qirat Api is onboard," Diamond said. "It would have been horrible if she'd been upset over what we're doing."

"I think she appreciates the chance to give Sham and her in-laws a bit of a middle finger. They certainly deserve it."

Diamond sighed. "I guess."

"Don't tell me you agree with their rules?"

"No, of course not. Those are awful. It's just... bro, you haven't known Qirat Api for very long. She's always been like my older sister. Diamond can't get over the fact that she's going to marry some guy she doesn't even like. Why is she doing it?"

"She feels like she must, I think. You're the one who told me about how Aiza Aunty's past affects both her and Beans."

261

"There are people in the world who wouldn't care," Diamond insisted. "Roshni Aunty is just in a rush to get Qirat Api out of the house. Anyway, Api would be better off not marrying anyone than marrying into a family that'll treat her like that."

"Maybe they think they're just being good Muslims."

"They're not, though. Those rules aren't about Islam. They're about control. That Sham, that family, they want to make sure they have Qirat Api under their thumb. Her mother can't be at the wedding? That's bullshit."

"I didn't say they were being good Muslims," I pointed out mildly. "I said they *think* they're being good Muslims."

"And I'm telling you they know better. And if they don't...fuck them, because they're still human and their demands on Qirat Api are not."

"What are you saying?"

"Diamond is saying that she shouldn't marry this dude. Obviously."

"I don't disagree with you. Why are you getting so worked up?"

"Because you haven't done anything about it, Niz. Don't you want to do something?"

I stared at him. "What could I possibly do?"

"You can talk to her. You convince people, bro. You convinced Beans to forgive me. To forgive Aiza Aunty. That's a miracle! You know words, man, and people who know words can work magic. Why do you think it's called *spell*-ing?"

"You're seriously overestimating me. Beenish and I have a...relationship of a sort. Qirat is my teacher. She's not going to listen to me."

"She might. And even if she doesn't listen, you'll have tried. Ultimately, there is nothing more a man can do and nothing less he can expect of himself."

"You were supposed to get some sleep, Arsalan. You look exhausted," Beans said as she pushed past me into the living room the next morning.

Nana—who was standing by the glass door to the back-yard, watching the birds he left breadcrumbs out for every morning—waved hello as Beans took off her windbreaker.

"How are your knockoff dinosaurs?"

Nana turned his attention back to his avian friends. "Getting ready to depart due to the coming winter. Not all of them will return, you know."

I barely registered the slight melancholy in his voice because I saw now what Beenish was wearing. She had on a robin's-egg-blue tank top with matching tights. The color complemented her dark hair and black eyes. Unusually, there was no writing to be seen anywhere. The outfit needed no words. Silence, it turns out, is perfectly capable of being extremely appealing and distracting.

I tried to keep my eyes focused on the top of her head. I wasn't entirely successful.

"You were thinking, weren't you?" Beans said, her tone accusatory. "What caught your attention?"

"Uh...just now?" I asked, scrambling to come up with a halal answer to that question.

Beans looked at me from the corner of her eye. "Last night. What kept you awake?"

"Oh. Another postcard came from my father. He's leaving LA."

"I'm sorry." She stepped closer and touched my arm.

I smiled and felt the urge to move toward her as well, like I was drawn to her.

I *was* drawn to her. I'd felt this pull many times, especially when we'd slow danced together. My body reacted to her just being there.

I guess your mere presence has completely altered the shape of our world, Qirat had said.

"Arsalan? What's wrong?" Beans asked.

I shook my head, not wanting to be distracted, but also not wanting to be pulled out of my train of thought. I just told her what I was thinking. "When I'm around you, I feel...I'm really aware of your being, of your body—"

"Dude," she whispered, "Nana is right there."

"What? No, Beans—I'm talking about science."

She folded her arms across her chest and muttered something that sounded like "I thought you said biology was a science."

I didn't bother responding. I was close to figuring out a

puzzle. "She gave me a hint. Forever ago, when you set up that lunch at the mall, she said that any answer I came up with would have to be universal, because the Earth isn't the only celestial body that is round."

"Who? What's even the question? You're not making any sense, which I'm obviously used to at this point, but in case you can't tell from my voice, is still super frustrating."

"Qirat. The physics extra credit assignment. Why is the world round? The answer is *universal*—not in the sense of planets and stuff, but in the sense of you and me. People are attracted to each other."

She sighed. "Not really at this exact moment, though."

"You have gravity, Beenish. I've known that since the day we danced together to Dean Martin. *Everything* has gravity. Drops of rain, blots of ink—"

"You're talking about adhesion?" Beans asked. "And cohesion?"

I nodded. "The pull of molecules upon other molecules. When a tear falls, it forms a circle on the surface it hits. Why? Because the molecules want to stay as close to each other as possible. They pull on each other."

"If a tear fell," Beans said, her brow furrowed, "in a vacuum—"

"In space," I added, "with no forces acting on it—"

"In three dimensions..." She grinned. "It'd become a sphere, like a little world of its own. Dude, that—"

"Took you unacceptably long to figure out," Nana called

from across the living room. "Really, Arsalan. That question has been hanging on the wall above your desk for months. I would have thought you'd find it rather elementary."

"I've been a little distracted."

Nana looked at Beans, who lowered her head and took a step behind me, so that she was partially hidden from his view. "Yes. I'm aware. I'm surprised you figured it out now. Not your finest moment, I must say."

"I'm sure Qirat will be more impressed," Beenish said, trying to soothe away the sting of my great-grandfather's irritation.

"Did I tell you Diamond wants me to talk to her?" I asked, eager to move on from the subject of how long the physics extra credit assignment had taken me. "He thinks I'll somehow be able to convince her not to marry Sham."

"Can't hurt to try," Beenish said. "God knows I have."

"It's not really my place. I should say nothing about her personal life."

She started to say something, almost certainly to tell me that I wasn't just a student in Qirat's life anymore, but Nana spoke first. "Nothing will come of nothing."

"What does that mean?" Beans asked.

"It's Shakespeare," I told her. After a moment, I added, "*King Lear* is a great play."

Beenish looked at me, then looked at Nana, then back at me again. She scowled when neither one of us offered a further explanation. "You know, I really hate you guys sometimes."

Two days later, I walked up to Qirat at the end of her physics class and handed over the extra credit assignment. The sheet of paper she had given me now read:

> Q: Why is the world round?
> Q: Why is the world an oblate spheroid?
> A: Gravity.

She looked at it for barely a second, then set it aside on her desk. "You didn't explain yourself."

"I wasn't asked for an explanation."

That drew a smile from her. "I'm asking you now."

I'd hoped that she would. "Every physical thing in the universe—stars, dust, light, us—is made up of particulate matter. Matter attracts other matter because these particles are drawn to each other, connected by an invisible force."

"Everything has gravity, you're saying?" Qirat asked.

I nodded. "Basically."

"Okay. How does that result in a round Earth?"

"Because particles are drawn to each other; they try to get close to each other." I held up a palm, then closed it into a fist. "A sphere is just the shape in which they can get as close to each other as possible."

She grinned. "Good work. But if everything has gravity, how come I'm not stuck to my chair, unable to get up?"

"A lot more stuff went into making the world than went

into making you or the chair. The chair doesn't have enough mass to keep you in place."

Qirat clapped her hands once. It wasn't applause. It was delight. "Brilliant. Good job, Arsalan. How did you figure it out?"

"Beans."

"She told you?"

I shook my head. "No. She has... There is a... When I'm around her, I noticed that—"

"You're attracted to her," Qirat finished. "There's no blushing in physics, Nizami."

"It got me thinking about people, you know, and how they have their own pull on us. Some of them barely acknowledge our presence, and we barely acknowledge theirs, like the sun and Pluto. Others draw you in so close that you become like Mercury and just burn."

"A scientist and a poet."

I shrugged. "The thing is that there are people in our lives who are neither stars nor the planets swaying around them. They are black holes. These people try to exert so much control over us that they begin to crush us. They absorb all our light and leave us with nothing. It would be best to avoid people like that, I think, if we can."

She folded her arms and sat back in her chair. "Are you trying to tell me something?"

"I'm simply talking about science."

"You're talking about relationships," Qirat countered.

"They're the same thing. It's just... my father is like that.

A dead star of a person. He sucked up all of my mother's brightness and he wasn't even there when she finally went out, because he's trapped himself, locked in a battle with his own demons."

"I'm sorry," she said quietly.

"I hope to one day achieve escape velocity. We'll see how it goes. It isn't easy. It's better, I think, to not get close in the first place, if one can help it, to that kind of toxicity."

Qirat shook her head. "You *are* trying to tell me something. Beenish put you up to this, right? Or was it Amma?"

"It was Diamond Khan, actually."

"Well...I guess I appreciate it. It's nice to be cared for."

"Yes," I agreed softly. "I have found that it is."

"This is personal," Qirat said, gesturing at the classroom around us. "And we aren't in the place for that, but we might as well talk about what we're talking about. I think you've valiantly stretched your metaphor as far as it'll go."

I nodded.

"I didn't know what Sham was like when I agreed to marry him, and besides that, saying no didn't really seem like an option, given my mother's past. I knew Roshni and my dad wanted me out of their house. And now that I do know what he's like...well...it doesn't matter. The wedding is too close. People have been invited, all this money has been spent....My father and Roshni would freak out. It would cost too much, in emotional and actual capital, to back out."

"Money doesn't—"

"Don't say money doesn't matter," she said. "People make it seem like material things are trivial, but they aren't always. You're in the same position as me, after all. You're putting up with your father to save your grandfather's house, aren't you?"

"I didn't know Beenish told you about that."

"We sisters share our pains. Anyway, you and I both have a little time left before our fates catch up with us. I'd rather not spend it dwelling on what's to come."

I nodded. "We've still got today."

"And no one knows," Qirat added, "if the sun will even rise tomorrow."

Chapter Nineteen

When I got home, Beenish was sitting with Nana in the living room, playing a ghazal on her phone. I couldn't understand many of the words or the crooning verses of the song, which was a little sad. My great-grandfather certainly thought that this kind of music was beautiful, and whatever his flaws, his aesthetic sensibilities were very refined.

He claimed that there was no language better suited to poetry than Urdu, with the possible exceptions of Persian and Arabic. I'd never asked him why, if that was true, he hadn't ensured that I learned it properly. I suspected he hadn't because my regular homeschooling had taxed his patience more than enough over the years.

Still, upon hearing this language that I should have understood, that had been the inheritance of my family for generations and which I had lost, it was difficult not to feel like something had been taken from me. Someday, perhaps, I'd have the chance to recover it.

"What's happening?" I asked.

"Your bean sprout is trying to convince me that this soulless reproduction of Mehdi Hassan's voice coming from her infernal contraption is superior to my vinyl recordings," my great-grandfather explained.

"And how's that going?"

"Awful," Beans admitted. "He won't listen to reason."

"Not usually," I agreed.

"I do not have to listen to reason," Nana declared, "for I know how to listen to music, a skill which apparently both of you lack. Otherwise, you'd abandon that portable misery generator in a heartbeat."

"This lets you listen to any song ever recorded in the history of the world," Beenish reminded him, waving her phone around for emphasis.

"What good is all that if it doesn't sound right, hmm? Besides, I already have all the music I like. I don't need to collect anything new."

Beans held up her arms in surrender. "I don't know how you live with this man."

I shrugged. "With difficulty."

"You're such a hipster, Nana," she added as a parting shot.

"I am not sure what that means," the old man informed her, "and I do not care to find out." He tried to rise to his feet, but I could tell he was having some trouble getting up, even with his cane. I moved toward him, but Beenish was closer. She got to him first.

"Thank you. I will retire now. Know that you were not entirely unpleasant company."

"I'm honored," Beenish said wryly as Nana walked away.

"You should be. That's the nicest thing he's said to any-one in years."

"I believe it. Hey, how'd it go with Qirat?"

I shook my head.

"Damn it," she said. "You two and your twisted determination to be martyrs is really messing up my life."

"So sorry to inconvenience you."

"No, you're not. Anyway, I'm glad you're back. I need to measure you."

I took a step back instinctively. "You need to measure what?"

"Measure you for your sherwani. Mom is having clothes made for me by Haniya Tahir. Can you believe it? This is one of the few times having a ridiculously extra parent pays off."

"I don't know what a Haniya Tahir is, but it sounds expensive. There is no need for—"

Beans thrust her phone at my face. "Here's what I'm wearing."

The dress on the screen was more than enough to quell

any further protest on my part. It was a satin, pale pink two-piece outfit. The top part, the choli, was full sleeved but daringly short and elaborately embroidered. The long skirt, the ghagra, sat low on the waist and flared out dramatically in an elaborate floral print.

The model who was wearing it looked regal. Beans would look perfectly stunning.

"It's...nice," I said.

"So for your sherwani, I'm thinking a shade of green or maybe a deep purple to match the flowers in the print? Would you wear a color like that?"

"I'll wear whatever makes you happy."

She grinned. It had apparently been the right thing to say. "I knew there was a reason I liked you. Okay, so I've got some measuring tape here. Go ahead and strip and we'll get started."

"Sure. Wait. *What?*"

Beans laughed. "I'm kidding, dude. You should have seen your face."

"No, thank you," I said, as she stepped toward me. "I'm satisfied with the view I have."

"By the way," Beans said over the phone, "Amma wants to meet Nana. I can bring her over tonight if that will work."

"Aiza Aunty wants to meet him?" It seemed like one of those "immovable object meets an irresistible force" kind of moments, an encounter the outcome of which could simply not be predicted. "Why?"

There was a long-suffering sigh on the other end. "Something about how if I'm spending so much time in his care, she ought to know who he is. She's on this maternal-concern kick, like I haven't been doing fine for myself for years. It sucks."

Even though Beans had forgiven Aiza Aunty, they were still getting used to being in each other's lives again. Qirat said this would be work, that it would take time and patience. An apology is not a magic elixir that makes things the way they were again. It is a seed from which trust grows slowly, if it ever grows at all.

"I'm sure that'll be fine," I said, even though that wasn't entirely true.

"See you then."

They came over around eight, with Aiza Aunty wearing an excessively ornamented maroon saree and so much jewelry that she could have probably used it to buy Nana's house. Her hair and makeup looked like they'd been professionally done.

Beans was wearing another shalwar kameez, off-white this time, with chikan embroidery of the same color all over it.

"You look nice," I whispered while Aiza Aunty exchanged pleasantries with Nana.

"For a guy who reads a lot of books, you give really awful compliments."

"What's wrong with my compliments?"

"They're so…bland. 'Nice.' 'Great.' 'Pretty.' It's super-generic stuff. You can do better."

I tried again. " 'Shall I compare thee to a summer's day? Thou art—' "

"Oh, shut up," Beans said. "Hey, look who's getting along."

I turned to see that Aiza Aunty and Nana were drifting toward the living room. I couldn't hear what they were talking about, but they seemed to be having an engaging conversation.

"Who would have thought?"

"I did," Beans claimed. "They're actually very similar if you think about it. She idolizes the past and he lives in it. Plus they're both ridiculously extra."

This was true.

"Diamond was right, by the way," she went on. "Bringing Amma in has taken this whole thing to a different level. Come on. Let me show you what she's planning for the stage."

When I got back home from school the next day, there were more cars in the neighborhood than I'd ever seen before. For a moment, I thought someone might be having a party. Then I realized that if there was a party happening, we were the ones hosting it. Nana's house was the center of all this activity.

A wall of chatter hit me as soon as I walked in, and a bunch of strangers nodded or waved at me, as if I was supposed to know who they were.

"This place is wild."

"Historic."

"Prehistoric even."

I figured there were around twenty or so people present, which was a lot for the small home. Despite the crowd, I knew exactly where I'd find Nana. He was sitting in his favorite chair, though instead of having a book in his hands, he had a glass of turmeric milk.

"Who got you that?" I asked. It was not the most pressing question in the circumstances but making that drink for him had been my job since forever. I'd ceased to imagine someone else could even do it. I nodded to Aiza Aunty, who was sitting next to him.

"Qirat did," Nana said. "A very nice young woman, that one."

"Yes, she's wonderful."

"Like you, however, I prefer the devilish one." He turned to Aiza Aunty and bowed slightly. "With all due respect."

"A matter of taste," she said languidly. "But know that your preference is for rocket fuel over a gemstone."

"Who are all these people?" I asked.

"My friends," Aiza Aunty said. "Who happen to be backup dancers. I sent them a video of you and Beans dancing, so they are familiar with the moves. They have been practicing on their own, but you do have to get some work in all together. You can hardly expect to be perfect otherwise."

"We can hardly expect to be perfect regardless," I pointed out.

Aiza Aunty tsked in that imperious way she had. "That's a disheartening statement. You must expect to be perfect. You will most likely not be, but you should aspire to it."

"Okay," I said uncertainly. "But how will you ever be happy if you're expecting to be flawless? Won't you always be disappointed in yourself?"

"The price of happiness," she declared dismissively, "is mediocrity. It's not worth the bargain."

I raised my eyebrows at Nana, who was repeating what she'd said under his breath. He was probably going to add it to his unending list of maxims for later use.

"Beenish is in—" Nana began but was interrupted by a huge cheer from the kitchen. A few seconds later, the song "Haye Dil Bechara" from *Parey Hut Love* started blasting through the house, followed by enthusiastic clapping. I knew the song well. It was one of the tracks Beans used regularly for practice.

"So it begins," Nana said darkly as I walked toward the source of the commotion.

As I got closer, I saw that the kitchen had become a battlefield. Qirat Api, lip-syncing to the music, was twirling around, bringing one hand above her head, one behind the small of her back, in a step I recognized from the music video.

Beans, who saw me approach, ran over and yelled, "You're on my team!"

I looked over at Qirat, expecting her to protest, but she just extended a hand and waved for me to come forward. "Bring it, Nizami."

I hesitated and looked at all the people around me—all the professional dancers. No matter how much practice I got, I'd never be as good as—

Beenish took my hand, and all of a sudden my entire universe was centered on her fingertips and mine. When our eyes met, she mouthed, "You're with me."

And I was.

She pointed up, which was her signal to listen for the next beat drop, and then we were dancing, our hands moving out in a wave and then to our hips. We undulated our arms in concert with our shoulders. It seemed like we'd done it at least a hundred times.

I held my hand out to Beans, and she took it briefly before quickly letting go and spinning toward me so that my arm was wrapped around her waist and her face was inches from mine.

"Oh," she said. "Hello."

I chuckled. "Hi."

There were a few whistles and some hooting as we stayed as we were for a beat longer than was absolutely necessary. I flushed not with embarrassment, as I'd feared, but with pride. This was going well...and it was fun!

Qirat was grinning as she clapped for us, until an absolute roar went up from people on the other side of the kitchen. We whirled around to see Aiza Aunty with Nana, who was leaning on a counter, but doing the best jig he could.

I stopped and stared. What was *happening*?

Beans, however, was not at all stunned or, if she was, she

recovered quickly. "My team!" she shouted again, rushing across to him. "Nana is on my team!"

"Hey," I protested being abandoned, but only half-heartedly, as I watched Beenish wrap her arms around Nana and him transfer his weight to her, trusting her to hold him up even as gravity tried to pull him down.

It was one of the best things I'd ever seen, those two dancing together, everyone clapping along to the music to encourage them.

It was the only time I ever saw Nana truly laughing.

"Today is a good day," Qirat said into my ear.

"The best," I agreed.

Thanksgiving was the worst day of the year. I used to love it. It was our one big, annual family feast, even though the food wasn't all that good. No matter what she tried, my mother never quite managed to master the fine art of making a turkey. Hers were either undercooked or too dry and chewy. Even so, every November, she rolled up her sleeves and attempted to climb her avian Everest.

It was, in her opinion, a truly American experience that Muslims could be part of. In another month, when Christmas came around, it would seem like everyone was celebrating except for us. At least, she told me, that is what she'd felt like when she used to go to school. Thanksgiving was a chance to belong.

Now that she was gone, our special dinner was store-bought pre-sliced turkey breast and mayo squeezed into a sandwich, along with a glass of cranberry juice. Nana did not complain. He'd never really liked the celebration anyway. He said the holiday called to mind the systemic oppression and destruction of people native to this continent, which was difficult to argue with.

I made a face at the apple I was cutting into small pieces. My theory, that placing slices of the fruit on graham crackers would essentially emulate a pie, had proven to be false. Unfortunately, I didn't have any better ideas for dessert.

The doorbell rang.

I frowned and went to the sink to wash my hands. I wondered if Nana was expecting someone. He hadn't said so, and I couldn't remember the last time he'd had a visitor.

Apparently, Nana had known the bell would ring, though, because I heard him open the door and greet someone. I couldn't remember the last time he'd done that either.

I heard them before I saw them.

Beans, Diamond, Qirat Api, and Aiza Aunty, each one holding a dish of some kind. It was Diamond, however, who held the pièce de résistance. Even though it was covered in foil, it was obvious that he'd brought an impressively large, cooked bird.

"Hey," Beenish said, shoving a barely warm casserole dish full of mashed potatoes at me.

"I...uh...yes, hi. What is happening?"

"It's Thanksgiving," she said, pointing down to her red shirt, which had a white crescent moon with a single star by it. I recognized the flag, of course.

"Droll," I said. "I know what day it is. I just...What are you doing here?"

"Diamond said you're an awful cook. So he asked us if we could prepare"—she paused significantly to stress the fact that she was about to be impressive—"a movable feast."

As incredibly sexy as a Hemingway reference from Beans was, I barely noticed it. Instead, I found myself shaking my head as everyone made their way to the kitchen, and Nana's usually silent home was filled with the magic of many voices.

As Diamond heaved the turkey he was carrying onto a kitchen counter, I asked, "This was your idea?"

"Yeah," he confirmed proudly. "Had a feeling you and Nana wouldn't have much going on today."

"How could you doubt my excellent culinary skills?" I asked, gesturing grandly toward my now-abandoned efforts at creating a pie.

"What is that?" Diamond demanded.

"Dessert."

He shook his head. "You weren't kidding when you said dinner around here sucked."

"When did I—" Then I realized that I'd mentioned it briefly when Diamond had invited me to the mosque. "I can't believe you remembered that."

"Don't be surprised, bro. Surely you realize by now that Diamond is a genius."

I didn't attempt to refute his claim.

In that moment, it would have been a task impossible.

Hours later, when it felt like I'd eaten more in one night than I'd eaten all year, I found Aiza Aunty in the kitchen, wrapped in an elaborate shawl, picking thoughtfully at a piece of pecan pie with a fork. She seemed surprised when, after cutting my own slice, I took a seat next to her.

"You're not playing?" she asked.

I shook my head. I'd surrendered my place at the Monopoly board after Beans refused to stop cheating. It was aggravating. Why even bother with a game if you are unable to follow the rules?

Besides, I'd heard Nana's long-winded thesis on the evils of unchecked capitalism, supported by the poetry of Faiz Ahmed Faiz, a few times before. Qirat Api might be content to listen intently, but I wasn't.

"You didn't want to sit with everyone?" I asked.

"I was just taking a moment. Solitude makes it easier to appreciate other people properly, don't you think?"

I could understand that. I started to get to my feet.

"No. Stay," Aiza Aunty said. It was probably a request, but in her commanding tone it did not come across as one. I sank back into my chair. "I would speak with you."

"About what?"

She sighed, as if gravely disappointed in me. "Direct and to the point. How very American all our children become,

283

hmm? Back in Pakistan, business is not done—was not done—in this way. First, there was tea, then talk, and only then did we speak about work."

"Sounds inefficient."

"Perhaps," she granted, as if doing me a huge favor. "But is the goal of a civilization to be efficient, or is the goal of a civilization to be beautiful?"

I didn't know how to answer that, so I helped myself to a bite of pie.

"Some people say," Aiza Aunty went on, "that the West is all about the right of the individual to be free of the community, while the East focuses on the rights of the community over the individual."

I'd always thought that the division of the world into categories of East and West was clumsy and too broad to be useful, but I didn't say so. Presumably, Aiza Aunty had a point she was trying to make.

"If that is true, perhaps I was born in the wrong place," she continued.

I assumed she meant her decision to pursue dancing despite the wishes of her society, her family, and, later, her husband.

"That is a prettier thought, isn't it, Nizami, than wondering if you're just an awful person? It puts the blame on God so one doesn't have to carry it."

"I'm...Honestly, Aunty, I'm not sure what you want me to say."

"I am not sure either," she admitted. "I'm just wondering

if what I'm doing—what I'm helping Beenish do—is worth it. It is an impertinent thing, this dance at Qirat's wedding."

"Beans is fond of giving people the middle finger."

"I'm her mother. I should put a stop to that."

I had personally grown to find this propensity of Beenish's endearing, but that was probably not okay to just come out and say to her mother.

Aiza Aunty delicately set aside her fork and pushed the pie she'd been toying with away. "Am I being selfish by allowing this dance to happen? The truth is that I want to be at my eldest daughter's wedding. My ex-husband and his new wife, not to mention Qirat's in-laws, won't let me attend. If this dance happens, however, they will feel my presence there. I'll win."

"That's what Beenish wants." I paused, then added, "It must also be what Qirat Api wants. She knows what we have planned. Did she tell Beans to stop once she heard?"

Aiza Aunty shook her head.

"Did you ask her why?"

She made an irritated sound at the back of her throat. "She said that everything worthwhile happens because human beings defy gravity. The Earth to which we belong can be allowed to hold us down, but not so tightly that there is no room to move."

I smiled. Qirat Api was standing up for herself....Well, she was letting Beans stand up for her, which was still something. "You've taught your daughters the value of freedom. That's not selfish."

"I don't want them to walk down the path I walked down."

"Maybe you just don't want them to go as far as you went."

Beenish's mother seemed annoyed at my response. "You know, you are much too young to be this much of an oracle, Nizami. Didn't your mother teach you not to be a know-it-all?"

"She tried," I admitted.

"Well, she didn't do a very good job of it." Aunty Aiza went silent for almost a full minute. "I don't want Beans to be whispered about her whole life, and the people she is surrounded by are very much the whispering type. I had to leave the circle into which I was born to find friends, to find a place in the world. It was... it has been lonely at times. My life would've been a lot more painless if I had been the good, quiet girl everyone wanted."

I considered her words. What she'd said was so close to the truth that I could see why she thought it was so. "I'm sure you're right, Aunty. It would have been an easier life if you'd stayed in the orbit that others wanted. But it wouldn't have been *your* life at all."

Chapter Twenty

A routine settled in over the following weeks. There was school, there was the gym, and there was practice with Beenish and sometimes the entire group. Under Aiza Aunty's guidance, we had danced to "Shakar Wandaan" so many times that it felt like the steps were carved into my bones. My body knew exactly how to move before any conscious thought was required.

The only thing that changed, really, were the locations from which my father sent postcards, like some kind of touristy countdown clock to his arrival. From Los Angeles he went to Santa Barbara, then to Bakersfield—why did

Bakersfield even have postcards?—to San Luis Obispo, up to Visalia and Fresno.

The closer Zeeshan Nizami got, the lower my heart sank. My grades took a further hit. I wasn't really pushing myself at the gym, but Diamond let it go. The only joy left in the world was on the dance floor, with music blasting through the air and pulsating through the ground at my feet.

"Let's get started," I told Beans, jumping up as soon as she stepped into the garage and turned on the light.

She frowned. "Were you just sitting here in the dark?"

"I was thinking."

"Was there another postcard?"

I nodded. "From Monterey. He's just three hours away. He could show up anytime."

She stepped toward me. "Arsalan—"

"It's fine," I lied. "Let's just practice."

"You don't need to practice. You need to talk to Nana."

"About what?" I asked.

She pointed to the walls around us.

"I don't think—"

"You should've told him already. If your father shows up and throws a will in his face, Nana will be devastated. It's not fair to him."

That was a good point. "It's just…how do you take the last thing he cares about away from a man who has lost everything in his life? I don't want to."

"You don't have to do this alone. Let me call Amma and Qirat. Let's all see if we can work out some kind of solution."

Beans held out her hands and I took them. "Things aren't like they were before. You're not alone anymore. We're with you."

I smiled for her sake.

"Also," she said, "Nana hasn't lost everything he ever cared about. Not yet."

An hour later, Qirat, Beans, and their mother sat in silence in Nana's living room, waiting for him to speak. I served chai. Every clink of glass seemed to highlight how quiet he had gotten since Aiza Aunty informed Nana that his beloved home actually belonged to Zeeshan Nizami. I hadn't been able to bring myself to say the words when the time came.

Nana hadn't moved since he'd found out. He was just sitting in his favorite chair, leaning forward, his chin on his hands and his hands on the top of his walking cane. It was only when I brought him his tea that he stirred, accepting it without thanks.

Finally, Beans gave a loud sigh, set her chai aside, and went over to kneel by him. "Nana, will you please say something?" she asked gently.

He mustered up a smile for her. She had that effect on people. "It is good tea, don't you think?"

"That's not what she meant," I said from across the room.

He glared up at me. "Boy, I do not require commentary from you at this time. I require answers. How long have you known that this was not my house?"

"Since right after Mom died. My father told me. You'd put the house in her name around five years ago, remember? It was right before your surgery for—"

"I recovered my health but failed to recover my property?" he asked.

I nodded.

He glanced at Aiza Aunty. "It appears, madam, that I have become an old fool."

"I know how that feels," she replied. "It happens to all of us, I think."

He grunted in acknowledgment, then turned his attention to me. "Why did you not tell me before?"

"Because you weren't going to lose the house, Nana. My father just wanted to—"

"He wanted to use it to control you," my great-grandfather finished grimly, "to continue to hurt you. Your mother's husband understood that you would do everything he wanted if the cost were my home."

"I was protecting you."

"*I don't need your protection!*" Nana shouted, so loudly, so suddenly, that Beenish yelped in surprise and I stepped back a little. Then he turned to Aiza Aunty, perfectly calmly, and said, "Excuse my tone, madam."

"By all means," she drawled, "do go on."

"Did it ever occur to you, Arsalan Nizami, that it is not your function to protect me, but rather it falls on you to receive my protection? I've been trying to keep you safe from the world to the best of my ability—"

"Too safe," Beans muttered.

Nana ignored that comment. "So many of my children and my children's children have lived here, and each of them had their own tragedies. I wanted to make sure you were spared. Now you tell me that you have been suffering on my behalf, on account of this"—he waved his cane around wildly at the entirety of his house, causing Beenish to duck—"box of wood?"

"You love this place."

Nana shook his head. "I love what has *happened* here. I love the times these walls have seen. I love the memory of my wife in that kitchen and of your grandfather playing in that backyard."

"Right," I said, "and I didn't want that taken away from you."

"I think," Qirat broke in gently, "that you aren't hearing what your grandfather is saying. The value of the home is the people who live within it."

"And," Aiza Aunty added, "that you are the most important person who lives within it now."

I looked at Nana, who nodded.

"Not to me," I said. "You don't get to tell me not to protect you. My opinion matters as well."

He scoffed. "Since when?"

I glanced at Beenish, who smiled at me, and Nana sighed.

"His balls have dropped since he met you," Nana told her. "I don't like it."

I resisted the instinct to be embarrassed at the mention

of my nether regions. Beans, of course, seemed utterly unaffected by it. "I get that this is bad," she said, "but being mad at Arsalan doesn't solve anything."

"She is right," Aiza Aunty agreed. "We should discuss actual solutions."

There was a long silence.

Apparently, no one had anything useful to offer.

Finally, Qirat said, "Maybe we should sleep on it."

"It would appear," Nana said dryly, "that we have no other choice."

The next week was typical for December in Sacramento, all gloomy rain and chill winds. Like my own spirits, the wattage on Qirat Api's smile kept dropping as her wedding date drew nearer. These were probably the last best days of our lives, but the shadow of the coming future had already fallen upon them.

With fourteen days left to go until Christmas Eve, we met to discuss Aiza Aunty's plan.

"The wedding is taking place in a hotel ballroom," she explained. "There is a much smaller conference room beside it, which we have rented. The partition between the two rooms is portable. We'll put a curtain up, take the divider down, and set up a stage behind the curtain, along with the DJ, the sound system, and all. No one at the wedding will even know we are there until the show is ready to begin."

"Also," Beenish added, "I won't be missed at the wedding

because I can just show my face there before coming over to change for the dance."

"Since we are renting the conference room," Heera added, "some gym friends and I can provide security. They'll keep anyone from coming over to our side to mess you guys up onstage."

Qirat sighed. "That sounds good in theory, but you won't be able to keep Roshni or Baba out. It's not like you can lay hands on them. They'll storm the stage and put a stop to everything."

"They'll be busy," Aiza Aunty said, "along with the groom's parents."

"What are you going to do?" Qirat Api asked suspiciously.

"I'm going to make a rather histrionic entrance to your wedding, my dear. I am known for being dramatic, after all."

"It means Amma will miss the dance, which sucks, but otherwise this is a good plan. If none of the parents are in the room for the performance, it'll buy us time to—" Beans was interrupted by the ringing of the landline. She hopped to her feet, declaring, "I'll get it. I always wanted to answer one of these."

Aiza Aunty apparently didn't think it necessary to pause our discussion as her daughter went to field the incoming call. "Your outfit for the wedding, Arsalan," she continued, "and Beenish's are in a DHL shipment that—"

"Sorry, Amma," Beans cut in, lowering the receiver. She looked at me. "It's for you. It's your father."

I met Zeeshan Nizami at a small, run-down diner at the edge of town. They had tried to spruce it up for Christmas, but any attempts to add cheer to this place were fruitless. It was the farthest spot my father could have picked from Eagles Nest, where Mom was buried. I wondered if that was a coincidence.

He looked thin, hollowed out, with hair that was cropped close in the military style he'd had since his days in the army. He was clean-shaven and his lips were chapped. I noticed his fingernails were a little long, and he'd used them to pick at the sides of his thumbs. The skin there was livid red, broken, and gashed. His eyes were hard and clear when he saw me. He got up from the booth he was sitting in, smiled wide, and moved forward to embrace me.

I held out a hand to him. His smile died. He sat again.

"We've just met and you're embarrassing me already, Arsalan," he said, his voice a little hoarse, but familiar enough. "You know I don't like it when people make a fool out of me."

I took a seat across from him and folded my arms.

"So this is how it is going to be? You're going to be a child."

I glanced away from him at the tired-looking waitress walking by. She smiled down at me. "You ready to order, honey?"

"I'm not hungry," I said.

"He'll have the French toast," Zeeshan Nizami told her. "I'll have the same."

She hesitated, almost as if she knew I hated French toast, like my father did. "Do you want to look at the menu?"

"He's fine," my father snapped. "Do what you're told."

The woman, who must have been in her mid-forties, stayed standing where she was, waiting for me to make eye contact with her. There was sympathy in her eyes when I looked up. No, not sympathy. Something deeper. Empathy. I wondered what those green eyes of hers had seen, what they understood about my father just from what had happened so far.

When I shook my head at her, the waitress nodded, touching my shoulder lightly as she left.

"Somebody isn't getting a tip," my father said loudly.

I hoped she would spit in his food.

"How is school?" my father asked.

"Fine."

"I knew it. I told Muneera she shouldn't homeschool you. 'Academic standards,' she said." He snorted dismissively. "Bullshit. You needed to be made tough. You can't make a man out of a boy if he's tied to his mother's dupatta."

"So you decided to be the one to make me tough?"

He drummed his fingers on the table. "You have to admit that whatever little strength there is in you is because of me. You are looking more confident. I was the one who raised you to have the courage to talk to me like this, like an equal."

I didn't tell him that he hadn't raised me, that he'd barely been there. I didn't mention Nana or tell him about Diamond or Beans. It was pointless to upset him further.

"Speaking of strength, you look like you've been working out. Is it for a girl?"

"No," I said immediately. Too quickly. He caught the lie. "Who is she?"

"No one," I said.

"You got a picture of her?"

I shook my head.

"What? I don't have the right to see what target my son has acquired? Oh. I forgot. You're living with that old fart in that stupid house. You don't have a phone, do you?"

"I don't."

Zeeshan Nizami chuckled. "It's weird, isn't it, Arsalan? For all of my demons, I'm freer than you in some ways."

"Hilarious," I said.

A silence descended between us. Then my father sighed and picked at the exposed flesh by his thumbnails on both hands. It had always been an old nervous habit. "I am sorry," he said. "This isn't how I wanted things to start off. It's just...you make me so angry, Arsalan. You're prideful and disobedient. It's your fault I get this way."

I put my elbows on the table and buried my face in my hands, eyes closed.

"We'll work on it. I'll help you be better. It isn't your fault Muneera gave you over to that superior jackass nana of hers and he made you into what you are. Tell me, do you even pray five times a day?"

I shook my head.

"He's always been an infidel, that one. He'll go to hell and take you with him. I pray all the time, Arsalan. You'll pray with me."

"What use are your prayers?" I asked, remembering a thought I'd had ages ago. "The Prophet said that mercy is not shown to him who does not show mercy." My father stared at me, obviously surprised I knew that. I allowed myself a little smile. "Academic. Standards."

Zeeshan Nizami slapped both his palms on the table with alarming force and jumped to his feet. Just then, however, the waitress came by with a jug of coffee.

"You leaving?" she asked.

My father pasted a grin on his face and sat down. "No, no. Of course not. Just a misunderstanding. No coffee for us, thanks." As she walked away, he rounded on me again. "There it is, that annoying cleverness of yours. You are always the smartest one in the room, haan? Well, when I leave here for Arizona, you're going to come with me. How's that for smart?"

"I have school."

He shrugged. "They have schools there."

"But this is my home."

"Your home is wherever I am. You are my child. You will do as I say."

"I won't."

He actually laughed. "There's a lot more fire in you than before. Did you catch it from that girl you found? Is she the reason why you don't want to come with me? Don't worry, we'll find you a better one there."

"I'm almost eighteen," I told him. "You can't make me go anywhere."

"Even if you were twenty, boy, you know the score. I own that old man's house. Your precious Nana would be begging in the streets if it weren't for me. I thought, you know, how long can he live? Let him die and then I'll sell the house." He leaned forward across the table. "But if you don't do what I tell you, I'll sell it tomorrow. And where will he live then?"

I sat back and stared up at the ceiling. This was going exactly how I had expected, which didn't make it any better at all.

The waitress served our food in silence. I watched as my father took a bottle of maple syrup and upended it over my plate until my toast was swimming in a lake of amber.

"Eat," he commanded.

I ate. I chewed my food and somehow managed to swallow it.

"That's good," Zeeshan Nizami said with a grim smile. "Very good. That's a good boy."

I forced myself to take another bite.

"How much you love that old man, haan? Too bad you don't care half as much for your father. All this time and not a single phone call from you. Shameful."

"I can't go with you," I said through the eggy sweetness of the toast, which had a bitter tang to it somehow. "Not for a while. I'm doing something that's important to me. A school...school event. A project. I can't let the people I'm working with down."

"When is it?"

"Christmas Eve," I told him.

"On Christmas Eve? You really think I'm a fool, don't you? It doesn't matter. We'll leave that day and you can just miss whatever it is you have planned. How about that?"

My fury fell from my eyes, leaving my face wet. My voice was soft when I asked, "Why do you hate me so much?"

"Because you ruined my life." He said it simply, without rancor. "You're old enough to know that now. We never wanted you, your mother and I. We didn't have anything. We were just two stupid kids in love. But after you, everything changed. I enlisted because of you, to support you. I saw what I saw because of you. I killed the people I killed because of you. I began drinking because of you. You've been a cancer since you were born."

My tears dropped into my plate, ripples in a sea of gold. "I'm sorry, Dad. I'm sorry."

"The worst of it," he continued, "was that you took your mother from me. I think she would've had more patience with how broken I was when I got back from Afghanistan if it hadn't been for you. But I resented you and that made her begin to resent me. I'll never forgive you for that. Not ever."

A few seconds after my father left me sobbing quietly at the diner table, I felt a hand on my shoulder again. I looked up, expecting to see the waitress.

"You okay, bro? That was nasty."

"Diamond? What are you doing here?"

Heera Khan slid into my side of the booth, forcing me to move over. He put a heavy arm across my shoulders. "I've been here the whole time."

I stared at him. "You followed me? Why?"

"Because it seemed like this was going to be some heavy shit, brother, and Diamond is your spotter, after all."

Chapter Twenty-One

King Arthur had a round table. I—being rather square and by no means a king—had a rectangular one. Aiza Aunty, Diamond, Qirat, and Nana sat with me. Beans was outside, too upset to stay with us after she'd heard what had happened at the diner. I'd wanted to follow her, but Qirat had stopped me, telling me to give her some time.

"Nana," Qirat now said quietly, "I know this is not the kind of thing one asks but...could you manage, financially, if you lose this house?"

He took a deep breath. "It would be very difficult. This one"—he pointed to me—"will be fine eventually. My life insurance will go into a trust if I die before he is eighteen, so that'll be safe from Zeeshan. Before I die, things would be... uncomfortable."

She nodded.

"If you don't think, boy," Nana continued, addressing me, "that I would pick up a bowl and beg in the streets for your sake, you don't know me at all. Forget me. Forget the house. Let that awful father of yours do his worst."

"I can't let that happen. Nana, I'm not going to be responsible for you losing your home."

"Yes," the old man said sarcastically. "Much better that I should lose you."

"I have some money I could help with," Aiza Aunty volunteered, "for a while."

Nana waved her off just as I started to protest. "We appreciate it, madam, but I do not wish to be a burden on you. I thank you, but I must refuse you."

"We could try to raise money online," Diamond suggested. "That works for some people."

"Maybe," Qirat said dubiously. "A lot of those campaigns fail. We'd have to get it to go viral somehow and—"

"This is temporary," I assured them. "My father's power over me, that is. I'll go with him. Once—"

"Once I am dead," Nana said, his eyes watery, "you might be free to come see me at the cemetery, like you visit your mother."

I looked away from him. "I should go check on Beans."

"It is a horrible thing to be saddled with rebellious

children, madam," Nana said to Aiza Aunty. "This one would have you put on my headstone that I died in comfort but in sorrow." Turning to me, he demanded, "Is that what you want? For me to die in this place by myself?"

"That won't happen," I told him.

I looked at Qirat and then at Diamond and then at Aiza Aunty.

They all nodded in response to my unspoken question.

Nana wouldn't be alone. They'd make sure of it.

I put my hand on my heart, unable to speak, and followed in Beenish's footsteps.

Beans was standing outside on the front porch, leaning on a worn gray wood railing. Her arms were wrapped around her torso to shield her from the cold, and her breath puffed out in front of her in little clouds. Her black eyes were fixed on the glittering lights that the neighbors had put up. Our home remained dark, illuminated only by a giant inflatable Santa towering over everything across the street.

"You okay?" I asked, stepping up beside her.

She shook her head. "You?"

"Same." I leaned forward on both my elbows and looked back at her over my shoulder. "What are you thinking?"

"I hate Santa Claus."

I blinked. "Really?"

"Yeah. When I was a kid, I'd get psyched for Christmas but, obviously, we never got anything. So one day I went to my father and asked him why. Why didn't Santa ever come to our home?"

"Because you were always naughty?"

"I'd at least get a lump of coal, then," Beans said with a small smile. "No, he told me it was because Santa didn't like Muslim children."

Despite everything, I laughed.

"That was the first time I realized that people might not like me because of what I believed or what my family believed. It was the first time I realized that someone might actually hate me. It was awful."

"I'm sorry," I said.

"Fuck it." Beans exhaled. "It was forever ago and I know better now, but I still don't like Santa. Parents do awful things to us, dude. They all suck."

"Some, I imagine, are better than others."

"I just hate that so much of life is random chance. Who would you be if you'd been born to Diamond's parents? What if he'd been born to yours? What if we'd been white or Black? What if we were born in somewhere else? What if we weren't Muslim at all? Our lives would've been totally different."

"I've told you this before: We live the life we're given. We make lemonade."

"This is a really shitty time to say I told you so, Arsalan."

"Sorry."

"Forget it," she said. Then after a pause, she asked, "So

you're really going to do it? You're going to Arizona? What's in Arizona?"

"A desert, I think."

Beans didn't seem to think that was funny. I suppose it wasn't.

"Listen," I said, "I wanted to apologize."

"For what?"

"I promised you I'd dance with you. I've never broken a promise before. If I was destined to break one...Beans, I'm sorry it was one I made to you."

"Hey." Beenish pulled at my arm, making me stand up straight. She moved close to me, her face turned up toward mine. Gently, she touched the side of my face, and I wondered if she was going to kiss me.

Instead, in a completely even tone, she asked, "What the fuck is wrong with you?"

I raised my eyebrows. "What?"

"Do you really think that I'm upset because of the dance? I'll manage, okay? I'll figure something out. Yes, I'll miss having you with me more than I've ever missed anyone, but this isn't about one night. It's not about one dance. It's about all of them."

"All of them?" I echoed.

"Arsalan Nizami," she said softly, her eyes wet with tears, "you have to know by now that you are in love with me."

"I am?"

"You are," she confirmed, even though it shouldn't have

been a question. I knew the truth. I had known for some time.

"Yes," I admitted quietly. "I am. But don't worry, I do not expect you to feel the same way about me."

Beenish groaned and looked up at the sky. "Seriously?" I realized she was asking Allah. "Of all the boys in the world, you had to make me fall in love with this one? He's such an idiot!"

"Wait," I said. "You—"

"Shut up," Beans advised, her lips moving toward mine.

The front door opened and the night was flooded with light. "Niz," Diamond said, stepping out, Qirat and Aiza Aunty behind him. "We're going to head out—what's going on?"

I tried to come up with an explanation as to why Beenish and I were standing so close. "Uh…"

"There's something in his eye," Beans said smoothly. "I was just—"

"That's the worst," Diamond said. Pushing her back gently, he roughly grabbed my head and dragged my face to the light streaming out the door. He peered at me closely. "Which eye is it? They both look red."

"It's the right one," Beans said.

"Actually," I started to say, "I think whatever it was is—"

Diamond blew into my eye hard. Some spit accidentally came along with his breath.

"Gross," I cried, wiping at my face and stumbling back a little.

"Sorry." He wiped at his mouth. "Didn't mean for that to happen. Let me try again."

"I think, Heera," Qirat piped up, "you got it."

"Yes," I hurried to add. "I'm good."

He clapped me on the back. "You're welcome, bro. Call me if you need anything, all right?"

"Yeah," I said.

Qirat gave me a knowing look, then grabbed Beans by an ear. "Come on, Juliet, before you get turned into a pumpkin."

"That doesn't even make sense," Beenish protested.

That left me on the porch with Aiza Aunty, who regarded me gravely.

"Um...we were just—"

"I think, Mr. Nizami," she said with her usual regal air, "that I've lived long enough to know what you two were doing. This has been brewing for some time."

I looked down at the ground, my face warm.

"May I give you a piece of advice, Arsalan?"

"Of course, Aunty."

"Find a way to stay. Don't leave Beenish if you can help it. It'll break her heart if you do. My daughter has...she has felt unwanted her whole life. Even when her father and I were together, we weren't there for her. Not really. And then...well, you know our recent history."

"I'm not choosing to leave her," I pointed out. "I have no choice."

"And rationally, she will know that. Emotionally, it'll

still gut her. I think what Beenish needs, maybe what we all need, is to be loved most and to be chosen first."

I gestured helplessly toward the house and the old man in it.

"I understand," Aiza Aunty said softly. "And I'm not really one for prayer—I know you aren't either—but maybe we should make some time for it tonight. This would be a good moment for a miracle."

'Twas the day before Christmas when Aiza Aunty's gift got to me. It was the sherwani she'd ordered from Pakistan. The note it came with was not from her, though. It was in a messy, barely restrained hand I recognized well.

I'm sorry I'll never get to see you wear it. —B

I'd spoken to Beans a few times since that night on the porch, but the unsaid goodbyes between us were growing in number. It felt like we were a little distant from each other already. Or maybe I was imagining it, and she was just busy with preparations for the wedding and her dance.

No matter what the reason, it seemed that I was more alone now than I had been before I'd ever met Beans.

I was still in touch with Diamond. In fact, he was coming over later today to take me to the mosque my father was staying at. He was planning on going to the wedding from there. I wondered what outfit he'd chosen to wear. I was pretty sure they didn't make sherwanis sleeveless.

Turning my attention to Aiza Aunty's present, I undid the zipper to reveal a gorgeous, deep turquoise, raw silk long coat along with an impossibly soft white kurta and shalwar to wear underneath. I ran my hand along the rich fabric, marveling at its elegance.

"It's beautiful, but I'm not sure when I'll ever get to wear it."

"It was made for you," Nana told me. "It ought to stay with you."

I set it aside. I'd think about taking it with me to Arizona. It wasn't as if I didn't have room in my luggage. I only had a few belongings. Most of the space in my duffel bag was taken up by what Beans had picked out at the mall when she'd given me a makeover. I had little claim to anything else in my life.

"Beenish is a gift too. A divine one. As, I would like to think, am I," Nana added. "But it appears you have decided to be ungrateful to your Lord."

"If you wanted to use religion to emotionally blackmail me," I told him, "you shouldn't have made me a skeptic."

"If you cannot find wisdom in things you do not believe in, then I've failed to educate you entirely."

When I didn't respond, he went on. "Even if Allah didn't make us share the same blood and the same time, even if he wasn't behind your meeting Beans, even if every good thing you have in your life is the product of coincidence alone, is it wise to throw it all away?"

"Nana, I—"

"You spoke to Beenish about the gravity that people exert on each other, Arsalan, but the truth has gravity as well. You should be drawn to it wherever you find it, whether in the Quran or the Torah or the Gita."

I sighed. "I understand that. What you seem to keep forgetting is that I'm doing this for you. So, in a way, aren't you the one who is being ungrateful?"

"You spend your entire life," he grumbled, "hoping your children are clever, until one day you realize life would have been easier if they were simple."

"Speaking of your children," I said, trying to change the subject, "I was going to go see Mom today. To say goodbye. Do you want to come with me?"

"You know I have no use for graveyards," Nana said. "All my ghosts are always with me."

I left him to those ghosts and went upstairs. I didn't have anything to do there, not really, but I also didn't want to be around my great-grandfather. His efforts to convince me to stay with him, to let my father do his worst and take this house from us, had gotten exhausting. I was doing something I didn't want to do because it was right. It would be nice if the person I was doing it for appreciated it.

My reflection caught my eye. I walked up to the full-length mirror in my room. Just a few months ago, the boy in the mirror had been nervous at the mere thought of speaking ~ Beenish Siraj. A week ago, he'd been moments away from . It was an amazing transformation.

At least, it looked like an amazing transformation.

What had really changed?

The hair, the clothes, the slight change in posture and physique—those were all surface-level things. Were the eyes different? Was the soul they reflected different? Or was I still the same scared little boy whimpering in a corner as his father raged on and on and on?

I stepped closer to my reflection.

Would that boy have gone back to Arizona with Zeeshan Nizami?

Yes. Absolutely. He'd been a coward. Before meeting Beenish, there had been no thought of standing against the world and throwing lemons back in its face. That boy would have kept his head down. He would have done what he was told.

There were tears in his eyes when he asked, "Isn't that what you're doing now?"

I turned away from him and he turned away from me.

"This is different," I reassured myself. "I'm choosing to do this."

But was I? Or was I just failing to stand up to my father, like I always had?

It was impossible for me to spare Nana pain. He'd either lose me or lose the house. The old man would get hurt either way. He'd told me, repeatedly, which wound he preferred. Was it right to take that choice away from him?

And what about Beans? In one of his attempts to convince me to stay, Nana had said, "I hope you understand that you will see God before you see another girl like that one."

311

That was a selfish consideration, and I'd disregarded it. But both she and Aiza Aunty had made it clear that by leaving, I was breaking Beenish's heart. It was the one thing I wanted to avoid the most.

I wasn't acting like it, though. I was acting like saving this house was the most important thing in the world to me, when it wasn't.

The question remained: Was I making a sacrifice, or was I accepting whatever the world did to me?

I turned back to face the boy in the mirror and considered reaching out and pushing him, just a little, so that he would topple over and shatter. If I did that, there'd be a million broken pieces of me scattered all over the floor and I'd have no idea how to put me back together.

Then my reflection would look how I actually felt.

The graveyard at Eagles Nest was silent when I got there. It wasn't pleasant and green anymore. There were no birds and no birdsong. There was just a profound, cold quiet.

We never wanted you

You've been a cancer since you were born.

"Is that how you really felt, Mom?"

There was, as always, no answer.

But I realized I didn't need one. I knew what my father had said wasn't true.

Search for love and you'll see. Life is beautiful.

I'd fixated so much on the first part of what she'd said, on her wish for me to find love, that I'd forgotten what she'd said next. Even as she was dying in that awful hospital room, despite how horribly broken her marriage had become, despite how hard she'd been forced to work and how little she'd slept, her last thoughts had not been dark. She'd seen past her own struggles, past mine and Nana's and Dad's, and she'd seen what was good in the world.

I closed my eyes.

I remembered Mom stroking my hair the day she'd died.

I remembered Diamond's arm around me at the diner, being my spotter.

Qirat lip-syncing as she danced in our kitchen.

Aiza Aunty crying as she held Beans in her arms after two years of missing her.

Slow dancing with Beenish in the garage, the gravity of her lips tempting mine.

Nana telling me to wear hats and that syllables were irresistible.

Beans informing me that I loved her.

"You were right," I whispered. "Life is beautiful."

Muneera Nizami smiled at me.

I don't know how I knew that, but I did.

"Should I stay? Tell me I should stay. Give me a sign. Mom, please. Help me."

It wasn't an entirely reasonable request. But I wasn't asking for gold or frankincense or myrrh. I just needed something. Anything. If a little rain had started, if I'd felt a slight tremor in the earth, if I'd heard a car horn honk or a bird call out, I'd have told myself it was a message from her.

But there was nothing.

I was alone again.

Darkness was gathering by the time I left Mom. In an hour Diamond would take me to Zeeshan Nizami. The drive home from the cemetery was to be my last ride in the Eldorado. I would miss the old Cadillac, but this had been an appropriate final trip with it. These were the roads it had most traveled in its time with me.

Diamond's car was already there when I got back. He was probably in a hurry. He had a wedding to get to, after all.

I sat back and exhaled, trying not to think about the fact that Beans was likely putting on her dress, that Qirat Api was about to get married, that Aiza Aunty was getting ready for her first great acting performance in years.

I tried not to think about how much I wanted to be with them.

Diamond was in the living room with Nana when I walked in. They were speaking, but so softly that I couldn't make out what their conversation was about. He stood up and held out a fist for me to bump.

"How is Beans?" I asked.

Diamond hesitated, then said, "Very quiet."

I looked away from him.

"Did Muneera give you any advice as to what you should do?" Nana inquired after a moment.

I shook my head.

"I have found the dead to be a quiet lot," the old man said with a tired smile, "though perhaps they do have ways of sending us messages. Your devout friend here has a story for you."

"It's about Nuayman ibn Amr. The Companion of the Prophet who had a drinking problem? I told you I'd find out more about him for you."

I sighed. I didn't have the patience or inclination for a religious lecture right now. "This isn't the time, Diamond."

"Yes, Niz. Now is exactly the time."

"Can we just—"

"Sit down," Nana commanded. "Let the pious have their say."

I rolled my eyes. "The pious always say the same thing. Respect your parents. Do what you're told. Keep your head down. I'm already doing that." But I took a seat as ordered.

Nana gestured for Diamond to go on.

"Obviously, bro, you know that drinking alcohol is prohibited in Islam. The problem for Nuayman was that he couldn't stop. He'd drink and he'd be punished. He'd keep drinking and he'd keep getting punished. One time after this happened, one of the Prophet's other friends basically said: Curse Nuayman. When will he stop drinking?"

"To which Muhammad replied," Nana chimed in, "Do not curse him, for I know nothing of him except that he loves Allah and his Messenger."

"And in the end," Diamond finished, "the Prophet has said that a man is with the ones he loves."

" 'A man is with the ones he loves,' " Nana repeated, "says Muhammad. Will you not heed your Prophet?"

I started to remind Nana that he had raised me to be a skeptic, but I remembered what he'd said earlier about accepting wisdom wherever one found it.

"Niz," Diamond said earnestly, "there's gonna be a cost to whatever choice you make today. You can go with your father, who—and I'm sorry for saying this, bro, but that guy is not a solid dude, you know?"

I nodded.

"He said himself that he never wanted you. I heard him. But we *do* want you. Stay with us—with me and Beans and Nana and Qirat Api. We love you. That's what your mom would want, I'm sure. I think it might even be what the Prophet would want for you."

I looked around the living room—a century of books, mementos, and memories was gathered here. "You'll lose your home, Nana."

Nana harrumphed. "What was the last thing your mother ever told you, my son? Search for *real estate* and you will find that life is beautiful?"

Despite the fact that I was seized by a sudden urge to cry, I chuckled.

"You did it, Arsalan. You did what she asked. Tell me, my son, is life not beautiful?"

Chapter Twenty-Two

"Took you long enough to get here."

I raised my eyebrows at Aiza Aunty. "You're not surprised?"

She shook her head, smiled, and brushed something off the left shoulder of the sherwani she had gotten me. "Qirat and I were both sure you would come. She said something about the pull of a heart being greater than the pull of a black hole. Do you know what she meant?"

"Yes," I said. "I do."

"You may explain it to me later."

I nodded and started to walk away from her.

"Arsalan," Aiza Aunty called.

I turned back to face her.

"My Beenish didn't dare have hope or faith. She is hurting. You will be kind to her, yes?"

"Always," I promised. "Are you ready to be dramatic?"

Aiza Aunty laughed. "Always. Now go. Run."

I ran.

I ran through the parking lot full of cars and through the five-star lobby glittering with women in lovely, elaborate, colorful clothes and men in somber-colored suits.

I ran over a red carpet, under crystal chandeliers, and past uninteresting, inoffensive paintings. I ran around gossiping aunties trying to wrangle their dupattas and uncles discussing workers compensation insurance premiums. I ran until I could hear desi music, until strangers became familiar faces.

Some of the backup dancers waved or shouted out their greetings. Diamond, who had gone ahead while I was getting ready, walked up and slapped me on the back so hard that I'm pretty sure he ruined the alignment of my vertebrae. He was wearing a black T-shirt with bold white letters on it that read INSECURITY. A gift from Beans, no doubt.

"Where is she?"

"Behind there," Diamond said, pointing at a giant screen. It would serve as the background in front of which we were to perform. From where I was standing, it hid not only Beenish but also our stage. Beyond it was a giant purple curtain, which would part before the dance began. "One of my friends is about to go tell Siraj Uncle, Roshni Aunty, and Sham's parents that Aiza Aunty is making a scene in the lobby. You don't have much time."

"I understand."

"And Niz?" He held out a fist toward me. "Diamond didn't tell her you were coming."

I ignored his offered fist bump. Instead, I stepped toward him and wrapped him in a hug.

God, he was wearing a lot of body spray.

Heera seemed surprised for a moment, then he squeezed back for a few seconds.

"Thank you," I told him. "For everything."

"Diamond told you the first day we met," he reminded me. "We're bros, yeah? No thanks needed."

I inclined my head, then turned and rushed toward the stage.

I caught enough of a look at the screen to see it had a Mughal theme. It would make us appear as if we were dancing in the courtyard of the Shahi Qila, the Royal Fort, in Lahore.

I didn't spare more than a glance for it, though. I had no time for the majesty of kings. Beenish Siraj was waiting for me.

She was standing in the middle of the stage, head bowed, arms folded before her, almost in prayer. The pale pink dress she'd shown me before was even more beautiful in person than it had been in pictures. The modesty of the high neckline and long sleeves of the choli made the choice to leave her midriff exposed seem more dramatic and daring than it actually was. It was the kind of outfit that would definitely give aunties something to talk about.

I went to stand beside her. She was so focused that she didn't even notice, until I leaned toward her ear and whispered, "You look like magic, Beans."

Beenish yelped, turned, and almost tripped backward. I reached out and grabbed her arm to steady her. She started to say something, obviously irritated, but then realized that it was me, and the words softened on her lips.

Her eyes suddenly shining, she whispered, "What are you doing here?"

I gazed down at her. Her long black hair was pulled back, held in place with clips. Whoever had done her makeup had left it light and managed, somehow, to both deepen and soften the mysteries of her dark eyes.

I reached a hand out to caress her face, but stopped millimeters short, uncertain if this intimacy was permitted to me. Beans stepped toward me and my finger grazed across the impossibly soft skin of her cheek. She sighed. Her lips parted a little.

"'A man is with the one he loves,'" I said.

Beans blinked rapidly and looked down, then shook her head and exhaled forcefully. "Ugh. You absolute ass," she said.

Admittedly, that was not the reaction I'd been expecting.

"Ohmygod you're going to make me cry. If you ruin my makeup now, Arsalan Nizami, I'll...I'll...'"

"Kiss me?" I joked.

She did.

Standing on tiptoe, she pulled my face toward hers. It wasn't a gentle or tentative first kiss. It was wild and fiery and a little clumsy because neither one of us entirely knew what we were doing.

It was a perfect expression of her soul upon my lips.

She was flushed when she pulled away. I'm certain I was as well.

"Yeah," Beans said, "that totally works. Not feeling like crying anymore. Feeling...other things."

"I lov—"

She kissed me again in a way that left me conscious only of her mouth against mine. For a few blessed moments, my world was nothing but her warmth, the feel of the skin at the small of her back as I drew her closer, of her hands running through my hair, the shocked gasps of uncles and aunties all around us, some wolf whistles, somebody shouting "Astagh-firullah" at the top of their lungs. Why was someone seeking forgiveness? What use was it? I was in heaven already.

"Shakar Wandaan" started blasting through the hall as the backup dancers flooded the stage. Beans and I stepped back and simultaneously turned to look at a stunned crowd of wedding guests staring back at us.

"Well...fuck," I whispered.

"Couldn't have said it better myself," Beans told me. She reached over, took my hand, and squeezed it. "Will you dance with me?"

I nodded. "Always."

Years later, when gaggles of aunties sat around to discuss that night—and they discussed that night ad nauseam—our dance was mentioned before our kiss. At least, usually. That is how amazing we were.

It was a production. Professionals had set up the sound, the lighting, and the background for the stage. The backup dancers, if they were surprised to see that Beans and I were not at our marks when the song began, didn't let it show. They did this for a living, and they were great at it.

Despite months of practice, I was still the weakest link, but my fatal flaw, which Aiza Aunty and Beans had worked with me to fix, had always been that I overthought what I was doing and became self-aware and awkward. That was not an issue on that night, not with memory of Beenish's lips a conflagration in my mind. I couldn't think at all, which was fine, because my body remembered what to do. It recognized the beats of the song, it knew when to jump, when to spin, where and how to move my arms.

Beans and I were in perfect sync and we knew it. I could see the delight in her eyes when we transitioned into steps where we were facing each other, either as I twirled her around, or as we moved past each other, our heads bowed flirtatiously close.

Out of the corner of my eye, I saw Sham attempting to muscle past Diamond and the "guards" he'd brought with him to prevent exactly that. The groom looked disheveled and furious. Qirat, struggling with her bridal gown, was trying to keep him calm.

There would be time enough for all that later. The future would come and some of it would be painful. For now, I had Beenish and I had music and I was dancing and my old soul felt young, my heart incandescent.

The world *was* beautiful.

And I was part of it.

As the song ended, the crowd broke into applause and cheering. Beans stepped to my side and, without thinking, I put an arm around her waist as she stretched to kiss my cheek. It would have been a nice ending to the night.

But there was a roar of fury as Sham broke free of the men restraining him and charged the stage, his face contorted with anger. He climbed up and stalked toward Beenish.

"You shameless whore!" he screamed, silencing the entire hall. I heard the main doors swing open and looked over to see Aiza Aunty rush in, followed by her ex-husband, his current wife, and Qirat's would-be in-laws. "How dare you? You think I'm a joke? That my family's honor is a *joke*?" Stepping forward, he raised a hand to slap her across the face.

Beans flinched as he swung his arm.

I caught his blow.

It sounds more heroic than it looked. I staggered back more than a little under the force of his attack, but I managed to keep him from hitting Beans, which was all that mattered.

Then, like a monster from the deep, Diamond Khan lunged up to the stage, grabbed the back of Sham's collar, and pulled him down. The crowd let out an "oooh" as the groom crashed to the floor with a sick thud.

In an instant, Diamond was over him, fist cocked. He looked around for someone, until his eyes found Qirat.

"Api," he asked, "is this your man?"

She looked down at Shamshir Inteha, then up to Beans and me on the stage. Beans had her hands joined together, silently pleading with her sister to give the answer we all wanted. When Qirat's eyes met mine, I placed my hand upon my heart.

"No," Qirat said, her voice clear and resolute. "I want nothing to do with him."

A shocked murmur filled the air. Sham twisted to look at the woman he'd planned to marry. "What?" he demanded. "How *dare* you—"

That was when, with one punch, Diamond Khan ended the most astonishing wedding the desi community in Sacramento has ever known.

Chapter Twenty-Three

"**I feel like we've spent more time moving stuff than we have** making out," Beenish complained as she stuffed yet another box of Nana's books into the Eldorado.

"We can start changing that," I told her, "anytime you want."

"Inappropriate," Qirat muttered, heading back to the house to pick up the few items that remained there.

"Totally," Diamond agreed, following her. "God is watching, you know."

"Ignore them," Beans said, skipping up beside me. She was wearing an I LIKE TO MOVE IT shirt. "We're adorable."

"I know," I said.

It was a beautiful day for the middle of February. California will do that to you sometimes. It'll surprise you just when you think you know what to expect from it.

The weather would probably turn tomorrow, but today the sky was clear and the sun was bright. Something about the last rain had left Nana's home—well, it wasn't Nana's anymore, hence the boxes—looking particularly picturesque.

"See?" Beans said brightly as I studied the beloved old house. "I was right. I told you everything would be fine."

I chuckled. "You and Qirat got kicked out. Nana and I are homeless. And, frankly, I'm not certain Aiza Aunty will be able to tolerate having all of us living in her apartment for very long."

"But you're free of your dad. You're eighteen now. He can't control you anymore."

I smiled at her. I wasn't sure, even on that day, if we are ever truly free of our fathers. I think people struggle to flee them or struggle to be them all their lives.

But I did have a respite from Zeeshan Nizami for the moment. He had flown out to Arizona, as scheduled. He'd called soon after, though, breathing fire, threatening to come back and put me in my place for disobeying him. When I told him I'd call the police on him, he'd hung up. It wasn't long before a law firm representing him had written to Nana, demanding that we vacate the house.

"Arsalan?" Beans asked.

I bent down and kissed her forehead. "You're right. Everything is going to be okay."

326

"I have become a vagrant," Nana declared as he stepped out the front door for the last time, dressed to the nines. "A drifter and a nomad. Yes, I am a wanderer upon this earth. But tell me, friends, are you something more?"

"Is *he* okay?" Beenish asked.

"It's Goethe. The last part is, anyway. He's paraphrasing—"

She made a huge show of yawning.

"Don't worry about him," I said, amending my answer. "He's just been hanging around Aiza Aunty a lot. He's getting a little dramatic."

"Fabulous," Beans muttered under her breath. "More people like Amma is exactly what I need in my life."

Nana walked around the front yard for a bit, gazed up at the sky, and then studied the gorgeous tree by the house across the street, to which the inflatable plastic Santa had been tied the night Beans had informed me that I was in love with her.

"I've been inside so long," he said, walking up to us, "that I'd rather forgotten what the world looked like. It is not bad." He took off the fedora he was wearing. "I must admit I've missed the feeling of wind in my hair."

Beans retrieved her phone from her pocket. "Why don't I get a picture of you guys with the house before we go?"

"A capital idea," Nana declared, grabbing my arm and pulling me forward. "Come along."

"All right," Beans called out. "On the count of three, say 'cheese.'"

"Wait. Cheese?" Nana asked me. "This is a significant

occasion. Surely with our vocabularies you and I can come up with something better than 'cheese.' "

"We could just say 'significant,' " I suggested.

"Lazy. Also, we must consider what our faces will look like when we're—"

"Guys," Beans said, "just say 'cheese,' okay? Everyone says 'cheese.' "

Nana and I looked at each other.

"We should probably do as we're told."

"I concur," Nana said, putting an arm around my shoulder. "I will accept the wisdom of the young. Very well. Proceed."

Beans raised her phone and started to frame the shot.

"Actually," my great-grandfather said, "I require a moment." He turned toward me and carefully placed the fedora he was carrying onto my head. "There. Now everything is perfect."

Acknowledgments

I write in the dark. That is to say that I write without a road map or compass. I stumble through a forest of words in the search of characters and a story, and simply hope I'll find them. This process means there are false starts and abandoned ventures and many ideas that simply go nowhere. It is an unpredictable journey that requires faith and patience.

Usually, this is a trip I take alone. Not this time. This time, my editor, Deirdre Jones, went through it with me. Thank you, Deirdre, for helping me figure out what story I was trying to tell, for reading beginnings without middles and ends, and for trusting that, eventually, we'd come to our destination. We can be sure, at least, that Nana would appreciate us not relying on devices (plot devices, in this case) and finding our own way.

I am, as ever, thankful for my extraordinary agent, Melissa Edwards, who believed first. This book was written and edited during a trying and unusual year where certainty was a precious, difficult thing to find. It was an incalculable blessing to have someone in my corner I knew I could rely on without doubt.

My thanks also to Megan Tingley, Alvina Ling, and everyone on the Little, Brown Books for Young Readers team. I'd like to especially thank Hallie Tibbetts, Annie McDonnell, and the book's designer, Angelie Yap. Thank you, also, Fatima Baig, for the gorgeous, gorgeous cover.

My gratitude, as always, to Madelyn Burt and Addison Duffy.

And to my wife, Saira Amena Siddiqui, my children, and my family, who are constant reminders that life is indeed beautiful when we are with the ones we love.